DEMISE OF A SELF-CENTERED PLAYBOY

PIPER RAYNE

Cover Design: by Hang Le

Line Editor: Joy Editing

Line Editor: My Brother's Editor

Proofreader: Shawna Gavas, Behind The Writer

You might be wondering how you'll know when your playboy ways are coming to an end. For some it might be an unexpected pregnancy (ahem... you know who), for others it might be finally landing the one woman you've always wanted (cough... I won't mention any names). For me, it was the death of my mentor and the subsequent reading of his will.

The signs were there, they always are. But I didn't notice them until it was too late, and my demise was complete.

Demise Sign #1 – You find yourself thrust into the land of responsibility and you don't immediately hightail it out of town.

Demise Sign #2 – Despite being stuck with the world's biggest Jekyll & Hyde, some sadistic part of you actually enjoys spending time with her.

Demise Sign #3 – Your family suddenly stops wanting to weigh in on every decision in your life.

Demise Sign #4 – Somehow you end up being the voice of reason in your tumultuous partnership.

Demise Sign #5 – You start thinking of other people before yourself.

Demise Sign #6 – You agree to put yourself in the middle of an Alaskan reality TV show that has both of you sleeping in the same tent.

Demise Complete.

Demise
of a
Self-Centered
Playboy

The Baileys

Austin Bailey - 34 years old
(Biology Teacher/Baseball Coach)
Savannah Bailey - 32 years old
(Runs Bailey Timber Corp)
Brooklyn Bailey - 29 years old
(Runs Essential Oil Company)
Rome Bailey - 27 years old
(Chef)
Denver Bailey - 27 years old
(Bush Pilot)
Juno Bailey - 26 years old
(Matchmaker)
Kingston Bailey - 23 years old
(Smokejumper)
Phoenix Bailey - 21 years old
(Student)
Sedona Bailey - 21 years old
(Student)

ONE

Denver

Death sucks.

It sucks mostly for the person who died. Yeah, okay, it definitely sucks most for the person who died. Or maybe it doesn't. Maybe there's nothingness after you pass and it's really the worst for all of us who are left behind, dealing with the gaping hole of the one we've lost.

But you wanna know what sucks worse than attending someone's funeral? The reading of their will. Not that I've been to many. This is my first.

And I can tell you, it's a complete waste of an afternoon.

Especially when the most important person who's supposed to be here, isn't.

I glance at the small gold clock on the wall. I wonder if Luther Lloyd, Attorney at Law, has a stopwatch so he can milk every cent out of his clients. At least this isn't costing me anything. Although it sure did cost Chip. Which sucks. The man died too young.

When Luther called and requested that I be present for

the reading of the will, I was surprised. Chip wasn't the type of man I'd think would leave a will. He was more the type of guy I'd think would leave a note that says, "Throw my ashes into Lake Starlight. I lived a happy life. I'll catch you on the other side." Not someone who picked out special items to leave to someone else who will class them as junk. I don't want his high school diploma, his coffee maker, or anything of his if he's not coming with it.

"How long do we wait?" I ask.

Luther checks his watch because he's the type of man whose life is dictated by a schedule. "I was clear about our meeting time on the phone with her. Let's give it five more minutes."

I nod, tapping my fingers on my Vans. Not the most practical thing for an Alaskan winter, but unless fresh snow is falling, I make them work.

"Do you have an excursion today?"

I shake my head.

"And how's business going?"

I shrug. I'd like to say busy, but sadly, it's not. And the fact that I'm going to watch Chip's company, Lifetime Adventures, be taken over by the woman we're waiting for makes me want to throw up in her Gucci purse. She's going to run it into the ground. Which means everything Chip wanted for the company will die right along with him. His legacy will end in either bankruptcy or awarded to the highest bidder.

"I know this is hard on you. You and Chip were close."

I shrug again. What does Luther want from me? Does he expect me to ask for a tissue while I lay my heart on his desk? Not gonna happen. I'm used to death. When your parents die when you're fourteen, it's a sledgehammer right in the heart. I quickly realized that all the happily-ever-after fairy tales are bullshit. I learned that life is fragile and there's no way to know when your time is up. Crap you shouldn't know at fourteen, when you still think you're invincible.

When Chip told me his COPD was worsening, the writing was on the wall—he was going to die. I stuck by him, helping where I could by taking over the excursions and day-to-day operations, because that's what you do for the ones you care for. I should feel some sense of relief today, because his daughter, Cleo Dawson, will be told she's inheriting the company and I can slide back into my easy life of bush piloting. But all I feel is dread at the thought of her ruining the company her father worked so hard to build and keep.

I glance to the clock again, which spurs Luther to look at his watch. With no hopes of having a conversation with me, he blows out a breath and opens Chip's file folder.

"How many of those do you have in there?" I nod toward his filing cabinet. Four drawers upright. Grandma Dori's will is probably in there, listing the percentage of Bailey Timber that will be split up between my eight siblings and me. My stomach twists with the thought.

He follows my line of vision, and his thick salt-and-pepper eyebrows scrunch together. He's probably wondering *What's wrong with you, Denver? You come in here wearing jeans, a sweatshirt, and a beat-up pair of Vans. You won't make polite conversation.* I'm sure he assumes I'm hungover. But then he'll remember my tragic circumstances and the pity will set in. The part where his eyes turn soft and he nods, gifting me with the "I know, your parents died much too young and it's fucked you up" expression.

I'm used to it by now. It rolls off my back.

Mostly.

"Almost all of Lake Starlight. Have you thought about writing a will?" Luther sits back, and the small uptick of the corner of his lips says he finds his question as funny as I do.

"We both know I have nothing to leave anyone."

"Everyone has something," he says, his hands holding the ends of a pen in a straight line in front of him.

"I don't own a house or have any money in savings." Unless someone wants my phone with a bunch of chicks' numbers, there's only my plane, which I'm still paying off. Since my twin, Rome, is engaged and Liam, my best friend, is a step away from the same with my sister Savannah, that phone wouldn't come in handy to any of them.

"What about personal items? I've mediated my fair share of fights between family members over something as simple as a television."

"I'm living at Savannah's right now. It's all her stuff."

He straightens in his chair. "You know what I mean."

The door opens, and Luther's eyes zero in behind me. I swear a cold chill wafts into the room with her.

Cleo Dawson.

Chip's daughter.

I don't have to turn around, because her heels announce her arrival. The only surprise, which shouldn't really be a surprise, is that her stepsister, her mother, and her stepfather are alongside her. God forbid she deal with this on her own.

Luther's smile fades as her entourage finds their seats.

She, of course, sits in the leather-bound chair next to me, crossing her legs. Only Cleo would wear high heels and a dress in the middle of an Alaskan winter.

"Denver." Her voice is cool with a touch of forced politeness.

I turn to her, her tanned legs making it clear she's from

the south. I'd be lying if I said the smoothness didn't appeal to me, but that's the thing about the devil—no one said he or she wasn't a temptress.

"Cleo." I nod.

"Miss Dawson, I'm afraid the will is set that it is only to be read before you and Mr. Bailey."

"Why?" Cleo asks.

Her stepfather gets up and rests a hand on the back of Cleo's chair. Her mother crowds me by coming on her other side.

"We're her parents," her mother says.

I examine Cleo's mother's mink coat. I bet she bought it specifically for this trip, since last I checked, Texas doesn't require bundling up.

"Cleo's over eighteen and an adult. I'll read the will and Cleo can discuss it with you after if she chooses to."

"This is ridiculous," her mother says. "He was my husband."

"Ex," I correct.

All their heads whip in my direction with horrified looks that I'd have the audacity to speak at all.

"Why is he even here? He's not related to Chip." Cleo's mom eyes me as though I'm small-town trash.

"Are you worried you can't strip him of his last dime?" I roll my eyes.

Cleo turns in her chair and puts her hand on her mother's. "Go ahead and wait outside."

"I should at least be able to be here, being her mother." She gives Luther an annoyed huff and the three of them leave.

"Think you can handle yourself alone?" I ask Cleo.

"I hope you have the keys with you."

I pat down my pockets. "Shit, I knew I forgot something."

Her eyes narrow. I watch her nostrils fill with air that leaves her body practically with flames.

"Okay. Let's just get started. We're already late." Luther taps his pen on his desk.

"I wonder why that is?" I sneer.

"It's not exactly dry weather out there. The roads are horrible." She swivels to focus her attention on Luther.

"You'd think by what you're wearing it was a balmy eighty degrees."

"You'd think by what you're wearing that you were on your way to the local skatepark."

I laugh and shake my head. "Let's have it, Luther."

Luther opens the file folder again and clears his throat. "Chip Dawson was my client, and I will be upfront in saying he changed his will two months ago, but he was of sound mind to do so. I suggest neither of you go and try to say otherwise. I made sure to have witnesses present."

"She might argue, but I won't." I don't even mention whatever he left me isn't worth anything anyway. Without Chip himself, it's all meaningless.

"Cleo, you are left Chip's house and all the belongings inside."

She straightens and eyes my pockets, silently saying, "Hand over the keys to Lifetime Adventures, fool."

"Cleo is also getting his truck," Luther says.

"I hope a stepladder comes with it." I chuckle.

She huffs. "You know, we can get out of here faster if you stop interrupting."

Luther waits a second, and I nod for him to continue.

He goes through all of Chip's financial accounts, and as expected, everything is going to Cleo. If we could get to my toaster or whatever he's giving me so I can get the hell out of here, I'd appreciate it.

"Now Lifetime Adventures." He taps the papers on the desk. My attention is piqued, because for the first time, I sense apprehension in his voice. "Lifetime Adventures is to be split fifty-fifty between Cleo Dawson and Denver Bailey. If one shall not want their portion, the other has first option to buy the other one out."

My stomach drops like the chunk of an ice cap into the ocean. Chip left me his company? What was he thinking? I look at Cleo.

Even with her layers of makeup, her face pales and her head tilts. "He left it to both of us?"

Luther smiles. "Yes, Miss Dawson. You both equally own everything that has to do with Lifetime Adventures."

She sinks back in her chair and her manicured nails land on her mouth. "I can't own a business with him. We'll kill one another."

I sit up straighter. Savannah's not exactly a billboard ad for all the great things in life that come with running your own company. She leaves Bailey Timber looking exhausted most days. I'm not meant for a life like that. Can I do this? Run a company when I hate anything that comes with strings? Lifetime Adventures comes with a whole slew of strings, Cleo Dawson apparently being the thickest and most binding of them.

Luther digs into the file folder and produces two envelopes and some paperwork, handing each of us a package. "I know this is big news, so he's written you both a letter. Why don't you take some time, read the letter, and let me know if you have any questions?"

We reach out at the same time. In Chip's handwriting,

'Cleo' is written on one white envelope and 'Denver' on the other.

"Why would he not leave it to me?" Cleo asks Luther.

"I'm sorry, Miss Dawson, I don't ask my clients why. Maybe the letter will provide a better explanation."

She stands and faces me. "I'll buy you out."

I'm sure she'd love to buy me out. I was unsure a second ago, but the thought of Cleo destroying what her father worked so hard for has me digging in my heels. "My half isn't for sale."

"You know as well as I do this will never work out." She crosses her arms.

The worst thing about Cleo Dawson, the thing that drives me insane, is that she's hot as shit, yet I'll never be able to lay a hand on her. She's always been miserable to me —why, I have no idea—but I'm happy to return the favor.

I stand, towering over her. "Well, we can give it the ol' college try." I nod to Luther. "Thanks."

Stuffing the letter into the back pocket of my jeans, I wink and sidestep her.

"Did you even go to college?" she calls after me.

"Don't worry, Cleo, we'll get to know all those fun details about one another working side-by-side." I walk through the door.

Her entourage stands, and I walk right by them.

The fun of sparring with her might be the silver lining to a shitty situation.

TWO

Cleo

Denver leaves with only the lingering scent of what I assume must be day-old cologne after a night of partying.

"Thank you, Mr. Lloyd." I nod and take the letter. The one piece of advice my dad gave me when it comes to the city of Lake Starlight is that you never know who you're talking to, so be polite. According to him, my mom made a lasting impression on this town. I never asked if it was when she showed up or when she fled.

"You're welcome, Miss Dawson."

I catch his expression. The one that says, 'I'm not sure why your dad left you everything he had when you couldn't even visit him.' He can think what he wants. It makes no difference to me.

My mom and Bridget are already standing. Phil is on his phone. His cowboy hat, pressed jeans, and button-down with silver snaps on the pockets says we're out-of-towners. I'm surprised he came today and that he didn't fly out right after the funeral. My mom stuck around because she wants to see what she left all those years ago. My stepsister, Bridget, would never allow me to deal with this on my own, so I expected her to stay.

Bridget slides her arm through mine. "He's kind of hot."

"He's the enemy," I remind her for the fourth time. "And now he owns half the company."

Bridget rips the paperwork out of my hands and reads it as though she understands the legal jargon. I'm not saying anything bad about her. It's just that people in her circle pay others to read the legalese to them.

We were sixteen when my mom married Phil. By that time, we'd each been through so many stepsiblings and step-parents, we decided to embrace one another rather than fight. It helped that she had a closet five times the size of mine. People in Dallas still comment about how surprising it is we turned out to be the best of friends.

When our friend Miguel is lost in half a bottle of Patron and has failed yet again to get either of us into his bed for the night, he always says that we should wait until the will is read. We'll hate one another then. But I don't really care if she inherits all of Phil's money. At least my mother wouldn't get what she married him for. A lesson she's yet to learn from her previous five husbands. I could dissect each marriage and why it didn't work out, but it's the same story for each of them—they weren't built on a foundation of love. Someone was always in it for the advantage.

My father was the first rung on Mom's ladder of marrying for money. Phil is by far her most successful catch, which is why it makes sense that she's still married to him all these years later.

"What do you mean he gets half?" My mom holds out her hand.

Bridget shrugs as though she doesn't understand any of the words written on the papers and hands them over to my mom.

"We own the company fifty-fifty."

Mom reads the papers, and I tuck the letter into my purse before she notices it.

"You're going to work side-by-side with that man every day?" Bridget obviously doesn't share my opinion that nothing could be worse. Her eyes soak him in across the parking lot. "I've always thought there was something about a man in a truck."

I look down the hall and see him nearing the stairwell and blow out a breath, ignoring the way his jeans hang off him. He makes fun of my heels while he wears those Vans. Idiot.

"He has that look like 'who gives a shit what life throws at you, I'll catch it with my bare hands.'"

"You mean the one that says, 'I dodge responsibility'?" I deadpan.

"No, the laid-back look."

Bridget's only accompanied me once to Lake Starlight for a week during my last summer with Chip, before I turned eighteen. But I've heard the rumors and seen Denver in action. A man who still behaves like a boy can only run my dad's company one way—into the ground.

"Do I have to blindfold you?" I say to Bridget.

She laughs as we descend the stairs. When we reach the bottom of the stairway, Denver pulls his truck to a stop in front of us. The sidewalk is wide so we're about ten feet apart at least but I glare at him, hoping he can feel the animosity rolling off me. Rolling down his window, his face appears from behind the tinted glass. He really is a beautiful man. Not that I'd admit that to him or anyone else.

"I'll be at Lifetime Adventures if you care to discuss anything, sweetheart." His smile is huge and his ego even bigger.

Anger spurs through me like a kickstart only he can ignite, and I straighten my back to walk over and give him a piece of my mind. He must see something on my face because he puts the truck into park to wait for me. Bridget's arm slides out from mine, and my mom and Phil stay behind, discussing the paperwork. Mostly, it's Phil explaining it to my mom. I guess she can only read a divorce decree like a pro.

I want to buy his half, but that entails asking Phil for money, which spurs an entirely different feeling in my stomach. "We need to set up a meeting."

"Watch out."

He points at the ground and I look down, losing my footing on a patch of ice. My purse flies in the air and the cold, hard, wet ground welcomes my ass.

Denver opens his door and climbs out like the gentleman I'm sure he is not. "If you're going to stay in Lake Starlight, you should go shopping for some new footwear."

Once he helps me up, I yank my arm out of his hand. As I straighten my jacket, Bridget hands me my purse.

"I'm Bridget," she says to Denver in her flirty bar voice —the one that earns her free drinks all night.

Denver looks over, shakes her hand, then turns his attention back to me. "You okay?"

"What do you care?"

Bridget is looking at Denver like *what the hell? Do you not see me standing here?* She might be a millisecond away from unbuttoning her coat to show off her figure. I love the girl, but she can be a tad self-involved.

"Hey, I know we don't see eye-to-eye on a lot, but I'm not a dick," he says.

"You aren't?" I ask.

I transfix on his lips. I can't help it. They're pink from a fresh swipe of Chapstick, and he runs his tongue over them. It's the way he moves one side up in amusement that does me in. It's sexy and tempting and I should not be having these thoughts.

Bad Cleo. I mentally slap my wrist.

"No. You wanna ask my sisters?" He steps forward to the side of me and leans around behind me.

I shift my ass away from his prying eyes. "What the hell do you think you're doing?"

"I don't understand," Bridget says to herself, probably still trying to figure out why Denver's tongue isn't hanging out of his mouth for her.

"I was making sure you weren't too wet. I have a blanket in the—"

I put my hand in his face. "Nope. I don't need anything from you."

He holds his hands in the air and backs away one step. "Have it your way."

Opening his truck door, he looks at the rented SUV with a driver that's pulling around from the parking lot out back. "I assume that's your ride?"

"Yes." I make my back ramrod-straight, so he doesn't think my ass hurts like a bitch right now.

"Like I said, I'll be at Lifetime for a few hours. If you wanna talk."

"Bye," Bridget says.

Denver lazily raises his hand to her, but his eyes remain on me. He's so doing it on purpose. No one ignores Bridget. She's like a shiny object. You can't look away.

"Put some ice on your ass." He winks and shuts the door before driving away.

As our car pulls up, my mom and Phil huddle inside.

Bridget stops me, placing her hand on my arm. "Am I too beautiful for this place? Do they like their women more outdoorsy or something?"

I should tell her ignoring her is probably Denver's plan. He seems like the type of man who always has an agenda. I just need to figure out what it is.

Then again, maybe he's already achieved it—he does own half of my dad's company.

TWO HOURS LATER, after a long lunch where I was too chicken-shit to ask Phil for money, we sit at the airport, waiting for his private jet to be ready for takeoff. Mom is grabbing magazines and trying to find some fresh fruit and vegetables. Bridget is at the desk, flirting with the guy who works there, still trying to prove that her attractiveness didn't vanish on the flight from Dallas to Alaska. Which leaves Phil and me alone.

"I can send the plane back whenever you're ready to come home," he mindlessly says, his eyes on his phone.

I cross and uncross my legs. "I have to clear out his house and stuff."

"Good thing you have time now." He smiles at me before burying his head back into what I assume are emails.

I could respond with a dig, because the reason I have free time is that he recently fired me from the ranch. Not that he didn't have a good reason. I accidentally gave our organic feed animals the feed with growth hormones. Yeah, not my brightest moment. But in my defense, they should mark the containers better. So Phil lost money since he can no longer say the meat he butchers from the poor animals is organic. He was nice about it but let me know in a kind way that maybe ranch life wasn't for me.

I'm a business graduate from the University of Indiana. After graduation, I interviewed at so many places, but nothing panned out. Finally, I hung my head and asked Phil if he knew of anyone looking. I told myself I was networking and using my connections like any smart person would do, but I hated having to do it.

My first job was in the mailroom of a large television studio. Two weeks in, I wheeled my mail cart into the studio. Delivering to the offices behind the set, I stopped my cart and got to chatting with a co-worker about the episode of *Roswell* on the night before. I guess I forgot to put the brake on the cart because a guy rushing around bumped it and it went rolling, so I ran after it. Luckily it stopped right before getting into a camera shot. After receiving scathing looks from the producer and cameramen, I tiptoed to retrieve it, but a cord wrapped around the wheel. When I yanked harder to free it, the mic attached to the camera fell, then the camera guy moved to see what all the action was about—putting me on live TV. My mom calls it my ten seconds of fame. It made the news that night in a funny blooper reel. Technically it was the guy who bumped the cart's fault, not mine, but I was fired.

My second attempt at employment came in the form of an assistant position. My boss always got the same thing every morning—a poppyseed lemon muffin and a large coffee. We were becoming friends, chatting about our morning commute and the weather as I set them on her desk. Except that morning I didn't double-check the order and she didn't bother to look away from her computer while grabbing a bite. Turns out it was a banana nut muffin. I know what you're thinking. So what? Who can't handle a different type of muffin? As I was calling 9-1-1 and stabbing her thigh with an EpiPen, I was thinking the same thing.

Add on the froyo place where I forgot to put the refrigerated items away at night or the bookstore where I was caught too many times in the corner of the romance section reading during working hours... things just haven't worked out for me. I'm determined to make my next job work, come hell or high water.

But I can't do that with Denver Bailey breathing down my neck, so I swallow past the big lump in my throat. "Hey, Phil?"

He peeks up and smiles. "I think this is good for you. You can figure out some things up here. Away from your regular life."

"Well, I can't do it with Denver Bailey." I lay down hint number one. I've seen Bridget coerce him into giving her money a million times. I'm a quick learner.

"Running a business isn't easy. You have to surround yourself with people smarter than you."

"Meaning?"

His smile grows. "Right now, that boy is smarter than you. He knows how to run that company. Knows everything involved. You have to find a way for it to work. Think about it." He taps his finger to his forehead. "You can't take people up to the mountains. You'd get lost or eaten by a bear." He laughs.

A tight smile strains my face. "Yeah, of course."

"Don't be all sour about it. Truth is truth. Facts are facts, darlin'. You'll find what you're meant to do one of these days but take your time up here. Go through your dad's things. Take some time to mourn."

"But don't run the company?" I should hide the bitterness in my tone, but I can't be bothered to mask it right now.

"If it was a coffee shop or a bakery, I could see it maybe. But an outdoor excursion company in Alaska?" His too-tanned face looks as though it might crack with how big his smile is. "I just don't think that's you."

So I guess that's a no to the loan then.

"Why do you look like you're sick?" My mom sits down next to Phil with nothing but a magazine in hand.

"I'm fine."

"We're talking about her future. I told her to take her time up here to figure things out."

My mom smiles at Phil as though he's as smart as Einstein. "Not too long. I'd hate for my daughter to turn into one of *these* people."

I slide back in my chair and pull out my phone to distract myself until they leave. Don't say I never bite my tongue.

THREE

Denver

Two hours after the meeting, I'm still sitting outside the small shack of an office building for Lifetime Adventures, reflecting on what happened in Luther's office. I haven't been able to bring myself to read the letter Chip wrote to me.

The office is located on a hill, the view spectacular. I don't know if Chip picked this location for that reason, but if you were considering touring the outdoors here, there's no better advertisement than the backdrop I'm looking at now. There are three drive sheds full of planes, snowmobiles, and other gear behind the small office. Now half of it is mine.

But I'm not sure I want it. Of course I told Cleo I did just to piss her off, but I'm not made to run a company. I don't even like to work for other people, let alone have people work for me. I like being my own boss of a solo operation. It's a big part of the reason I went into bush piloting. I dictate my hours, my trips, and my time.

I decide that now is as good a time as any to read Chip's

final words to me, so I grab the envelope off the passenger's seat and tear it open.

Denver,

I'm going to be cliché in saying if you're reading this, I've lost the battle. Also, if you're reading this, Luther just informed you that half of Lifetime Adventures is yours and the other half is Cleo's.

You and I have had a lot of talks around campfires and plane rides over Alaska. I know where you stand and where you see your life going. And I realize that this sends you in a direction you never wanted to go. You're probably cursing my name right now. Hear me out before you sign your half over to Cleo or the two of you decide to sell.

You came to me wanting to learn to fly. I told you that you were too reckless, because we both know your reputation in Lake Starlight throughout your teen years. But you came back again and again, agreeing to pay off the lessons by working at Lifetime. You had the drive to keep going, and through all the skills I've taught you, I've seen something inside you I'm not sure you know is there. You deserve this opportunity, and you should take it.

Plus—and I'm going to be an overprotective father here—I'm going to ask you a favor. Cleo is lost, much like you were when you came to me. She has no idea where she fits in this world, and I have an inkling she could fit right here in Lake Starlight. The warmth of the people in this town will do her good. But there's no way she can do it on her own. She doesn't have the skill set. So please take a chance on her like I did you?

I could never repay you for these last few months. Thank you, Denver. You truly are an amazing person, and I hope you find the happiness you deserve. Fly high, my friend.

Love,

Chip

P.S. I want you to fly Cleo up north and let her choose where to spread my ashes. Have her pick somewhere that speaks to her heart, somewhere beautiful she'll never forget. No rush, whenever she's ready. I'm not going anywhere. ;)

I blink a few times to keep the tears at bay. *How the hell am I supposed to say no now, old man?*

My phone rings over the Bluetooth, and Savannah's name runs along my dashboard screen. She's the only person who probably remembers today was the will reading. I bet she uses nine different colors in her planner for each of our siblings' schedules. These days she must be using ten to account for Liam—my best friend turned her boyfriend.

"Hey, Sav," I answer.

"I'm glad I caught you. I didn't know if you had an excursion or something for Lifetime Adventures."

I tap my fingers on the steering wheel. Does she really not remember what was going on today? "No. It's winter and Chip hasn't—didn't do a great job of booking trips, what with him dying."

Savannah is quiet for a moment. "I'm sorry."

"I know you are."

There's another long beat of silence that I don't fill.

"I wanted to check a date with you for another eighties movie night, but you've got a lot going on. It can wait."

"You're being nice," I say with suspicion in my tone.

"I'm always nice these days."

One good thing about my best friend shacking up with my sister is that he dug so deep inside her, he brought back the Savannah who doesn't take everything so seriously—the one from before my parents died.

I say nothing, waiting for her to ask about the will reading.

"Actually, time to be not so nice. When do you think you'll be getting me the rent?" she asks.

I guarantee Phoenix hasn't paid her either. "I don't know. I haven't been able to pilot because of the excursions, but you remember his will reading was today, right?"

My question is met with silence.

"Shit, I forgot. I should've been there with you."

Before Liam, she would have. Not that she needed to though. I can handle myself fine with Luther Lloyd. "It's okay."

"No, it's not. I should—"

"Stop it, Sav. You have a life, and besides, I'm twenty-seven. But there is something I wanted to talk to you and Austin about." My two oldest siblings are like my pseudo parents. One of them will tell me what to do.

"Okay," she says warily. "How about dinner? We can meet wherever. I'll call Austin."

"Sure. How about six o'clock at Terra and Mare? I want Rome in on this too."

"Okay."

"See you then."

"Denver?" Her voice holds that soothing tone she uses when she fears something is wrong.

"It's all good. Just need some advice."

Another few seconds of silence. "I'll see you tonight."

"Thanks."

We hang up and I file out of the truck, my feet crunching on the snow as I make my way to the office doors. I lose my traction but recover before falling on my ass, which brings back memories of Cleo's fall from hours earlier.

Maybe she's not the only one who needs to get new shoes.

AT SIX-FIFTEEN, I walk through the back doors of Terra and Mare. Rome is in the kitchen wearing his chef jacket and hat, looking professional. It still takes me a second sometimes to remember that he's done a lot of growing up over the past couple of years.

"Where's my favorite niece and nephew?" I ask, stealing a piece of beef and sliding up on the counter.

Rome eyes where my ass is on the counter and rolls his eyes. "They're upstairs with Harley. Did you forget you said six to everyone?"

Colin returns from the walk-in refrigerator and I fist-bump him.

"It is six," I say around the piece of beef.

"It's six-fifteen," Rome says.

I look around for a clock and find one over the doorway to the dining room. I shrug. "Close enough."

Rome blows out a breath and Colin chuckles as he cuts peppers. I snag a piece of red pepper and Colin slides a pile over to me on the corner of the cutting board. Colin's good people.

"Let's go. Sav and Austin are already here." Rome grabs a plate with beef and a potato dish on it. "You good, Colin?"

"Yeah," Colin says, and Rome looks back at him with gratitude.

I jump off the counter, smack Colin on the back, and pick up a few more red peppers. I shouldn't have skipped lunch.

The dining room is three-quarters full, and my oldest sister and brother are in the corner table by the street, talking to one another.

"What's up?" I ask, sliding into a chair next to Austin.

"Isn't that the question we should ask you?" Austin says.

Savannah sips her wine and leans back in her chair. She's dressed as though she came right from work, and Austin is in his classic jeans and button-down after teaching biology at the high school. Rome places the dish down and holds up his finger to go to the bar.

I should be thankful I can call a last-minute meeting and my family comes. They're the only ones I can ever count on.

Rome returns with a beer for me and water for him. He dishes out food while Sav and Austin focus on me.

"Chip left me half the company," I blurt.

Savannah blinks in surprise. "And what about his daughter?"

"She got the other half." I take a pull off my beer.

"Oh." She sighs and sips her wine again, looking over the rim of her glass at Austin.

"And?" Austin asks.

"And I'm not sure what to do. She comes from that rich family and I know she wants to buy me out. We all know I can't buy her out. Not that I'd want to run a company on my own. But I don't even know if I want to run a company at all, let alone with her."

Rome finishes dishing out the food and is surprisingly quiet, putting his napkin in his lap and positioning his silverware on either side of his plate.

"Well, let her buy you out then," Austin says and eyes Savannah.

She shrugs. "If you don't want to do it, then sell it to her."

I have to admit, I thought there'd be some pushback. They all have their opinions on my life, wanting me to strive to be more responsible, to do something more. I thought maybe this would be the ideal opportunity for them to push me.

"Rome?" I ask.

He stares at me with eyes that match my own. "I'm not sure why you want any of our advice. We're not the ones who'll have to live with the decision."

That's not the answer I thought my twin brother would give me. I get that parenthood has changed him, but since when doesn't he have an opinion?

"Hey, how is Holly feeling?" Savannah asks out of nowhere. "She looked a little pale the other night."

Austin cringes. "She's fine. Maybe it was your cooking." He laughs, tipping back his beer bottle.

"Funny, jerk." She picks up her fork and stabs a piece of meat.

"Can we please get back to me?" I ask.

They all turn my way.

"What do you want to do? This isn't about us. We can't give you the answer." Austin picks up his fork and eats.

"Sure, you can. What do you think I should do? I mean, Savannah, running a company sucks, right?"

Rome buries his head in his meal. What's up with him tonight?

Austin glances at Savannah.

She shrugs, finishes chewing, and sets down her fork. "Rome, this is awesome. Can I order a to-go for Liam? He's at the shop and I was gonna stop by there after."

"Can we please stop talking about your significant others?" My voice is loud enough that the table beside us glances over.

It got my siblings' attention though.

Savannah gives me her motherly eyes. "Running a company sucks at times, but there're a lot of benefits as well. Truth is, I love that we're able to give people employment. That something I do affects this town in a positive way. It sucks when it's negative and those days are hard, but as much as I sometimes hate it, I'm not sure I would do anything different."

Of course, she's anal and OCD. Plus, she went into an established company. Chip let this one idle for too long and it has languished. I suspect he was sick for longer than he let on.

"But you get to do it all by yourself."

Savannah tilts her head. "Have you ever heard of someone named Grandma Dori?"

I cut into my beef. "I get your point. But if I can't buy Cleo out, I'll be doing it with her, and she's just terrible."

Austin snickers, and when I look his way, he deflects by shoving a pile of potatoes into his mouth.

"Are you asking us for a loan?" Savannah asks. "Because Bailey Timber can't invest in anything right now. Maybe Wyatt?"

"I'm not asking my brother-in-law for a loan." I shove a piece of meat into my mouth.

Damn, my brother can cook. This is delicious.

"Sorry, bro, I can't," Rome says. "Between the restaurant and the kids, we're strapped."

"Here's an idea, maybe you guys use protection," Austin comments with a sour note to his voice, which is weird.

"For your information, we were using protection when both our kids were conceived. My sperm are just so powerful that they conquer anything in their path." He looks at me. "Watch out, dude."

"I've been lucky up until now." I take another swig of my beer.

Austin grumbles while Rome sips his water.

"I have to get back into the kitchen. Sorry I can't loan you." He stands and squeezes my shoulder.

"Jesus, I'm not asking for a loan. I'm asking for some advice, which you all have been happy to give me until I find myself in the middle of a fork in the road."

Rome sits back down, and his shoulders fall. Savannah's lips turn down, and Austin keeps eating.

"Listen," Rome says, "there's a reason Chip left you half the company. I've seen you run away from responsibility your entire life. Maybe this is the one time you don't run."

"We can't decide this for you," Austin adds. "Consider this a giant leap into maturity."

Rome pats my shoulder and walks back into the kitchen.

I put my head in my hands.

"Denver," Savannah sighs, but I'm not picking up my head.

"Excuse me?" Someone comes to the table. "I just wanted to say how happy we are that you've stepped up to take over Lifetime Adventures. Chip was such an integral part of this town, I can't imagine losing the business too."

I raise my head to see who the voice belongs to. I don't know the man standing at the end of the table, but I remember seeing him at the funeral, talking to Cleo. "You knew him?"

"I did. He was a great man."

I pick up my beer and raise it. "That's for sure."

The man smiles. "Have a good night."

With that, I watch him walk out on to Main Street as if he was a mirage.

"How did he find out?" I wonder.

But my question gets answered when the cocked eyebrows of my brother and sister imply that I'm stupid.

Austin pulls out his phone, hits a few buttons, and hands it over. The Lake Starlight Buzz Wheel is on the screen, and the local gossip blog has a picture of Cleo and me on the steps of Luther Lloyd's office building.

Which means if I turn this opportunity down, I don't only disappoint Chip, but the entire town.

Perfect.

FOUR

Cleo

Phil gives Bridget a hug as my mom and I embrace, then we switch partners before we watch our parents walk onto the tarmac, out to the plane, and up the stairs. Neither of them give us a look back or one last wave. Not that I'm surprised.

When I went to college, I was put on a plane with a suitcase and a promise that my stuff would be delivered the next day. I arrived on campus and watched everyone's parents crying, the moms clinging to their children until the last possible second, while I pretended I was the lucky one because mine hadn't come.

"Just us now!" Bridget slides her arm through mine like she always does, and we watch the engines start and the plane roll down the runway. "Daddy said I can stay as long as I want."

Truth is, I'm not sure how long I want Bridget here. I like to do things on my own, whereas Bridget likes people to do things for her.

"Let's go back to the hotel and do a spa treatment and order room service." Her eyes are already rolling back into her head and her voice lowering to a whisper as if she just dipped into the warm water.

"I have to go to my dad's. We can stay there."

Her arm slides out of mine. "I'm not staying there."

"Why not?" My forehead wrinkles.

"How do you even have to ask that question? It's dark and dirty and messy and just no."

I try not to get my back up. My dad and I weren't overly close, but I'm still dealing with the loss of him and her comment comes off as insensitive.

"And to think people say you're snobby," I say as we climb into the Uber I called for.

"I'm not snobby."

I say nothing because we don't lie to one another. Plus, I have bigger things to worry about right now.

Bridget leans forward to tell the Uber driver, "Glacier Point Resort in Lake Starlight."

"He knows. I had to tell him when I put it in the app."

Bridget smiles widely at the guy.

"Sure thing. I'm from Lake Starlight, so no worries," he says. I look at the guy's security uniform, and he catches me doing so in the rearview mirror. "Security at the airport and an Uber driver. I'm sorry about your father, Cleo." He turns in his seat and puts out his hand. "Duke Thompson."

I shake his hand. He could've gotten my name from the Uber app, but he would've had to know my dad to know about me.

"How do you know about her father?" Bridget asks.

Duke chuckles. "Your dad never told you?"

"Told me what?"

He pulls away from the curb, but we immediately stop

at a light. "Buzz Wheel. There's an online blog that reports the town news. You and Denver Bailey are gonna run Lifetime Adventures together, huh? My bet was on Denver, but—"

"I'm sorry, what is Buzz Wheel?" Bridget looks as if we asked her to go work in a fast food joint. Her small nose crinkles in my direction and she mouths 'Buzz Wheel' to me.

Duke passes his phone to us, and Bridget snatches it before I can. She laughs and turns the phone to me.

"You're famous, sis," she says.

I take the phone from her hand, and sure enough, there's a picture of Denver Bailey and me. Actually, I'm on my ass on the sidewalk and Denver is looking like a saint, holding out his hand for me. Great first impression.

I start to read the article to myself, but Bridget grabs the phone back. "Let me read it. To practice for the weather girl job."

I suppress my eye roll. Bridget called in a favor with her dad and is going to be interviewed for the weekend weather girl down at a Texas news station.

She clears her throat. "'No surprise that Denver Bailey would run to a woman in distress.'"

"Distress? I wasn't in distress."

Bridget nods. "Definitely not in distress." She glances from me to the phone, asking for permission to continue. "'But the fact that the woman is the late Chip Dawson's estranged daughter—'"

"Estranged? I wasn't estranged. I've been up here. Just because I don't attend the stupid Founder's Day parade—"

Bridget puts her hand on my thigh to stop me. It's then that I notice my heartbeat is at max pace.

"Go ahead," I say.

"Okay, I'm going to start at the beginning. Try not to interrupt, you're ruining my flow."

I roll my eyes and nod, watching the snowbanks at the side of the road whizz by.

She clears her throat again. "'No surprise that Denver Bailey would run to a woman in distress. But the fact that the woman is the late Chip Dawson's estranged daughter, who just inherited all of Chip's assets, is the surprise. Rumors spread while Chip was ill that these two don't see eye-to-eye. No one really knows why there's so much tension between Cleo and Denver, and more rumors have spread around town today that the two of them are now business partners. Chip left each of them fifty percent of Lifetime Adventures.

"'I think I speak for all of us when I say that it will be interesting to see how it plays out. Denver Bailey, who can't commit to a goldfish, and a woman who hasn't a clue how to dress for an Alaskan winter and probably shouldn't be the leading authority on how to survive it. At least we know one thing—it will be entertaining to watch these two from afar.

"'I do wish them luck. We lost Chip Dawson too soon, so the fact that his company will live on can give us all comfort.

"'In other news, there must be something in the Bailey genes, because pictures were snapped of Savannah Bailey and Liam Kelly making out outside his tattoo shop the other night. As lifers of Lake Starlight, they should know that even at one in the morning, there are eyes everywhere.'"

Bridget hands the phone back to Duke but quickly pulls up the site on her own phone. "Savannah and Liam sound like my kind of people." She leans back into her seat and studies the screen for a moment. "I want to make it in there." She squeezes her head between the two front seats. "How do I get mentioned in there?"

Duke laughs. "Most people don't want to be mentioned in there."

"Oh, Bridget thinks the Kardashians are goals," I say.

Duke laughs again. "Don't worry, Cleo. It's only up for twenty-four hours, then it disappears and a new one is put up."

"Thank God," I say. "At least there's a small silver lining."

"I hate when you say that," Bridget says.

"I don't care."

"You always look at the bad side of everything. Your dad died. That does suck." Her hand finds my leg again and she squeezes. "But he left you his company."

"Half."

"Half with a hot guy who owns the other half."

I blow out a breath. She doesn't understand. She has her trust fund.

"I mean, you're the baddest bitch I know. Come on. Stop moping. Who the hell cares about this Buzz Wheel thing?" Bridget asks.

"You seem to care." I look at her and raise an eyebrow.

She shrugs. "You know what I mean. Go in there and show that Denver Bailey who's boss."

Bridget's little pep talk has me feeling hopeful for the first time today.

"Be done with the negativity. It doesn't make up for losing your dad, but he obviously thought you could do this. We're going to spend the rest of the day relaxing at the spa, and you're going to wake up tomorrow ready to win this war."

Duke's gaze pings from me to Bridget and back to me, a small smile tipping his lips.

"How? He has the survival and piloting skills I don't."

"Remember that time we went camping?" Bridget asks. "With everyone after we graduated?"

"You mean when you and Miguel rented an RV for all of us to 'camp' in?"

"Yeah, and we only had that one bathroom and shower for all of us?" Her body shakes a little as though she has the heebie-jeebies. "You're the one who started our fire."

"With a match," I deadpan.

Duke swerves a bit on the road from laughing so hard.

"And when we got lost after Miguel wanted to try hiking because he'd just bought all that new North Face gear?"

"What about it?"

She nudges me. "You got us out of there."

She has a point but being a survivalist for eight spoiled rich kids isn't the same as being dropped somewhere deep in the woods and finding your way out. I'm not even sure I'd want to get on those small planes. "I don't know the first thing about—"

Her hand covers my mouth. "That sounded like negativity to me."

I yank my face away from her hand. "It's the truth—" She pinches my arm. "Ouch!"

"Every time you say you can't, I'm going to pinch you."

"That's abuse."

She shakes her head and her auburn hair swings side to side. It always looks as though she's had it professionally done every day. "No, it's sisterly love."

"Technically, you're not my sister."

Her lips turn down and she pinches me again.

"Damn it!" I put my hand on my arm. "Stop it."

"I'll stop it after you start finding the positivity in this situation. You got this, and I'm going to stay here as long as it takes."

I smile at the best thing that came from my mom deciding her life's mission was to marry rich. "Love you," I say with tears in my eyes—everything from the past week catching up with me.

She lays her head on my shoulder. "Love you back."

We're quiet for the rest of the ride to the resort.

I love Bridget and her rah-rah cheerleader attitude, but Bridget can stay on Daddy's dime as long as she wants. We might've grown up together, but we live different lives and sometimes she forgets that I don't have a safety net. Especially since my dad just died.

FIVE

Denver

Since my siblings didn't offer much advice about the boulder that landed in my lap, I head down the street to talk to Liam. Surely my best friend, who is an entrepreneur himself, will have sound advice. Bonus, he knows me as well as anyone.

The problem is that Savannah, my sister and now girlfriend of Liam, is walking beside me, carrying his dinner. "I really think Liam is going to love this dish. The other night—"

I hold my hand up to stop her. "I don't wanna hear about how you paint one another and roll around as foreplay."

She scoffs, but believe me, they've done it. Liam's found a freaky side of Savannah I never thought existed. Since I'm speaking as their previous roommate, you don't need a second opinion.

She wrinkles her face. "I'd never share that with you."

I wiggle my body as though I'm trying to get a bug off

me and jump up and down. "Jesus, Sav, I don't wanna picture that."

"You and Liam used to swap stories all the time."

I stare at her for a long, drawn-out second. "He wasn't screwing my sister at the time."

"If you don't want me to share, then don't share with the rest of us."

"I don't share."

"Um. Do you know how many girls I had to listen to scream my brother's name or—and this is the *pièce de résistance*—the girl who was so explicit in telling you exactly what she wanted that I went out for a run at one in the morning and almost got eaten by a bear?"

"Let's get one thing straight, she was telling me to keep doing what I was already doing. I don't need that much direction—I've got it covered." We stop at Smokin' Guns and I hold the door open for her. "And... slight exaggeration."

"Maybe the bear part, but do you know how many times I slept with my earbuds in?"

Our conversation dies with the sound of tattoo guns and chatter. Liam peeks up from where he's bent over a sketchpad and then smiles the smile he only seems to use on Savannah.

"Hey, babe," he says.

"I brought you dinner." She holds up the Terra and Mare box.

"I'm starved. Thanks." He stands.

She waves to Rhys and Moose, who each give her a nod. My sister and Liam disappear into the back. I don't even wanna know what they're about to do.

Then I notice a dark-haired girl lying with her chest on

the table, only in her bra and pants. Something seems familiar about her, but I can't place it.

"What's up, Moose?" I grab a spare chair and roll it over.

"Nothing." He sneaks me a sly grin then peeks down at the girl.

Does he like her? Moose is an overly tall bald guy who has barely an inch of skin without ink. He got his nickname because he has the same demeanor as a moose—he's grumpy and can't stand people. If you provoke him, you'd better run as fast as you can. His size alone fits the name.

I look at the girl again. Cute ass, but I'm a breast man, so I shrug at him like '*sure, whatever gets you off.*'

When I think about breasts, Cleo comes to mind. Another downfall of hers is her great rack. I know it's crude, but damn, she's blessed with more than a handful. If I didn't loathe her as much as I do, I'd totally take a chance and ask if I could cop a feel.

Fuck. What am I doing? I need to straighten out my head.

The brunette turns her head with Moose's direction, and that same experience with Savannah where I felt as if I had spiders crawling all over is repeated.

"Shit. Ew. Moose just had me check out your ass." I stand, the chair hitting something behind me.

My sister Phoenix looks at me with her evil dark eyes and smirks. "How did you not recognize me? You see me every day."

"I don't look at your ass!" I say.

She and Moose share a "got him" expression, and she laughs. It's then that I finally look at her back and see a familiar blackbird tattoo.

"You got the same tattoo as Brooklyn and Juno?"

"Yeah, I'm kind of pissed that no one told me we have a family tattoo."

"We don't."

"Rome, Brooklyn, and Juno all have the same one."

"And there's nine of us, so that's only a third."

Rhys slow-claps behind me. "Look at the mathematician."

I flip him off behind my back.

"I love that it represents Mom and Dad, so I got one. Why haven't you gotten one?"

I grab the stool and wheel it back over. "Because I'm not a follower."

She rolls her eyes. "That's weak."

Moose continues with her tattoo. I can't deny that I love the blackbird design. When Rome got it done, I almost got the same one, but we're twins, so that would've been freaky.

"I told Sedona, so next time she comes back to town, she's going to have Moose do hers."

"No offense, Moose, but why didn't you get Liam to do it?" I ask.

Liam is our family tattoo artist. Well, he's mine and Rome's. Brooklyn and Juno were both a one-and-done.

"He said he didn't want to chance Savannah being mad at him because he really likes getting laid every night."

I shiver. Again. "Can they not keep their sex talk in the bedroom?"

"You'd brag too." Liam comes in from the back and sits down with his sketchpad. "You're all just jealous."

"We're not jealous," Phoenix and I say in unison.

"I am." Moose raises his hand.

"I get laid every night." Rhys laughs.

Moose coughs out, "Bullshit."

"So I heard you want to talk to me?" Liam says to my back.

I push back on my heels, wheeling myself over to him. "Savannah's got a big mouth."

He cocks his head. "Remember, I love you like a brother, but she's number one now." I pretend to throw up, and he balls up the sketch he was working on and throws it at my head. "Stop acting like you're thirteen."

Unraveling the paper—because anything Liam draws is a damn masterpiece—I look at a picture of a flower with a stem that looks like an infinity symbol. "Has dating my sister made you soft?"

"It's an orchid." He looks back toward the office. "I'm trying to convince her. It means love, beauty, and strength. The infinity symbol is obvious."

I put it on his bench. "Sav get a tattoo? Yeah right."

Liam shrugs. "I gotta try."

"Well, you've definitely found a Savannah I never knew, so I shouldn't say never."

Just at that moment, Savannah joins us, and Liam taps his lap. She sits down and finds the orchid sketch on the table in front of them. She studies it for a moment then looks at Liam.

"Just a thought," he says.

Her gaze moves to it then to me. I raise my eyebrows and she looks at Liam. "We'll talk about it."

Liam kisses her cheek as if she said yes. I have to be missing something. How can her '*maybe*' give him such joy?

"You'd get a tattoo?" I blurt out.

She smiles at Liam. "Who says I don't already have one?"

They're playing some game I'm not playing, and irritation grows inside me from watching them together. Back in the day, this place was my safe haven. Liam and I would've already been halfway to fixing my problem. But now he's had to eat his dinner first—which I hope didn't include any part of my sister's body—and I've had to wait for him to come out, and now she's sitting on his lap, monopolizing his attention.

"Okay, you know what? It's Denver time."

I stand and take her hand, but Liam pretends to hold her to him. When I tug harder, he growls like a dog and Savannah cracks up. I look around the room as if I'm in a parallel universe, and everyone must share my thinking.

"My advice wasn't good enough," she says, standing.

I catch Liam tapping her ass. If I make it through today without throwing up, I'll be shocked. Savannah disappears into the back room, and Liam taps his work bench.

"What?" I ask.

"It's been a while, and you know the table and ink helps you solve your problems. You trust me, right?"

With my life. And he's not lying about a new piece of ink helping me figure out my shit. When I graduated high school not knowing what I wanted to do, I was Liam's guinea pig, which resulted in a kickass anchor with a compass face that said I'd always find my way home. He's tried to get me to cover it up but the hell if I will. It's a Liam Kelly original. I think he knew what I wanted before I did.

He gave me a horseshoe on my right shoulder blade after my plane went down a few years ago and I almost died. Then an olive branch along my right ribcage when Rome met Harley, and I struggled with becoming second in my twin's life. The only part he hasn't touched is my chest.

Isn't this the reason I came here?

I toss my shirt and lie on my back. "How did you know?"

Just like the moment when we were six, and we agreed to have a toilet paper party in the library bathroom. We're always on the same wavelength. Well, except for Savannah. We're definitely not on the same wavelength there.

Moose finishes up with Phoenix, and she says she's going to go bother Savannah about something in the back. Liam and I share a look that says we know the screaming between the two should commence in five minutes.

The idea of being a business owner is my sole focus as Liam washes his hands, puts on his gloves, does the stencil, and returns. Can I do what Chip asked of me? He did so much for me over the years. Is there even a part of me that could say no?

"Give me a con," Liam says, starting the outline of the tattoo stencil he chose for me.

"It'll be restrictive, cut into my lifestyle."

"How so? You'd still get to spend time outside. You could book as little or as many clients as you want." Liam never looks at me, keeping his eyes on the ink he's gouging into my skin, wiping every so often with a precision he's perfected.

"I'd have to keep things afloat. That's a lot of pressure."

I can't tell because he's quiet, but I assume he's got his classic smirk. We both know people would never rely on me.

"True, but you enjoy the excursions, don't you?"

I wince when he hits my rib. "I do, but there're so many what-ifs. Plus, it's not even just me. I have to run it with his daughter."

He nods. "Cleo Dawson. Sav says it's half and half?"

"Yeah."

"She has no experience."

"Exactly. She mentioned buying me out."

His eye catches mine as he dips the gun into the ink. "And you're cool with that?"

"I'm not sure. I mean, I hate the thought of Chip's company failing. There's no possible way she can keep it going on her own. I saw the books when I was managing things for him while he was sick. He's barely making payroll at this point. Plus, let's be honest, it's super outdated. Survivalists want thrills these days."

He's quiet for a moment. "Sounds to me like you've given this a lot of thought?"

"I have. The reason I love bush piloting is because of the places it takes me. I can fly to places few people have ever been, and it's something I don't want to give up. Leading excursions is okay, but not as thrilling as bush piloting."

"Maybe you can do both or combine them somehow? Maybe you're the man to give Lifetime Adventures a new start."

"But?"

He dips the gun into the ink. "Listen, let's cut the crap. We both know you wanna do it, but you're scared. I get it. When I opened this place, I was scared shitless, but I couldn't be happier being my own boss. You keep going around asking everyone for their opinion as though you want someone to tell you not to do it."

I turn my head away from him. The truth he's spilling is hard to hear.

He busies himself with my tattoo while I think of the last time I asked anyone for advice. I do what I want, damn the consequences most of the time. Chip was always one of my go-to guys, and I already know what he thought.

Why am I so quick to push people to tell me not to do it? Liam's right—I'm scared to fail. I like my life simple and easy.

As everything runs through my mind, Liam finishes the tattoo and sits me up to look in the mirror. I examine the blackbird tattoo right under my left pec. Along my ribcage are two blackbirds sitting on a branch. *Damn, Liam.* He's way too talented for his own good. He figured out a way to give me the blackbirds without copying what my sisters have.

He smiles at me over my shoulder. He doesn't say anything about the symbolism of having the two blackbirds right next to my heart.

"Thanks, man."

As I'm about to sit back down for him to bandage me up, the door of Smokin' Guns opens, and in walks none other than Cleo Dawson.

SIX

Cleo

"Isn't that...?" Bridget elbows me in the rib, and I step to the right, holding my side. She had way too much red wine at the restaurant.

How did I not know Denver has ink? And why do I find that so damn attractive? Other than our friend Ford, who went rogue from the country club crowd, no one in our circle has any tattoos. Tatted skin has had a soft place in my heart for years, and now I'm staring at the man I hate and all the blood in my veins is zeroing in between my legs.

"Cleo Dawson." Denver's gaze follows the curves of my body in my fitted coat as if he knows what I look like naked, and my body responds with shivers.

"Denver Bailey." I purposely add a cold tone to my voice, but the way Bridget is staring at me, she knows it's forced.

Her eyes widen as though she's silently asking me why I never told her that I wouldn't mind screwing him too.

"Can I help you ladies?" A clean-cut guy with dark hair and no piercings or ink steps up to the desk.

"I'd like a tattoo," Bridget says with the bravado of a veteran customer.

I shake my head at him behind her. I brought her in here to humor her before we go to the hotel, where I'll give her a few more glasses of wine before she passes out. When she wakes in the morning, I'll tell her that I saved her from permanently marking her skin.

"What are you looking for?"

I shake my head more firmly, but the guy isn't paying any attention to me. If Bridget was worried at all about whether she's considered attractive in this town, this guy is ready to prove to her that she's a ten. He's gawking at her like most men do, which means he'll please her and go against my wishes.

"Something cute and feminine," Bridget says.

He nods. "A flower? A heart? Where do you want it?"

The door opens and five people come into the shop, each of them with a plethora of tattoos. Yeah, we're definitely like nuns at the *Playboy* mansion in here.

Bridget leans over the counter. "Somewhere private."

I reach for her. "Really, Bridge, let's go. You do not need a tattoo."

She slides her arm out of my hold. "Yes, I do."

"Isn't there some sort of law about tattooing people under the influence?" I plead.

"It's not a law," the guy says with a shrug.

"Rhys." The guy who was with Denver comes over. I realize we met before when he came into Lifetime Adventures asking for a donation to a charity auction when my dad was sick. I'm not sure of his name, though.

My eyes betray me as I watch Denver put his shirt back

on, a bandage over where he got his tattoo. With his shirt on, he's back to being a clean-cut guy.

"She's had a lot?" Rhys, as I now know him to be, asks.

"Just some red wine." Bridget can't hold back her slur.

The guy who came over looks at me. "Cleo Dawson?"

I blow out a breath. "Yep."

"Liam Kelly." He puts out his hand. "We've met before." Jeez, I forgot how good-looking he is. What's in the water of this town to make everyone so beautiful?

I shake his hand. "Good to see you again."

"I'm this one's best friend." He nods toward Denver.

Figures.

"So you heard we're hot news in Lake Starlight, right?" Denver joins the two men on the other side of the desk.

I narrow my eyes. "It's ridiculous. I never even knew that thing existed."

"I just saw another one of you. You're a chef?" Bridget points at Denver.

"Twin, remember?" I tell her.

She looks quizzically at me then nods like 'yeah you're right.'

I know I'm right.

"Why don't you go help those people over there, Rhys? I think they're your next clients." Liam points at the people scouring the board of tattoos on display.

"You can take them, I'd rather do this one." Rhys's gaze hasn't strayed from Bridget.

"You haven't had your fill of flowers this month?" Liam says to Rhys.

"It just makes me her best option. I'm an expert." Rhys leans on the counter, and I send a pleading look to Liam.

"Rhys, go." Liam nudges the guy away, then he turns to my Bridget. "Listen, I'd love to give you a tattoo, but you're going to bleed so bad, it'll look shitty when it heals. So if you want to come back tomorrow, I'd be happy to tattoo you."

"I want him to tattoo me." She points at Rhys.

"Sure, he can tattoo you... tomorrow."

Bridget turns to me, but her gaze detours quickly back to the guy giving her all the attention. "When do you get off?"

Rhys sends a desperate look to Liam.

Liam is definitely the boss then.

"He has a few more customers, but you're welcome to hang around here." Liam smiles then shoots his gaze to Denver and me. "If you two wanna talk?"

"*No*," we say at the same time.

"Okay. Well, I have to get to another customer. Nice seeing you again. I'm sure I'll see you around." He walks from behind the counter and signals to some guy to come over.

"Wait for me? I'll be a half hour tops," Rhys says to Bridget.

"We're going to the hotel," I tell him, sliding my arm through Bridget's.

"I'll wait," she says, ignoring me. "Can I watch you work?"

"Sure." Rhys opens up the little half door of his station, and Bridget saunters in.

"Bridge."

She turns around and smiles at me, holding up her finger. I've been in this situation more than once, and after everything over the past couple weeks, I don't have any fight left inside me. When I turn my attention away from her, Denver's staring at me.

"What?" I ask him.

"Still going to buy me out?"

"You said it wasn't for sale."

"Maybe it is for the right offer."

I definitely don't want him to know that buying him out isn't a possibility. "Maybe we should find a buyer together."

He sits on the stool behind the counter. "You go from buying me out to getting out altogether?"

"I'm just saying. I have access to his accounts." I look around and lean forward. "He had no money."

"I figured. I mean, I've been in charge these past few months and the company was barely making payroll."

My shoulders slump. I'd hoped the company was thriving and Dad was taking too little for himself. The idea of him struggling makes me want to burst into tears, but I won't do that here. "Are you telling me we inherited a broke company?"

"It's not like it can't bounce back." He props his feet up on the edge of the counter, and I notice all the doodling and writing on the piece of wood.

"How's that?"

"Without your involvement." He lays his arms lazily around his knees and his long fingers tap on his shins to the beat of the music coming from the overhead speakers.

It's Imagine Dragons, but I can't remember the name of the song. Not that it matters.

"You forget that you need my involvement," I say.

"Not really. You know you don't want it."

"Why do you say that?"

He laughs and his gaze falls to my peacoat. "How warm are you right now?"

"I'm warm."

He nods toward outside, where flurries drift down. "Warm enough to spend the night out there?"

"I don't have to do the excursions, so what does it matter?" My fists clench at my sides.

"You wouldn't last five minutes without complaining about how cold you are. What on Earth makes you think you could run an excursion company that isn't headed to some rich beach resort?"

Denver's right, but I'll never tell him that. I should've tried to learn more from my dad, but Denver underestimates my desperation. I have nothing except this. Failure isn't an option.

"And you couldn't stay on schedule for five minutes. Not to mention a daily routine probably wouldn't work for you."

His feet drop and he stands.

Oh, I hit a nerve. Good.

"Don't get all your facts about me from Buzz Wheel," he says.

"So what's your goldfish's name then?"

He studies me for so long my straight back almost falters, and when his hands land on the edge of the counter and he leans forward, my breath hitches for a moment. His earthy, clean scent reaches me.

"Just sell off his shit and leave town," he says in a low voice.

"Not gonna happen. If anything, I'll stay to piss you off."

"You know I could drive you off." His cocky stance says he believes what he's spitting out.

"How do you figure?"

"Why would I tell you? That's like giving away my secrets."

I narrow my eyes, but he meets my challenge with a smirk. Bad energy surrounds us as if we're in the middle of a tornado that's picking up speed the longer neither of us speaks.

"This how you want it to go down?" He crosses his arms then winces and drops them.

"Oh, poor baby, graze that fresh tattoo?"

"Don't worry about me, princess, worry about yourself."

"*Ugh!*" I want to scream and yell and punch. Out of all the men I could be stuck in this situation with, it has to be him—an arrogant, cocky son of a bitch who wants to stay an adolescent child for the rest of his life.

"Okay, you two. Now you're disturbing *my* clients." Liam comes over, grabs my upper arm and Denver's, and leads us to the back hallway. He stops us and opens the door at the end of the hall.

A cute blonde with a messy bun who looks familiar peeks up from her computer with a pen in her mouth.

"Sorry, babe, these two need privacy," Liam says.

She smiles, shuts her computer and drops her pen, standing. "Cleo Dawson? Nice to see you again."

I give her a tight smile.

"Savannah Bailey." She nods at me.

"Of course. Another Bailey. You people are everywhere." I yank my arm from Liam's with unnecessary force because his grip was feather-light. If Bridget wasn't flirting with Rhys, I would've walked out of this place.

"Let them talk," Liam says.

Savannah slides between us. "Sure."

Liam pushes Denver into the office, and he catches his footing before his forehead meets a filing cabinet. Too bad. That would've given me great pleasure.

Before I can step inside, Savannah rushes back in, grabs her laptop, and smiles at me. Then the door shuts with a bang and we stand there quiet for a moment. Denver sits on the desk and puts his feet on the chair.

"What a gentleman you are."

His confused expression when he looks up says I have to explain myself.

"You don't let the lady choose her seat first?"

He kicks the chair my way. "By all means, princess. Sit."

"I'm not a princess."

He doesn't argue, instead blowing a frustrated breath from his mouth. "I don't wanna fight with you, but this is never going to work between us." His voice is calm and assured. "We can't both run the company."

I sit and cross my legs. His eyes follow my movement. I'd be lying if I said a thrill didn't shoot through my veins.

"I can't buy you out. That's not an option." I hate admitting that, but what choice do I have?

"Really?"

I meet his gaze so he knows I'm telling the truth, no matter how embarrassing it is. "Really. So unless you can buy me out, there aren't many options at the moment. Except sell it outright."

He studies me for a minute. "Why do you want the company?"

He asks the question I wish I had the answer to. I could give him lots of reasons—from my dad's legacy to wondering why the company always felt more important to my father than I did, to me finding my place in the world and how maybe I've been looking in all the wrong places. But for some reason, I choose to tell him the truth. "I don't know yet. You?"

He blows out a breath like he didn't like my answer. "Have you read your letter?"

"Yes."

"And?"

"And what?"

"What did it say?"

I uncross and cross my legs, shifting in my seat. "None of your business."

He nods, but his usual smirk shines bright. I'm assuming our letters are similar. If the reasons he gave Denver are as valid as the ones he gave me, we should be finding a way to save the company together instead of arguing about all the reasons the other person can't run it.

His shoulders slump. "Listen, your dad was my mentor. He taught me so much, so I'm gonna stick around and get this company to where it belongs, where he deserved for it to be. I can't commit to anything, but I can commit to that."

I blow out a breath and tip my head back.

"I'm trying here," he says.

He is, and I'm being the difficult one. "I can commit to that as well."

"So we're really going to do this together?"

"I guess so."

"If all else fails, we can sell," he says.

"Already getting your exit plan in place, I see?" I stand from the chair to head to the door.

I don't reach the door before his hand cups my elbow. He stands behind me, his breath uneven. "I'm offering suggestions. Believe me, if I do this, I'm all in. I'm not a half-assed kinda guy." He sounds sincere but quiet, as though he doesn't want anyone to know that about him.

"I'll see you tomorrow, Denver." My hand is on the doorknob.

"Just to show you how great of a partner I'll be, I bet I can get your stepsister out of here."

I turn around and he's still so close, his lips front and

center. I'd only have to rise on my tiptoes and mine could meet his. I bet he knows how to take care of a woman, knows his way around. God, it's been way too long for me. "Winner gets coffee?"

"I like cold brew, black." His hand twists the doorknob, and he steps out into the hall.

I'm not even out of the room when the fire alarm goes off and everyone scrambles. Bridget is frantically looking for me when I reach the front of the shop. I might not agree with his antics, but he was successful. Liam glares at Denver, and I think I'll get out of Dodge before the fight starts.

Denver winks at me as Bridget slides her arm through mine and we walk towards the exit. He mouths "cold brew, black" once more to make sure I understand he won that round.

SEVEN

Denver

Nancy is sipping her coffee, reading the *Lake Starlight Journal*. I swear, she, Grandma Dori's senior center, and Liam must be the only ones keeping that newspaper in business. She lifts her head up.

"Good morning," she says, placing her reading glasses on the paper and heading to the coffeepot.

"I'm going to say this again. You're not my personal assistant." I drop my computer bag and run over to the coffeepot before she can pour me a cup. My move strips her bright smile off her face.

"I always got Chip's coffee."

We've been over this, but I also understand that she's missing her twenty-year sidekick. I miss him too.

"Okay, but don't feel like you have to get me my coffee every morning."

She smiles and knocks me out of the way with her hip. "Black?"

I haven't had the heart to tell her I like cold brew. I'm

not really a hot drink kind of person unless I'm camping. Today isn't the day to mention it though, considering her red-rimmed eyes. She's grieving. We all are. Some of us just hide it better than others.

"Perfect," I say with as much of a smile as I can muster.

She pours it and hands me one of Chip's mugs. It's white with bold black writing that says, 'Best Boss Ever.' I reluctantly accept it to make Nancy's day slightly better.

"I'll be in the office. We don't have anything planned today, but I'm pretty sure Cleo will be in."

"I'll ring you as soon as she arrives."

"She's part owner, so she can just come in." Although I imagine for a moment Cleo's reaction if Nancy stopped her and said she had to buzz me first. A satisfactory gleam must hit my face because Nancy's smiling from ear to ear when I look at her. "If you could get us last year's financials, that'd be great."

Her back straightens. "Yeah. Of course I can do that." She practically runs behind her desk. "Just give me a moment to boot this up."

We both look at the computer from the early two-thousands. It's on its last leg, and when she hits the start button, a buzzing sounds from it.

"That's typical. Ol' Faithful is pesky but reliable." She sits, putting her reading glasses on and closing up the newspaper.

I've never seen someone so enthusiastic to work. "Great. Thanks, Nancy."

"My pleasure." She hits a key over and over. The screen blinks on then turns black again. "Honestly, we're good. You go get your day started."

I nod and hesitate before I walk into the office, or what Chip referred to it as. I haven't done anything in here other than shift the paperwork to the side of the desk. Old maps are rolled up in the corner, and paper, now tinted yellow, hangs on the walls, advertising adventures with people from the eighties. It's an office. A small one with the stale scent of cigarette smoke, and I anticipate it'll feel even smaller when Cleo arrives.

I drop my bag in one of the two chairs around the table used for client consults. I wonder when the last time Chip had anyone come in here to book a trip? In this day and age, people plan these trips online. Going through his papers, I try to make sense of it all, but the bills with red stamps don't have to be explained to me. Chip didn't ask me to handle any of this when he was sick—I just had to take out the tours he was already committed to. I knew Lifetime Adventures wasn't doing so hot, but from the looks of these, we're a second away from closing our doors.

The office door opens, and a dick-raising scent hits my nostrils before I can look up.

Cleo stands in the doorway with a tray of cold brew coffees, one a caramel color and the other one midnight black. She's in jeans and a sweater, but her flats with no socks scream she's not a local.

"They're all I own, okay?" She comes in and I realize how much shorter she is without her usual heels on.

I shake my head at her. "We need to go shopping."

"Hey, is Nancy okay?" she whispers, searching for an empty place on the desk to put the coffees. "I walked in, she looked at my tray of coffees and started to cry. I brought her one, and I told her I wouldn't be offended if she didn't like it."

I lift my Best Boss mug. "She's missing your dad."

She purses her lips and nods, takes her drink and sits on the chair, legs crossed. The way her jeans are molded to her legs fills my mind with unwanted sexual thoughts of wrapping those legs around my waist. "So recruiting her to help me at his house isn't an option."

I lean back in my chair. "I'd say that's a negative for the moment."

"Do you think they..." She sips her drink, her eyebrows rising to her hairline.

"No. I don't think so." I rack my brain to remember their interactions. Nothing sexual comes to mind, but I tend not to notice everything around me. "I guess I could see it though. She's been single. He was single."

"Both of them being single doesn't mean they were together," she says using a tone that suggests I'm such a sleaze.

"Lonely people might, and I think they were both kind of lonely."

Chip always said he only needed a hot cup of coffee, a warm fire, and a sunrise every morning. He never mentioned wanting a warm body next to him, but who could blame him?

"Even if I was lonely, that doesn't mean I'd sleep with someone just to sleep with them."

"Are you throwing daggers my way?"

She smiles sweetly. "I have no idea what you mean."

I nod and let the topic go. We have a lot to go through. "I asked Nancy to bring in last year's financials. And side note, she'll need a new computer."

She nods. "She was pressing some button on the keyboard over and over when I walked in."

"Yeah, well, your dad never adopted new technology."

"You think? He still had a flip phone."

"Every time I texted him, he'd—"

"Call you?" She laughs a little. "Me too."

"I tried to text once from his phone, and it was a skill. Pressing a button three times before one letter came up?"

She shakes her head. "I never understood him." Her face falls, and she distracts herself by taking in the pictures on the wall.

I let a few moments of silence pass because I'm not sure what to say. I didn't understand my parents, but I was thirteen and selfish when they died.

I pick up the stack of bills. "Well, there're a lot of past dues here. I'm starting to think we might not be able to save this company."

She blows out her breath. "Nothing we can do but see how bad it is."

She slides her chair up to the other side of the desk, pulls her hair back into a ponytail, and takes a stack of papers to get started.

TWO HOURS LATER, we have two stacks of papers. The higher one being unpaid bills. The smaller one being invoices paid. A kindergartener could see where this company is going.

Nancy brought in the financials for not only last year but the last five years.

"Two years ago, he was going strong. It dwindled, but it got really bad once he got sick," Cleo says.

"I feel guilty. I should've been recruiting business. All I did was take out people he'd already booked. I could've actively been trying to get new business."

Cleo swivels her computer in my direction and leans back, propping one leg up on the edge of the chair. "There's not a ton you could've done. He not only doesn't have decent Wi-Fi in this office, his website is a disaster. He was working entirely on word of mouth."

I click a few things, but other than the same eighties pictures that adorn the wall, there's nothing that would make anyone choose this company.

"His name is huge on the professional survivalist network." Chip Dawson is a name most extremists and survivalists recognize. But as time goes by, new people in the industry might not be as familiar.

"We need to appeal to a more family-friendly crowd. Or do workplace team excursions," she says. "There're so many possibilities, but I think the client base is too narrow right now."

"Let me guess, you have an MBA?"

She shakes her head. "Just my bachelor's degree."

"I think Chip has a niche that we should maintain but find a better way to advertise to them."

She's already shaking her head, and I blow out a breath before having to listen to her disagreement.

"We need excursions for the non-thrill seekers. The ones who want to take a bus ride to tour a glacier or hike a trail, not climb a mountain."

"That's not Lifetime Adventures."

"But maybe it should be." She lets her hair out of her ponytail, and I watch it swing back and forth like a pendulum. I wonder if it's as soft as it looks.

"That's a different company than this one."

"That's because you're a thrill-seeker. You want the rush of being on the brink of death."

I tilt my head. "Had one of those already. I'm not looking for a repeat."

The accident I was in a few years ago shook me so hard, I almost quit bush piloting. My heart still flutters when I fly over the same spot where Griffin Thorne and I went down.

"Oh yes, I forgot you were famous for a few seconds."

"It wasn't me. It was the music producer I had on my back. You know, from saving his life."

She laughs, but her amusement says she's getting used to my dry humor. "That had to propel that ego of yours up to the same level as Mount Everest."

I shrug. She would never understand how profound that moment was to me.

"Anyway, we need to decide what we're going to do," I say. "After paying these bills, we need two months of clients solid in order to keep going. We can't be looking to change the way the business is run. We need to get in the black."

"Maybe we should sell?" She brings her knees to her chest and holds them tight to her body.

"Maybe," I agree and her gaze darts to mine. "What? You said it first."

"Because I want you to object."

"Why would I object?"

She rests her chin on her knees. "Because you love this. This is your thing."

"Not exactly."

She shifts her head so her cheek lies on her knee. She's as sad as Nancy, but she's trying to hide it.

I shake my head. "Let's just get this business into the black. I have a few connections I can call who might want to take a trip with me."

"And what about me?"

"You can stay here and be the pretty face." Her eyes narrow to slits and I kind of want to laugh, but I keep my composure. "I'm kidding."

"You know, I can survive the wilderness."

"Really?"

"Yes." Her non-verbal cues don't match her words in the slightest.

"Then when we go up to spread your dad's ashes, we can stay a few days."

"That's not for a few months."

"Perfect opportunity for you to watch the Discovery Channel and get some tips then."

She picks up a pen and throws it at me. The phone on the desk rings, and we both stare at it like, 'who the hell is calling?' Then I see it's the front desk.

"Hey, Nancy," I answer.

"There're some people here for Chip?"

Cleo and I look at one another, then at the phone as if it's going to give us all the answers.

"Who?" I ask.

"Selma Torres with *Uncovering America's Beauty*."

"Why's she here?" Cleo asks, and we stand at the same time.

"Let's find out."

EIGHT

Denver

Apetite woman who's dressed the complete opposite of Cleo stands in the other room. You'd think we're in the Arctic and preparing for a month-long blizzard. She's wearing a huge parka that reaches her ankles, where there are rubber-soled boots lined with fur.

"Chip?" She smiles and extends her hand.

Nancy cries, and Cleo slowly steps in front of Nancy's desk to block her from disrupting the conversation.

"Denver Bailey actually." I shake her hand. "This is Cleo Dawson."

"Nice to meet you." Cleo shakes her hand, but the woman looks confused.

"Are you Chip's wife?"

"No," Cleo answers but offers no explanation.

Great. I see this is all on me.

Two men stand behind Selma and can't stop looking at Nancy as she loudly blows her nose, adding to the stack of tissues next to the newspaper I'm sure she was reading when they came in. Great impression.

"Would you like to come into the office?" I ask.

"Can I ask what this is about?" Cleo asks before Selma can respond.

"We have business with Chip Dawson. I'm confused. This is Lifetime Adventures, right?" She looks around the room for a sign of some kind.

There isn't one, of course. Chip must've thought that once people got in here, they knew where they were.

"It is, but um…" I glance at Cleo. Nancy has stopped sobbing, so we can have a conversation right here. "Chip passed away two weeks ago."

A loud cry from Nancy echoes through the room.

Both men stare at her, one inching closer. "Is she okay?"

"She is," Cleo says. "Actually, maybe I'll take her to the restroom."

I grip her sweater before she can get away, and I tug her back to my side. She's helping me with this whether she likes it or not.

"Oh, I'm sorry for your loss," Selma says. "He put his name in to be part of a reality TV show based on excursion companies in Alaska. When we couldn't get ahold of him, my boss, who's familiar with Chip's reputation, asked me to come up here and find him."

I knew Chip was well-known in his circle, but not that his name alone could get him cast in a show. He didn't have an over-friendly, peppy personality, and his threshold for drama was minimal.

"Apologies," I say. "If we'd known that he'd had this going on, one of us would've contacted you." I look at Cleo, who hasn't added one thing to the conversation.

"Apology not necessary. I'm sure you've been busy with

other things given the situation." Selma nods to all three of us, including Nancy, who's trying to get herself together. Selma's comment only spurs another round of tears and uncontrollable crying.

Selma turns and talks to the younger guy of the two. "Zeke will be saddened by this news. We'll call him back at the hotel. Shame, the money might've been able to spruce up this waiting room."

The younger guy laughs. Yeah, it's not the Ritz Carlton in here. Not that I'd know because I've never been in one. But I'm sure Cleo has.

"Money?" I inch forward. "Chip was going to get paid to do the show?"

The guy with the gray beard nods with an eager expression as if he wants me to ask about it. But I think he'd do about anything to get Nancy to stop crying.

"Of course. Did you really think reality TV stars weren't paid? Every episode," Selma says. "Lots of them amp up their personalities to stay on air so they can keep the paycheck."

Cleo and I look at one another. All I can think about are the red past due stamps and the fact that our saving angel, named Selma, is standing in our waiting room. Cleo nods as if she can read my mind.

"We're the new owners." I wag my finger between us.

Selma's eyes shift from me to Cleo then to the younger man with her, who's also dressed for the tundra. "Are you a couple?"

"Hell no," I answer.

"As if," Cleo says with an eye roll. "I mean, no. We barely know one another."

Selma smiles and looks at the guy again. Like Cleo and I just did, they have a silent conversation of their own. "I don't know. Zeke was set on Chip, and you two don't look like you have much experience. Maybe if you were a couple. America loves to watch couples work together. Even better if there's trouble."

Growing up with sisters, I've seen my share of reality television. I know it skews toward the dramatic.

"How about I take you to lunch? You can see the town. Believe me, there should be a reality show based on it," I say. She continues to stand there, and I take that as a good sign. She's letting me convince her. "I'm one of nine kids."

"You are?" Cleo asks.

I nod. "Each of us are named after the city we were conceived in."

"You were?" Cleo asks again.

I nod. "My parents died when I was thirteen."

Cleo's shoulders fall and her hand touches my forearm briefly. I look at her and nod that it's okay.

"My brother raised me. He's a teacher married to the high school principal. My twin brother owns a restaurant in town." I think of anything else I could tell her. "My brother-in-law owns Glacier Point Resort."

"That's where we're staying," Selma says.

"Me too!" Cleo says, pointing at herself.

"Let's see, what else can I tell you…" I rack my brain for anything else that might be juicy and interesting enough to get Selma to consider us.

She looks at the young guy one last time. I want to step between them and ramble on all the reasons this could work, but before I have a chance, the outside door bursts open. A gush of cold wind enters the room, then someone pushes the young guy out of the way.

G'ma D stands in front of Selma, looking her up and down. "Oh, sweetie, it's Alaska, not Siberia." She approaches me and kisses each cheek. "I'm here to offer my business expertise. Savannah said you needed me." She unwraps her scarf and unbuttons her jacket. "Oh, Cleo, welcome back."

My grandma knows Cleo?

"Hi, Dori."

My grandma steps over and kisses Cleo's cheeks. "You need better shoes. Denver will take you shopping."

I roll my eyes.

"Oh, Nancy." G'ma D rounds the front desk and hugs Nancy. She shoots me a look to say, "Poor baby."

"Who's that?" Selma asks.

"That's my grandma," I say.

Selma nods, but her eyes won't stray from Dori. "Give us a minute, okay?"

She holds up her hand and signals for the two men to follow her outside.

G'MA D STAYS with Nancy while Cleo and I move back into the office to discuss if this is something we want to do. I mean, the money has piqued our interest, but we could fail on national television.

"What if it doesn't work?" Cleo asks. "I'd be the laughingstock of Dallas."

"Better than being the laughingstock of Lake Starlight."

"Hardly comparable." She sits in her chair and crosses her legs. Does she have to purposely do things to draw my attention to her body?

"You have read Buzz Wheel, right?"

"You have no idea the circle of gossip that surrounds Dallas," she says.

"Then I guess we have to decide whether it would be worth it," I say.

I'm not stupid, I know I'm a react first, think later kind of guy. I made peace with that a long time ago. When you pull as many pranks as I did growing up, you figure that out pretty quickly. I never meant for Principal Gregory to find Rome's jockstrap in our English teacher's desk and threaten to fire her for assuming she was sleeping with a student. Nor did I think when I threatened to shave Juno's head with clippers that young Sedona would pick them up after I wrestled Juno to the floor and shave a reverse mohawk down the center of her head.

"Do we have any other option?" she asks.

"We're in the hole. We can do some hard work to try to dig ourselves out, but this is our best option."

She thinks it over. "I'm not even sure she'd take us."

"Take you? Who?" G'ma D enters the room with a semi-happier Nancy.

"The woman you insulted is a television producer for *Uncovering America's Beauty*," I say. "Chip was supposed to be on the show."

"One of those shows where stupid people purposely get in fights so other people think their lives are better?" G'ma D asks.

"It would showcase the company and the excursions. We'd get paid and..." I look at Cleo, and she inhales a deep breath as though she's seven and preparing to jump off the high dive. "It would be great publicity for the company."

G'ma D scowls. "I don't like it."

Of course she doesn't. She hates all reality TV, which surprises me since she's usually the center of gossip in Lake Starlight.

Selma and the two men walk through the office door and Cleo stands.

"Well, Zeke is intrigued. He said we'll film one and see what happens on camera. But he wants to try to get someone well-known to star on the first episode to draw in the viewership. Tommy"—Selma thumbs toward the younger of the two men—"has a few connections through a friend of a friend, so he'll see what he can do, and we'll be in touch."

Cleo's lips tip down. I feel the same way. I don't want some spoiled Hollywood starlet risking all our lives out there.

"That's not necessary." G'ma D steps up between Cleo and me. "Denver knows Griffin Thorne, the music producer."

Selma's eyes widen as do Tommy's, which says Griffin is a better catch than any of his prospects.

I swing my arm around G'ma D's shoulders. "She's right. I do."

"Call him, sweetie, I'm sure he'll do it." She nudges me with her elbow.

"You still talk to Griffin Thorne?" Cleo asks. I kind of like the way she sounds impressed.

"He saved him a few years ago. That man would've died if not for my boy there to pull him out," G'ma D brags.

Selma, as well as Cleo, eats it up as I step aside and call Griffin.

Griffin answers on the second ring. "Denver, how the hell are you?"

"Remember that favor?"

Griffin laughs. "What do you need?"

"Well, it's big."

"I said anything, and I meant it. Spit it out."

I take the same breath Cleo took earlier, and I mentally jump off the diving board, preparing for the plunge into cold water. "How do you feel about doing another survivalist trip, but this time it would be filmed for a new reality TV show?"

I hear him blow out a breath. "I'd say if it helps you, I'm in. Just let me know the details and I'll arrange my calendar."

I fist-pump in the air. "Thanks."

"Let me call you later tonight. I'm in the middle of something."

I hear loud people in the background. He's probably in the middle of recording or something. "Yeah, definitely. Thanks, Griffin."

"Any time. Talk to you tonight."

The line dies, and I pocket my phone. "He's in. We just have to give him the dates."

Selma's wide eyes say she was ready to call my bluff. "Awesome. Okay..." She looks at Tommy and the gray beard guy now talking with Nancy. "I'll head back to LA and we'll be in touch." She puts out her hand. "This is great. Griffin Thorne. Amazing." She's talking more to herself than any of us.

When they leave, I pick up Cleo and swing her around the room. We're both squealing when I realize she's in my arms, her tits pressed against my chest and we're actually enjoying one another's company. I drop her to her flats and draw back.

"Okay, my work here is done." G'ma D buttons her coat as though she had any idea Selma was here. "Now, don't forget Sunday dinner."

"How could I forget?"

She pats my cheek. "I'm talking to Cleo. Please join us. It's at Austin's—well, Denver can bring you."

Cleo looks at me and laughs at my scrunched up forehead. "I'd love to, Dori, but I have a friend with me."

"Bring her. The more, the merrier. I have another grandson, Kingston." She leans in close. "He's a firefighter."

"And in love with his high school—well, it's complicated," I say.

"I'll think about it."

G'ma D hugs Cleo. "No thinking. Just come. You two are business partners now, so you're family."

Cleo draws back and nods. "Okay then."

I'm stunned, watching G'ma D walk to the door. "Oh, and Denver, next time, you come to me for advice, not your siblings. I'm the smart one." She looks around and out the window at where Selma is smoking a cigarette by her car. "But you did good here. I'm proud of you."

Cleo glances at me with a soft smile. G'Ma D's compliment shouldn't hit me right in the heart, but it does. It's been a while since anyone was proud of me for anything.

NINE

Cleo

That Sunday, Bridget and I wait in the bar of the Glacier Point Resort for Denver to pick us up. He gave me an out every day this week, but because he appeared so worried that I'd be coming to his family's Sunday dinner, I kept insisting that I'd love to come. Irritating him is becoming a bad habit of mine.

"You said Denver has brothers?" Bridget sits on the bar stool beside me, nursing her glass of wine. She's dressed as if she's going to an upscale restaurant for a five-course meal. A fitted dress shows off her long legs and three-inch heels, and her makeup is so thick that if I ran my nail down her cheek, it'd look as if she had a scar. But she's still the most beautiful girl I've ever known.

"Yeah, but I think majority of them are spoken for."

"Well, you know I can change that." I send her a look that says, 'please don't' and she laughs. "Come on. You know I would never."

Truly, she wouldn't. Her mother cheated on her dad,

which sent him into a spiral of quick marriages and even quicker divorces. To this day, she never talks about her mom. But I've seen her toe the line with guys who were involved with girls we knew. She's always had that itch to be the center of attention.

"Just please don't embarrass me," I say, wishing I wasn't so nervous and could've worded it better.

"Embarrass you? Since when do I embarrass you?"

See? Why didn't I think more about her feelings? "Not embarrass, but you tend to hit on every man around and if Denver's brothers look like him—"

"We know one does," she says with a twinkle in her eye that puts me on alert.

"Just stick to the single ones, okay?"

"I thought we went over this. I don't go after taken men. Jeez, Cleo, maybe I shouldn't go." She brings her wine glass to her lips.

"That's not what I meant. I just... look at you." I point at her entire outfit. "And look at me."

"You're wearing leggings and a sweater with boots. You look like we're going shopping."

I lift my spiked heeled boots. "These are not shopping attire."

She shrugs. "Do you want me to change? Would that make you more comfortable?"

I blow out a breath and push her wine closer to her. "No, you look great. Just forget it. I'm nervous."

She sips her wine and leans back in her stool. "Nervous about seeing Denver?"

"No," I say as if I'm offended she'd even ask.

"Come on. He's a hottie, and I know you like him. Every night this week, you've come back to the hotel room, and it's been all Denver this and Denver that."

"Because we're working together. That's all." I stare at the door of the bar again with the hopes he walks through just to get this evening started so it can end quickly.

"Are you sure it's not because he knows Griffin Thorne? I saw on your computer that you were looking up articles about the accident."

I open my mouth then close it. "It's called curiosity. I wanted to know what happened so that when I meet Griffin on the excursion, I'll have something to talk to him about."

She holds up her perfectly manicured hand. "Wait. You're going too?"

"Yeah, that's the stipulation from the show. Denver and I have to go on the excursions together with the guests. I think they're hoping we fight and make for good TV. You know, the more drama, the better."

"Please, I'm the queen of reality TV viewing. You should watch Bravo. Find out what those people are doing so you can replicate it and make sure your show gets picked up."

Bridget *is* a reality show junkie. She can tell you all the info on each housewife and knows every person from the *Bachelor* franchise and where they are now. Do you know how long it took me to convince her that *The Hills* was not reality?

This is probably not the best time for me to ask her this, but since I'm staying on her dime here, I kind of need an answer. Bridget tends to live according to whatever she's into at the moment, and it's great that she loves Lake Starlight so much right now, but her interest will wane eventually.

"When do you think you're going back to Dallas?" I ask, my finger following the grain of the wood top bar.

She huffs. "First you tell me not to embarrass you, and

now you're asking when I'm leaving? Way to make a girl feel wanted."

"No," I sigh. "I'm asking because when you leave, I'll need to find a place to stay." My eyes scour the chandeliers, the million-dollar view of the lake, anything other than her face. "I can't stay in a hotel for the rest of my time here. I thought I could stay at my dad's, but…"

I tried to go there the other day and I couldn't even bring myself to go inside. At some point I need to deal with everything at his house, but until I'm ready, I'll need somewhere else to stay.

"I'll charge the suite to my credit card even if I leave. No need to worry." She shrugs.

I shake my head. "I can't let you do that."

She sulks, but ever since we because stepsisters, I've made it clear that I might take what she's offering when we're together, but I won't take anything if she's not with me. "You're so difficult sometimes. I have to go back next week for my weather girl interview."

"Oh, right. Are you excited?" With everything going on, I'd completely forgotten.

She smiles. "Sure. We'll see what happens."

I shake my head. I guess it's easy to be *laisse faire* about how a job interview will turn out when you have a trust fund to fall back on.

She takes me in for a minute, turning somber. "I fear that with you doing all this up here… I'm going to lose you." Tears well in her eyes.

I place my hand over hers. "You'll never lose me."

There's so much more I want to tell her. About dad's letter, or that I'll probably be back in Dallas soon because I'm going to fail, but Denver walks into the bar. He's wearing jeans, boots, and a skull cap. When he takes it off, a few snowflakes shake off, and he eats up the distance between us with his long strides.

"You guys ready?" His gaze falls over us, and he shakes his head.

"What?" I stand and grab my coat off the back of the chair.

"You do know it's snowing out?" He eyes outside.

I look too, and the window shows it's flurrying, but it's not that bad.

"Aren't we just going into a vehicle and out of a vehicle?" Bridget asks.

"And the pavement you have to walk on to get to the vehicle is slick," he says to Bridget as though she's an idiot.

"Hey," I say.

Denver shakes his head. He can't have a problem with Bridget—I figured she was his type. "Sorry, but you girls need to go shopping."

Once we've buttoned our coats, he waves like the gentlemen he is not for us to go first.

"Well, thank you," Bridget says, and I say nothing. We reach the door and Bridget stops abruptly, staring at the snow accumulating on the ground. "That's a lot."

"Eh, not horrible." Denver opens the passenger door and the back door for us.

"Um..." Bridget stays put right outside the sliding door to the resort.

I walk out and slip on the slick pavement right away, but Denver grabs my elbow before I completely fall on my ass again. He shoots me a look that says, 'Go shopping and buy some real shoes.'

"Yeah, I'm out. I'll eat at the restaurant," Bridget says.

I look at Denver after he gets me upright, and I walk

only on the balls of my feet over to her. "Come on. It's just snow."

She leans to the side of me, looks behind me, and comes back to face me. "Yeah, no. You two go. Really, I'm good here."

"Is this about earlier? I didn't mean anything by what I said." My shoulders sag.

I could hit my forehead for doing that to her. She gets enough shit from Phil. She doesn't embarrass me. I mean, other than the time she sneaked into my economics class in college and proceeded to flirt with the TA for the entire class and ended up going back to his apartment with him. For the rest of the semester, he kept asking about her and I had to skirt the topic so he didn't fail me for saying she had just been into guys with glasses that week.

"It's not that." Her body language says she's telling the truth.

"Then I'll stay too."

Denver blows out a breath, and I turn around to give him the evil eye.

"No, you go. I'll be fine. I have to balance my checkbook anyway." I tilt my head, and she laughs. "Go. Denver, take her."

She lightly pushes me, but I'm not prepared and I practically skate into Denver's arms. Damn, I hate that he's so strong. He wraps his arm around my waist, and I take the opportunity to smell him.

Bad idea.

"Bridge..." I say, but she's shaking her head.

"Me and snow *no bueno*."

"But there's been snow here the entire time," I say.

She points. "Not like that."

"My family will make you a to-go box and Cleo can

bring it back," Denver says, shutting the back door and holding the passenger door open for me.

"Great, thanks." Bridget smiles and waves, walking back inside. The doors slide shut, and she pulls her phone from her purse.

I climb into Denver's truck. When my phone vibrates in my purse, I pull out my cell.

Bridget: *You can thank me later and I won't be waiting up for you. ;)*

I shake my head as I see her laugh inside the foyer. The girl is unbelievable.

"Let's get this over with," Denver says, starting his truck and putting it in drive.

"Maybe I should stay with her."

I shift my weight toward the door, but his hand lands on my thigh. Big, strong fingers slightly imprint on my inner thigh. I look at them and realize that I'm way too horny for him to be touching me like that.

"G'ma D will kill me if you don't show up with me." When I don't move, he squeezes my thigh once more. "Please."

I nod and relax in my seat. "I get to pick the music then."

He removes his hand from my thigh and motions to the radio. "Be my guest."

And just to piss him off, I hook up my phone to his Bluetooth and play the Spice Girls. Of course I sing along over his grunts and groans. Why do I get so much enjoyment out of his displeasure?

TEN

Cleo

Denver turns down a long driveway surrounded by woods on either side. When the dense forest clears, a beautiful two-story house comes into view.

"It's stunning," I whisper—though I'm guessing not too quietly, because Denver turns toward me briefly before parking alongside another truck that reminds me of the ones in Dallas. The expensive trucks with all the extras that never get used. Not that Denver's truck is bad. It's not ancient or anything, but it doesn't have a million bells and whistles. You can tell he uses his truck for more than just driving around.

"This is where I grew up," Denver says, interrupting my internal comparison between Dallas and Lake Starlight.

"Really?"

He turns off the engine. "Did you envision a shack?"

Before I have a chance to respond, he's out of the vehicle and grabbing something from behind the driver's seat. I climb out. Thankfully someone here salted the driveway, so my boots don't slip too much. Denver holds up a big bag with Lard Have Mercy printed on the side of it.

"What's that?" I meet him at the back of his truck.

"Pies. Everyone has to bring something and since I don't cook, I bring dessert. Store bought."

I glance into the bag. "They look yummy."

He smiles at me for a moment.

"What?"

"I practically placed the dagger in your hand, and you didn't throw it." He grabs my hand and leads us up the driveway.

Again, I concentrate on standing on the balls of my feet. "Why are you being so nice?"

"Because you're being nice. I'm nice when you're nice," he replies quickly, as though it needed no thought.

"I'm being nice because I'm walking into your family's home. They're having me over and you're the only one I know."

He stops at the bottom of the steps and drops my hand. Snowflakes land on his long eyelashes. Without blinking them away, his gaze remains glued to mine. "You do know Dori, correct?"

"I met her at my grandma's house a few times back in the day, but I'm surprised she even remembered me. Of course, being splashed on some gossip blog has allowed the majority of this town to refer to me by name." A smile tips my lips. My grandma passed away well over a decade ago, but the few memories I have of her make me smile.

"She likes you," he says.

"I like her too."

His hand lazily runs down my arm and captures my hand again before he leads us up the stairs. "She's trying to fix us up. Consider yourself warned."

We don't reach the door before I pull him to a stop. "What?"

He laughs at my expression, which I have to imagine looks horrified. "She's been playing matchmaker for a few years now. Pushes one of us siblings toward someone."

"Why?"

He stares at me, and I notice his eyes crinkle on the sides when he's deep in thought. Why is it cute? It's not cute.

"I guess she just wants us to be happy?" He knocks on the door. "I knock to be polite now that Austin lives here with his wife."

"Yeah, okay." I'm distracted and still rolling over what he said about Dori's matchmaking. I hear movement on the other side of the door and my stomach fills with unease.

"Oh, and don't worry, I'm not settling down any time soon. No matter how hard she tries, you're in the clear."

My mouth hangs ajar as the door opens and a dog flies out, jumping like a spaz. I step closer to Denver and the dog follows, sniffing obsessively and pawing at me.

"*Myles!*" the man in the doorway yells.

"I thought it was only Wyatt he loved so much?" Denver says, trying to barricade me between him and the porch railing, away from the dog.

My boots slide, but I'm thankful for the salt, so I don't embarrass myself too much by falling on my ass.

"Apparently he's got something for the rich people," the man at the door says.

"I'm not rich," I say.

But they're both too busy trying to wrangle the dog to pay any attention to me.

"Myles!" a woman inside says calmly. "Treat."

Myles stops and looks at me as though he's debating if

I'm worth risking his chance for a treat. Thankfully, I'm not, and he jets off inside the house.

"Sorry about that." The guy sticks out his hand. "Austin."

I shake his hand. "Cleo."

"Yep, I know. Welcome to Lake Starlight, where you can't sneak into town without being mentioned in Buzz Wheel. My wife made her debut there, and so did Harley." He steps aside.

Denver motions for me to enter ahead of him. I unzip and slide off my boots before placing them next to a bunch of outdoor boots similar to the ones Denver is wearing. Clearly, this is a 'one thing isn't like the others' situation. Denver laughs, putting his boots next to mine, and quirks his eyebrow. Surprisingly though, he keeps his mouth shut.

"I'll take the pies." Austin grabs the handle of the bag. "You can show Cleo around and introduce her to everyone. You're last to arrive, as usual." Austin walks around a corner.

"Not a very timely guy, huh? Somehow that doesn't surprise me," I say.

"Are we off the polite train so soon?" Denver falls in line with me.

The laughter leaking out of a nearby room nauseates me, and I shrug. "Sorry."

"I could leave you to the vultures if you're not careful." He speeds up and rounds the corner but at the last minute stops.

I run into his back before sliding to his side. All laughter in the room stops.

"What's everyone's deal? It's just Cleo Dawson," Denver says.

Everyone laughs and rises from where they sit around a

large harvest table and rushes over. Denver gets crowded out as everyone introduces themselves.

By the end of it, Savannah, who I remember from the tattoo place, puts a glass of white wine in my hand. "It's Holly's staple."

The tornado of people has me so turned around, I couldn't put name tags on any of them if I tried.

Denver returns to my side. "Ready to hop on board the polite train again?"

"Please." I cling to his arm for a second.

"Okay, let's do this quick and efficient." He extends his arm and raises his voice. "In the kitchen, the auburn one is Holly, and you met Austin. This is their house. Their delinquent dog Myles was the terror at the front door, and his doggie wife is Daisy. They're in the mudroom, probably humping because that's all they see their owners do."

Austin flips him off, but Holly laughs, waving while pouring a glass of wine.

"Then you have Savannah and Liam, who you met already."

Savannah's on Liam's lap. They drag their attention away from each other to wave to me.

"Sitting next to them is my twin, Rome, but the uglier version." Rome flips him off, but Denver says nothing. "His fiancée, Harley."

A cute brown-haired girl runs over and hugs Denver's knees.

"And this is their daughter, Calista. The boy stuck in a wrap his entire life is Dion."

"Uncle Denver?" the little girl asks, her eyes on me.

"Yeah?"

"Is this Wednesday night girl?"

Although she's hard to understand, I think I caught that

one correctly. The laughter from everyone in the room says I did.

Denver glances at me. "This is Cleo. Can you say hello?"

She waves to me. "Do you like 'Baby Shark'?"

"That annoying song that never seems to stop?" is the response I want to give, but I have manners. "One of my faves."

Her cute face lights up. "Play it," she says to Denver.

He pulls out his phone and hands it to her. "It's all yours, kiddo." He ruffles her hair, and I swear I just heard my ovaries sigh.

Calista runs off into the family room. Soon I hear the beginning of the song and everyone groans.

"All of our phones are 'dead,'" Rome says, making quotation marks around the word dead before his forehead hits the table.

"It's a phase. She'll grow out of it." The brunette stands and comes over to me, holding a chubby little baby boy on her hip. "I'm Harley and this little guy is Dion."

"Hi."

She detours over to her daughter, dancing on the way but trying to convince her that Uncle Denver needs his phone for emergencies.

Denver's hand lands on my back and he leans in closer. The fresh smells of soap and man awaken my girly parts. "Phoenix is around here somewhere, and her twin is still in New York, at college. My brother Kingston is on shift in Anchorage right now as a firefighter. Then you have my sister Brooklyn and her husband, Wyatt, who you might recognize from Glacier Point." He leans closer and whispers, "He's the owner." Pointing at me, he yells, "She's one of your guests, so don't embarrass yourself tonight."

"You've been staying at Glacier Point? This entire time?" Rome asks.

I nod. No need to mention that it's on my sister's dime. "Yes."

Rome looks at Wyatt, who I realize I've seen walking the halls of the resort, usually in a suit. "She's probably richer than you, Whitmore."

Wyatt raises his beer bottle and chugs it, not fazed in the least. He probably knows who's paying my hotel bill.

"You can't stay at a hotel forever." Dori comes from out of nowhere. "You could always stay at Savannah's. Denver and Phoenix are there now."

Everyone cracks up.

"Stop fixing everyone up. You'd never think with the way you keep pushing people to live in sin, that you were in your seventies." Savannah wraps her arms around Liam, and he kisses her cheek before whispering something in her ear that makes her blush.

"Oh hush." Dori grabs a carrot and dips it into what looks like hummus set out on the large island. "Come, Cleo. Away from Denver." She waves me over.

I step forward, but Denver wraps both arms around me, securing me to him.

"Don't listen to anything she has to say. I'm not a good guy," he whispers and releases me.

Still I surge forward, and she turns me around toward the living room, where Calista is replaying "Baby Shark" as if it's her job and she's being paid to do so.

"Calista, be a dear and go to the basement," Dori says. Calista's bottom lip sticks out, and Dori changes her tune. "You can sit in here, but we can't have the song on, okay?"

"Okay." She drags out the word and rolls her eyes.

Calista picks up a doll that's been discarded on the floor and puts her in a stroller before she leaves.

I watch Harley and Holly go upstairs while Rome and Austin head outside. Dori sighs. Is there some family drama that I don't know about? Savannah comes over, sits on the floor by us, and puts Dion between her legs before spreading out some toys that go right into his mouth.

"I'm so sorry about your father," Dori says. She told me this same thing at the funeral.

"Thank you."

"How are you liking Lake Starlight?"

"Other than being in the Buzz Wheel, I'm liking it."

They both laugh.

A dark-haired girl comes over. "What's the secret about?" She nods toward the stairs where Holly and Harley just went upstairs. "Phoenix, by the way."

"Hi, Phoenix."

She doesn't really pay attention to me though. Her attention is on Savannah and Dori.

Savannah looks at Liam, who is trying to be discreet in looking at her. They share a glance at the stairs and door as though they're worried about impending doom.

"Nothing," Savannah says without looking at Phoenix.

Phoenix curls into the big oversized chair. "How nice it must be to know all." She rolls her eyes.

This family is fun. Not like Phil's, with their stuffy "it's impolite to pry" mentality.

"Now that you have the TV show coming, I assume you're staying for a while?" Dori asks.

My eyes zero in on Dori's bluish tinted hair. Did she just get it done?

Phoenix's back straightens like a guard dog's ears. "TV show?"

Savannah mouths "sorry" to me.

"Denver!" Phoenix jumps up and heads into the kitchen and gets right into Denver's face. He must fill her in about *Uncovering America's Beauty* because she hits him in the stomach and jumps in the air. "Griffin Thorne!"

He dodges her and comes my way with the bottle of wine.

Phoenix follows and jumps in front of him. "You have to get me an introduction. He has to hear me sing!"

"No," he says, sliding by her and coming over to me. "It's not *American Idol*."

He holds out the bottle, and I lift my wine glass so he can refill it. Look at how cordial we're being.

The front door opens and Austin barrels up the stairs, but Holly and Harley are already on their way down. Harley meets Rome at the bottom of the steps while Austin whispers to Holly. She smiles and puts her hand on his arm, almost reassuring him that she's okay. Was she sick or something?

"Hey, everyone!" Holly yells to grab the household's attention.

Once it's silent, Denver looks at his twin brother and takes in the whole scene. "Oh fuck," Denver says under his breath.

"Harley and Rome have an announcement," Holly continues.

As an outsider, I take in everyone's non-verbal cues.

"Are you moving?" Juno asks then laughs.

"Are you finally gonna tie the knot?" Phoenix says.

Harley's eyes shift from Holly to Rome, almost pleading with him.

"We're pregnant," he says.

Holly claps and screams *woohoo*, but as I clap in

congratulations, I'm hyper-aware of everyone in the room. Why aren't they all hugging and carrying on?

"Come on, everyone. Congratulations are in order! I'm going to open the champagne." Holly flees to the kitchen, but when everyone stays seated, she turns around. "*Hug them!*"

Everyone scrambles to their feet and hugs the couple on their third baby.

Denver leans into me as we wait in line for our turn. "I'll fill you in later."

ELEVEN

Denver

If Dori knew that Rome and Harley were going to announce their pregnancy and she purposely asked Cleo to come to dinner, she and I are going to have to have a serious conversation. Things were awkward all night—Holly acting as if it's the best news ever and Austin's perma scowl. Harley was practically in tears and Rome ran his hand through his hair so often it was sticking straight up by the time I said we had to leave.

"We could have stayed longer," Cleo says in the seat next to me.

"We should get you back before the snow gets worse."

She doesn't say anything more, and my silence doesn't help the situation. I'm lying about leaving because of the weather. The two of us have had a nice evening where neither of us nitpicked the other. I should just be truthful, but I'm always gun shy about revealing family gossip to anyone not in our circle.

I take a deep breath and plunge forward. "Holly and Austin were married last year."

"They're a great fit."

She's lying, because they weren't their usual so-in-love-it-makes-you-sick tonight.

"They've been trying to have a baby for a while now," I say.

Her long, slow nod says she's placing all the pieces together. "Oh, that's hard. Not that I would know or anything. I'm not getting ready for a baby or..." She stops and I laugh at her rambling. "Not sure where all that came from."

"It's okay." I touch her thigh. I need to stop myself from touching her so much, but I can't seem to hold my hands back when they reach for her.

Cleo and I are about as compatible as a crocodile and a bird, and we switch places daily on who's the grumpy one.

"I just mean that it's hard for all of them. But man, Harley and Rome... three kids so close together."

I blow out a breath. "Supposedly they use birth control." I quirk an eyebrow.

"She must be fertile myrtle." She laughs.

"It's scary as hell for me, I tell you."

She tilts her head as if she's doesn't understand.

"I'm his twin. We must have some super powerful sperm."

She laughs again, but harder this time. So much, in fact, that she bends forward and can't stop shaking her head. "Only you."

"What does that mean?" I stop at an intersection, and the red glow of the light allows me to see her wide smile.

She is so gorgeous. I thought she knew she was, but I'm beginning to think she doesn't.

"You have such a big ego, it makes sense that you'd think you have sperm so powerful it could break through a condom."

"Supposedly Rome's did. And I do enjoy competing against him."

A look of fear crosses her face. "Do yourself a favor and don't tell that to a girl until you put a ring on it."

"I'm sure there're women out there who would love to bear my children."

"Not because of some immature competition. You're already three behind him." She giggles.

I can't help but laugh too, because imagining me spitting kids out with a wife is an absurd thought. "You think I couldn't do it?"

This is fun. Not something I'm used to when it comes to having a woman in my truck. Her hand isn't on my junk. Her lips aren't on my neck. And it's the most fun I've had in a while.

"Oh no, I think you could. That's the scary part."

Her eyes dart to the road and her laughter slowly dies, leaving us with an uncomfortable silence because on the right, we're going to pass the road to Chip's house. When I decided to take an alternate route, I forgot we'd pass it.

"So you don't want to be that girl?" I ask, but from her shaking her head absentmindedly and her eyes still pinned on the street we're approaching, my attempt to distract her fails.

"I haven't been able to go in." Her fingers graze the glass as we're about to go by.

I brake and turn the truck onto the road.

"No, Denver." She shakes her head. "Not now."

"I haven't been either. Not since they put him in hospice." I swallow a lump in my throat.

She doesn't say much else until the truck lights shine on his drive and I pull in, illuminating the small log cabin that could use some love. Chip never cared much for how he lived. He spent the majority of his life at the office or out in the wilderness.

"Do you want to go in? I'll go in with you." I kill the engine which grabs her attention because she shifts her gaze to my hand on the keys.

"I should do it alone." She doesn't move.

"Why?"

Her gaze refocuses on the dark house. "Why what?"

"Do it alone."

Her head slowly twists in my direction. "Because he was *my* dad."

"So?"

Her hand moves to the truck door, and my own heart rate picks up from watching her convince herself to do it. I can almost see the same war that was inside me five years after my parents' deaths when I finally went to their grave.

"It's my job," she says.

I wish we were closer and I could tell her it's not all on her, that it's okay to lean on me. She might hate me, but if she needs someone right now, I can be that person.

"What about Bridget?" I ask.

She shakes her head. "I love the girl and she'd help me if I asked, but she'd have a hard time walking around in there without judging. I just can't bear to hear it."

I open my door, the interior light blinding us for a moment. "I'll go with you."

"Okay," she says in a quiet voice.

As I round the front of my truck, she's still inside. I open her door and her cold hand lands in mine. She slowly steps down from the truck and pulls keys out of her purse. But before we hit the porch, she stops.

"I'm not ready," she says, retreating to the truck.

"Okay."

A minute later, we're back in the truck and I'm turning around in the driveway to get back on the road.

She says nothing for five minutes. "Why didn't you push me?"

"Push you?"

"To go in. Most people would've tried to pressure me into doing it. You just said okay, and we got back in the truck."

I pull up to Glacier Point and stop in the valet section. "You said you weren't ready." I place my hand on her leg again but retract it right away. I need to work on my self-discipline. "But you will be one day."

She stares into my eyes, and I allow her to see the truth I'm speaking. I've been where she is. She'll find her way one day.

"Thanks."

"You're welcome."

She nods and opens the door. "I'll see you tomorrow."

"Yep."

We stare at one another for a few heartbeats, and an energy fills the cab. One I'm not used to with her. If she wasn't my business partner, I might break the tension by pulling her into my side to kiss the hell out of her. Her tongue slides over her bottom lip. For a moment, I think she's thinking the same thing I am—until she hurries out of my truck and shuts the door, never looking back.

This relationship between us is taking a turn down a forbidden path, and we need to get back on the main road so we're walking alongside one another, not crossing over into other parts of each other's lives that could make everything messy.

As I pull out of Glacier Point, I remind myself again that Chip's business and legacy is what matters here. My dick doesn't get a say this time around. It'd be easier if I'd trained him better in the past.

TWELVE

Cleo

Bridget isn't in the suite when I get back, but her dress is balled up in the corner of my bedroom. Her makeup is spilled out on the counter in the bathroom, and a wet towel lies on my bed. There's a note on my pillow, so I step out of my boots and pick up the piece of paper.

Met a hunter down at the bar. I'll see you in the morning or hopefully the afternoon. ;)

I BALL up the note and miss the trash can by a good foot.

Falling onto the plush mattress a high-end hotel like this one offers, I stare at the white ceiling. I inhale deeply and close my eyes, imagining what would've transpired if I'd kissed Denver Bailey in the cab of his truck minutes ago.

His soft lips touching mine, his tongue slowly sliding into my mouth while his large hand lands on my back and nudges me as close as our bodies can get. I bet he's perfected the move of sliding his seat back to make room for me to straddle him. I can almost feel the steering wheel pressed into my back while his hands skim up the hem of my sweater.

I arch my back while he casts kisses along my jaw, and I grind along his length, pressing against the denim of his jeans. The steamed-up windows. Our sweaty bodies with clothes half on and half off. Him unable to stop kissing me.

My phone vibrates next to me and I sit up in a panic like someone knew what I was thinking.

Grabbing the phone from my purse, Denver's name appears and I can't help but feel like he knew I was a second away from sliding my hand under my leggings.

Denver: *Griffin is in town. He's coming by tomorrow.*

I send a thumbs-up as a reply because my hands are shaking.

I don't want a man like Denver Bailey. Someone who thinks he has Olympic-level sperm and could impregnate me from across the room. A man who views commitment as a life sentence without parole.

As I try to convince myself, his imaginary lips skitter up my bare shoulder and his hands explore the rest of me. I relish the strong build of his chest.

No. Stop.

He's a disgusting man who doesn't respect women. But even I know that's a lie. I know little about Denver, but I'm realizing I might be in deep trouble if I can't stop this sexual energy from challenging my hatred for him.

I WALK into Lifetime Adventures armed with Brewed Awakenings cold brews for Denver and myself. I added a hot coffee to my order today, because although Nancy always politely accepts the cold brew I buy her, I caught her heating it in the microwave the other morning.

"Hi, Nancy," I say.

She looks up from her newspaper over the rim of her reading glasses. I hand her the hot coffee, and she smiles and thanks me as she always does then places it next to a cup of cold brew.

"You like the cold brew?" I ask. Maybe I was wrong.

She waves me off and sips the coffee I brought her. "Denver brought me one earlier."

I nod and allow us both to pretend she'll drink it.

I step into the office that we've only been able to half clean out. I keep meaning to come in one night and finish the job without Denver. He's a little like Chip—a hoarder. Denver is leaned back in his chair, his feet on the edge of the desk and a phone to his ear.

"No way, Phoenix. He's here for Lifetime Adventures." He rolls his eyes and they close briefly, so I sneak into the room, shutting the door. "Maybe if the topic comes up. Just let me get through this and then we can revisit him listening to your demo."

His eyes pop open, and when he sees me, a smile quickly hijacks his mouth. Damn, a girl could get used to that greeting. I put the tray of drinks on the desk but see a caramel-colored one on my side and a black one on his side. He got me coffee too.

He laughs, looking at my tray, and I mouth thank you, getting a nod as a response.

"You need to chill out," he says into the phone. Another pause.

I pick up some papers and boot up my laptop, hoping the website is loaded like our new designer promised.

"I gotta work. Bye." He hangs up and puts his fingers on his temples, massaging them.

"Why are you so against introducing her to Griffin?" I sip my drink while my fingers slide around the trackpad, searching out our website.

"I'm not against it, but I just asked the guy to risk his life for us. I'm not about to say, 'And by the way, how about checking out my sister, the aspiring singer?'" He turns his attention to his computer. "It's up and looks awesome. People aren't in neon colors sporting mullets anymore, so that's a good start."

He swivels his laptop my way. We had Wi-Fi installed last week, so we don't have to hotspot through our phones anymore, much to my data plan's relief.

"There was a message from Selma on my phone this morning. I wonder if that woman ever sleeps?" he says.

"What did she say?" I continue mindlessly searching the website to make sure all the changes I requested are complete. Everything looks awesome. Now we need to move on to advertising, which is hard when you have no money to advertise with.

"She said they want to see how the taping with Griffin goes, then they'll show it to a test group. If the response is good, we continue. They're committing to six episodes if all goes well, but after that, they'll see how the ratings and fanbase are."

I lean back from my computer, pulling my cold brew to my chest. "I'm a little worried."

"Worried about?"

Needing to stand, I get to my feet. I shouldn't admit this

to him, but we're in this together. He needs to know my weaknesses as I do his. "I'm not like you."

"You might not have an ass like mine, but your rack is better."

I spin around. He winks, and I shake my head at his need to use humor to deflect whenever someone is vulnerable with him.

"I'm not outgoing and personable. I can't come up with one-liners on the fly. Why do I have to film too?"

He leans back, his arms resting on the arms of the chair. He's so relaxed. How can he not have a care in the world? "You hate me. Let that shine through. The audience will love it."

I shake my head. "But—"

"Oh crap, don't tell me I'm growing on you."

Oh no, not at all. I just masturbated to thoughts of you last night.

"As if." Even I'm not convinced of my answer.

"Don't worry, I'll do enough to piss you off, but maybe we should figure out our roles before we go?"

"What do you mean?"

"Research. Selma said the camera crew will be up here next week, so I have to send them all the details of where we're going. We have time to figure out who we want to be on camera. I say we watch the most famous reality couples and pinpoint why they're successful."

The fact that he's not smirking says he's serious. "But it's *reality*. Why can't we just be ourselves?"

"You think reality stars don't act? Remember Selma said some of them amp up their personalities to stay on the shows?"

I chew on my nail. He has a point. Could I really act like someone else and not come off as fake?

"And we're in agreement, what we get paid goes into the company?" I ask.

He nods. "One hundred percent."

So I'm doing this for my dad's company, which is the whole point anyway, even if I have no idea what's going to happen after we turn this place around. "Okay, that's a good plan. Let's start tonight. You can come to my hotel room."

"Um, no, you can come to my house. I'll even order in dinner." The phone on his desk rings and Denver presses the speakerphone button. "Hey, Nancy."

"Mr. Thorne is here to see you."

"We'll be right there." He presses the button and keeps his eyes on me. "Tonight at six?"

I nod, still nauseated about the idea of being on camera.

"Then let's see the man who's going to make it rain for us." I circle toward the door, but Denver puts his hand on the door, stopping me from opening it. When I look up, he's looking at me with earnest eyes. "I won't let us fail."

My breath hitches and I nod, unable to say anything. Is he purposely coming close and saying nice things to me? Oh shit, he could be playing me. Masking himself as someone he's not, just to steal the company from me.

He opens the door before I have the nerve to ask him and smacks on a huge smile that seems genuine. "Griffin, it's been too long."

They shake hands and shift into a manly hug where none of their body parts actually touch.

Griffin's eyes zero on me over Denver's shoulder. "And who's this?"

Denver steps back from their embrace and puts his hand out toward me. "Cleo Dawson, my business partner."

"Business only?" Griffin asks.

"Yes." I step forward and shake his hand. It's soft. A

complete contrast to his messy shoulder-length, dirty-blond hair and more-than-scruffy beard. He's a total heartthrob.

"Nice to meet you, Cleo." His eyes lock with mine, and I might imagine our wedding for a moment.

"Dad!"

That imaginary walk down the aisle comes to a screeching halt.

"Maverick, come here." He waves a kid over from the old quarter-for-a-handful candy machines.

I'm sure the candy is ancient. *Note to self, get rid of them.*

"They got candy," Maverick says, not moving.

"Yeah, yeah, in a second." Griffin looks back at us. "I'm divorced," he says a little lower, presumably so his son doesn't hear. "He's six, so we switch midweek right now."

"I want it now!" Maverick says.

"And I told you in a second." Griffin walks over and physically picks him up, which spurs Maverick to kick him in the shins.

"I have some candy in here." Nancy rounds the front desk, holding out a wrapped butterscotch candy.

Bless her heart.

"Here you go, Maverick." She holds it out for him.

He stares at it as though it's a ticking time bomb. I peek at Denver, and we make eye contact. He understands exactly what is about to transpire and my heart is already breaking for Nancy.

Maverick knocks the candy out of Nancy's hand with a slap. Griffin sets Maverick down and lowers his voice. Nancy looks at the boy as if he's the spawn of Satan, a tear in her eye, and disappears to the restroom. Denver and I awkwardly stand around and try to act as though we can't overhear Griffin scolding his unremorseful son.

"Sorry, we're still treading the waters of divorce and Maverick is adjusting. He's really not a bad kid," Griffin says.

We nod as if we're in agreement.

"Yeah, I tested my limits too," Denver says.

"Still does," I say.

Denver nods like 'good one.' All I can think of is how these are going to be our new roles. Do I need to mentally come back with one-liners for us to be successful?

"You're funny," Griffin says.

I straighten my back. "Not really."

"She's funny at my expense," Denver says.

I pinch his cheeks. "It's too easy."

"You sure you're not a couple?" Griffin asks.

"*No!*" we screech in unison.

He holds up his hands and steps back. "If that's a fact, maybe try not to be so defensive about it."

I'm not about to explore what he said. "He's like a little brother," I lie.

"Bigger brother."

"Older?" I offer.

"I prefer the word bigger."

I roll my eyes. "I think little is a better word."

Griffin laughs and Denver puts me in a headlock, giving me a noogie. When did we turn into a brother-and-sister duo? I'm not sure, but maybe it will help push away my disturbing urge to mount him.

THIRTEEN

Denver

Wok For U has delivered the food, and I went through Phoenix's DVR recordings earlier to pick the reality shows we should watch. I purposely didn't buy any alcohol because my attraction to Cleo is growing, and just like prescription drugs and alcohol don't mix, Cleo and alcohol won't either. That combination would most likely result with us in a bed or her knee to my nuts when I tried something. And I kinda like my nuts where they are.

Phoenix walks down the stairs and rounds the corner, eyeing me putting the food on the counter. "Date night?"

"Don't you have somewhere to be?"

She steals a piece of orange chicken and flops down on the couch in the family room, grabbing the remote. "Nope. That's the great thing about being the most unsuccessful person in your high school class—you never have anyone to hang out with."

"You have siblings. Eight of them actually."

She puts her hand toward me. "And I'm hanging out with one right now."

"Where are the rest?"

She licks her fingers, cleaning them one by one as if she's eating barbeque. "I can't hang with Juno and Colton anymore. They're getting annoying, constantly acting like they're just friends."

"I think they are just friends."

She rolls her eyes. "We both know they aren't. Though I did hear Colton talk about going out on a date."

"What did Juno say?" I put out some plates.

"She said she thought it was a great idea." She rolls her eyes again.

I'm used to Phoenix's marble eyes. The girl used to be so sweet and kind, but after adolescence, a different Phoenix emerged.

"Well, it's her business. Stay out of it," I say.

"So I heard a rumor that Griffin Thorne was in town today. Thanks for nothing, big bro."

She refuses to look at me this time, and I blow out a long breath. This is going to be a problem with us.

"Where did you hear that?"

"I'm stalking Griffin." Her sarcasm is not welcome. "Where do you think?"

I pull out my phone and open the Buzz Wheel website. There I am, front and center again. Well, Cleo and me.

"It's a cute picture though," Phoenix says.

The picture is of me holding Cleo up outside my truck when she almost fell on those ridiculous boots with spiked heels. I skim the article about how a reality TV show is coming to town and Griffin Thorne is going to save Lifetime Adventures. The picture they use of him is from the Grammys two years ago. Of course it also mentions how

Cleo and I have been seen joking and smiling as of late. I might have to have a conversation with Nancy about gossiping about us. Then again, what do I care? I've been in Buzz Wheel ever since it started. I'm sure it'll even report my death someday. Who gives a shit? I'm not that interesting of a person.

Phoenix stands and heads back to the counter. "So you like her?"

"She's okay." I shrug as I grab the silverware.

"I don't remember ever sliding my hand along a person's thigh if I thought they were just okay." She plucks another piece of orange chicken from the container, and I take a fork and pretend to stab her hand.

"She's hot, but I'm not going to do anything about it."

She nods. Her expression screams '*yeah right.*'

"I'm not. I want to get this company up and successful for both of us."

"And then what? Like, what's the game plan here?"

I lean back. What is our end game? Sell? Buy one another out? Work it together? "One step at a time. We're just trying to get it profitable right now."

The words from Chip's letter resonate with me again.

The doorbell rings. Although I wish Phoenix had anywhere to go but here, there's no reason she can't hang out with Cleo and me. So I allow her to answer the door since she's like a dog wagging its tail to play.

"Hey, Cleo," she says.

Standing in the doorway of the kitchen, I look down the hall and see them hug, which surprises me. Phoenix doesn't get attached easily, but I could tell at the Sunday dinner she liked Cleo. Probably why she caught me touching Cleo's thigh at the dinner table.

"Hi, Phoenix." She holds up a bag from Liquory Split. "Are you twenty-one?"

"Just celebrated with my twin in New York three months ago." She takes the bag and eyes me.

I pray there're only wine coolers in there, so I have no temptation.

"Hi, Denver," Cleo says, walking by me in another pair of skinny jeans and a short sweater.

I've never been so turned on when there's this much clothing on a woman. Following her, I inwardly groan from staring at her ass.

Definitely no alcohol.

"I got Chinese food. Hope that works?" I ask.

"Perfect. I love it."

Phoenix dishes herself a plate and holds one out to Cleo. "So you scoured through my DVR and didn't pick any of the reality music shows?" Phoenix sits on the comfy chair and picks up the remote.

"We need drama. We want to find out what people love about them," I say, handing Cleo a fork.

She thanks me, and my eyes zero in on her lip gloss. It's like runway lights and those lips are waving at my lips to land.

"I'm pretty sure I'm boring as far as reality TV goes. I once tried to watch one about a group of people who were stranded on an island. They either came off as arrogant, stupid, or crazy." Cleo sits on one side of the couch and tucks her bare feet underneath her, placing her food on the side table.

I dig through the bag she brought, finding a six-pack of beer and a bottle of wine. *Shit.*

"Okay, girls, what do you want?" I hold them up.

They point at the wine before continuing to talk to one

another. Phoenix is pleading her case as to why I should introduce her to Griffin, and Cleo's nodding in understanding as if I'm the Grinch stealing Christmas.

Once we're all settled and I'm on the opposite side of the couch—as far as I can get from Cleo—Phoenix presses Play on the first reality show. One revolving around a small southern town and a group of friends. I try to concentrate on the arguments and the bickering, but my eyes stray to Cleo's bare feet with pink toenail polish snuggled under her perfect ass.

Damn, I'm screwed.

THREE HOURS LATER, I've heard more bitching and moaning than I did living with my five sisters in their teens. I'd say I'm done with reality TV for right now.

Cleo and Phoenix are heavy into the one about the housewives, Cleo remarking on how similar some of them are to her mother and her friends.

It goes to commercial. Phoenix is refilling her glass of wine, and neither Cleo nor I get up to retrieve the remote to fast forward.

"Do you miss Dallas?" I ask.

She shrugs and sips her wine, the residue of her lip gloss on the edge of the glass. "Not really."

"Your mom?"

"I should, but sadly, not really."

"You aren't close with your mom?" Phoenix sits down in the chair and faces Cleo. Either she's doing all this to butter her up to talk to Griffin about her music or she genuinely enjoys Cleo's company.

"We're really different."

"Well, you're not like those women." Phoenix points at the television. "You don't seem as plastic as your stepsister either."

Cleo laughs and nods. "*Mean Girls?*"

I'm clearly not in the loop, but I'm not going to interrupt them to find out the piece I'm missing.

"She's not a mean girl," Cleo says. "She's just grown up with privilege and money—an enormous amount—and never worries about not having it."

"You did too though?" Phoenix poses it more as a question.

I slide a little closer because I assumed the same.

"I lived in the same house. My stepdad bought me a car at sixteen. My college was paid for. I reaped a lot of benefits, but it's not like I have her trust fund money. When she turned twenty-five... well, let's just say she doesn't have to work for the rest of her life if she doesn't want to."

"And she doesn't?" Phoenix asks.

Now I'm glad she joined us. I never wanted to pry into Cleo's life—God knows I hate when people pry into mine—but I'm happy for my sister to.

"She wants to be a weather girl, so we'll see. She really is awesome. Her good side gets hidden by the effects of her upbringing sometimes, but her heart is good."

I smile at that. At least she has Bridget if she doesn't have either of her parents.

"What's it like to live a life like that?" Phoenix has leaned in, her eyes wide.

Cleo laughs. "Like what?"

"With kids who have access to everything?"

Cleo's smile wilts and my heart tugs. "It's hard when you're not one of them. They accepted me because of Bridget and my stepdad, but I heard the murmurs about my gold-digging mother. Girls are mean, and as soon as any guy showed me a little attention, their claws could be sharp."

"But you got to go on vacations and spend four hundred dollars on a pair of jeans."

Phoenix is enamored with the high society life. I worry that's one reason she's chasing singing. Her star has always been brighter than the rest of ours. Her voice is unparalleled, but maybe because she was so young when our parents died, she missed the one lesson they always taught us. It's not the quantity, it's the quality of friends.

"I just never fully fit in there." Cleo twirls her wine glass.

Phoenix remains quiet. I wonder if she feels as if she doesn't fit in here and understands how Cleo feels. I've always loved Lake Starlight and never dreamed of living anywhere else, even with how tempting running sounded. Especially after Rome ran away to Europe.

Phoenix turns in her chair. "Well, you're fitting in here."

"Except when people look at her feet," I joke.

Cleo laughs and punches my arm. "I like my shoes."

I like them too. Especially her heels. But she's not going to be able to hike up the mountain next week in those.

She and Phoenix continue to watch the reality show and joke about who Cleo could act like and whether we should pretend to be a couple, which sounds appealing only because spending the night in a tent with her sounds like winning the lottery right about now. To have those smooth feet with pink toes running up and down my legs... maybe Phoenix has a point.

"Maybe we should?" I say out loud before thinking the whole thing through.

"Should what?" Cleo asks.

"Act like we're a couple. Our fights will make it all the more appealing to people."

"Or you could toe the line of are we, or aren't we?" Phoenix suggests. "You can be annoying like Juno and Colton and act like you don't love one another."

Sleeping in the same tent with Cleo sounds much more appealing than what my sister is suggesting. "Nah, I say we go couple."

Cleo pales and she bites on her lip as though I'm not selling her on the idea. "Um."

"It's perfect," I urge.

Cleo looks at Phoenix, who's crazy enough to believe it's the right choice. She nods.

"Are you doing this to get me to sleep with you?" Cleo asks.

Man, she knows me well.

"Well, I can't lie that there's a bonus to the arrangement."

She drains the rest of her wine as if she needs the liquid courage, then she nods. "Okay."

I lean forward, puckering my lips. "Let's seal it with a kiss."

She puts her hand over my face and pushes me away, but her smirk says she might've considered it for a moment.

My parents really should've taught me not to play with fire.

FOURTEEN

Cleo

Five days later, I have to say goodbye to Bridget. I'm sad, but it's a blessing since she thinks the new arrangement with Denver is an excuse to screw him.

"It's not like he's a monogamous guy anyway." She nudges me with her elbow. "Might as well enjoy yourself."

"Safe travels." I kiss Bridget on the cheek and walk her to the private entrance leading to Phil's plane. "Good luck. You totally have this."

"I'll be back before you know it."

I hug her tightly. "Get the job first."

Truth is, she's probably already got the job. The interview is a formality because Phil's connections are concrete.

"We haven't really been apart since college." She steps back, and her pout that's usually reserved for her fake persona is there, but it's okay. Bridget has a hard time being real with people. It's why we get along so well. Neither of us calls out the other on our issues. "I paid you up for the rest of the week, and I don't want to hear anything about it. I would've done it for longer, but I know you."

I giggle. "Thank you. I think there's a B & B I can stay at that's a little cheaper, but I really need to go to my dad's place and stay there."

"Well, you have a week. If you need more, just call."

I nod, smiling. "You're the best sister."

The flight attendant calls her and Bridget throws herself into my arms. "Don't go staying up here too long."

I swipe a tear. "As if I could live in this small town for long."

She stares through me. Although nothing about my future has been set in stone, there's an underlying conversation happening between us. "Yeah, this is the worst place for you."

"Exactly."

She uses the heel of her hand to wipe her own tears. "Love you, sis."

"Love you," I say.

She picks up her bag and walks away, never looking back. I rush to the window and watch her climb the stairs of the private plane. Right before she ducks in, she turns and waves. I wave back, pressing my hand on the window. The ground crew member retracts the staircase, and I watch the plane head toward the runway.

Loneliness creeps inside my gut. The last normal part of my life has left, and I'm on my own. I'm going to do what my dad's letter asked. I need to strap on my courage and give it everything I have.

And if that means acting like Denver Bailey's girlfriend, then I guess that's what it means.

WALKING into the hangar on Lifetime Adventures' property, I find Denver clad in jeans and a T-shirt drenched in sweat. Six huge duffels full of I have no idea what surround him.

"I got you a present." He grabs a retail bag set off to the side and walks over with his hands behind his back.

"A sexy nightie is not part of the deal."

He chuckles. "You really are funny."

That shouldn't make happiness sprout inside me, but it does.

"Close your eyes and put your hands out."

"Nope." I cross my arms. "If you think you're going to do some initiation thing where you put a scorpion in my hand, I'm not falling for it."

His laugh gets louder. "This isn't Australia. If I could put a bear in your palm, I'd be a magician." He raises those dark eyebrows that are natural and not perfectly groomed like the guys back home. "Trust me. Have I steered you wrong yet?"

"Fine, but my leg can reach your balls and I will kick if I feel threatened." I close my eyes and put out my hands.

"Noted." All I hear is something coming out of a bag, then his breath is closer.

Every sound and smell is stronger with my eyes closed. His minty breath. The sound of him swallowing and his tongue licking his lips. Lips I want on mine. Wait, this is Denver. What is he up to?

"You're not going to put your dick in my hands, are you?"

"Fuck, Cleo. What kind of guy do you think I am?"

My eyes pop open and there's a big box in his hands.

He shoves it toward me. "It's a damn pair of boots."

The hurt in his gorgeous brown eyes unnerves me. The

fact that I'm the cause of that look winds a tight knot in my stomach.

"Dick would've been better." He splashes on a big smile to mask the pain, but I can't unsee it. It's an expression I've never seen on him before.

I bend down and open the box, revealing a pair of boots like the ones that were lined up at Austin and Holly's house. They probably have some kind of custom logo on them the way people love this family. But instead of brown or black, the fur that lines the inside is hot neon pink. "Thank you."

I toe out of my sneakers and slide on the boots, sitting down to lace them.

"You have to get them tighter." Denver bends down on a knee, lacing my boot as if I'm a child. He does it with a diligence I admire.

"Thank you, Denver," I say.

He must catch the hitch in my voice because he glances up at me and his expression softens. The same one that Bridget heard when I had to ask her for money during my junior year in college because I'd gotten laid off.

He finishes tying my boot, takes off my other shoe, slips on the boot, and ties that one before even looking at me. Sitting back on his heels, he stares at my tied boots like a work of art that took him five years to finish, then his gaze slowly moves up to mine and holds there. "You're welcome. We have to get you snow gear still. Even my sisters don't have a ton of stuff that will keep you warm the entire time up there."

I nod, unable to say anything. My apology for thinking the worst of him rests on the tip of my tongue.

He stands. "We can do that tomorrow."

My ass grows cold on the concrete floor even though the

hangar is heated. I stand, wipe off my butt, and pick up my sneakers, heading into the office to let him pack all our gear. I'll find a way to apologize to him at some point.

AT THE END of the day, I enter the lobby of Glacier Point Resort. I'll only be here for three more nights. Stopping at the reception area, I inform the employee that I'll be checking out—because I'm not spending Bridget's money when I won't even be here, but on a mountainside. Bridget knew I was leaving, but she'd think nothing of paying for a room I wasn't actually sleeping in for nights on end. Just as I'm telling the resort employee my plans, Wyatt comes out of the office that says Manager on the door.

"Cleo!" He looks as if it's nine o'clock in the morning the way his suit is still wrinkle-free and his tie in a nice Windsor knot. Even his hair is gelled back. "I heard you and Denver are heading off on an excursion."

I nervously nod while mentally repeating to myself that I can do this.

"And with Griffin Thorne?"

"Wyatt, do you read Buzz Wheel by chance?"

He laughs. "Once you're in it, you kind of relish when you're not the center of it."

"Okay, we have you all set to check out in three nights," the front desk clerk says.

"Three nights?" Wyatt asks, looking over his shoulder at his employee. "I just made arrangements with Bridget for the rest of the week."

"I'm leaving in four days for the excursion, so there's no reason to keep a room."

He scratches his head. "Where will you stay when you return?"

"I haven't figured that out yet. But I can't afford it here."

The employee politely steps away, and Wyatt motions for me to follow him to the side of the long counter. He seems like a good guy. The Baileys love him. Brooklyn is over the moon in love with him, that much is obvious.

I'm sure he's about to offer me a broom closet or, knowing this town, maybe even a room in his house, but I straighten my back and lift my hand. "Before you offer something, I have to decline. I'll find somewhere. If need be, there's always my dad's place."

He steps back and lets my words soak in. I feel like a scorned student. I want to raise my hand and admit I've yet to go to my dad's because I'm a chicken-shit.

"Brook will kill me if you end up in a box on Main Street." His lips lift. I definitely see how his smile could draw Brooklyn to him.

I put my hand on his arm. "I promise I won't end up in a box. I doubt anyone in this town would allow that to happen."

He nods. "Well, let me know if it changes. You're practically family."

I cough out a laugh. "Um, not really."

He winks, grabs a messenger bag, and touches my arm. "At least I know with Denver, you'll be safe up there." He says goodbye and steps away toward the front door.

Thinking about Denver, my stomach rolls with excitement. I place my hand over it.

"Oh, Cleo?" Wyatt turns around in the middle of the lobby that's more like a grand foyer. "You had a bunch of boxes delivered today, so I had Mac put them in your room."

"Boxes?"

He nods. "Yeah. Someone loves you." He winks then waves goodbye to the young bellhop, Mac, and disappears through the doors.

The woman behind the counter steps back over. "Anything else, Miss Dawson?"

"No. Thank you."

She nods politely and goes back to doing whatever they do between guests.

Heading to the elevator, I have no idea who would send me something, but it's the first thing in weeks I've been excited about—besides seeing Denver. And the former needs to change.

When the elevator doors open on my floor, I'm skipping like a toddler on her way to a toy store. Using my key, I open my door and blanch. When Wyatt mentioned boxes, I thought some Amazon boxes, not moving boxes.

All of them have a company logo I'm not familiar with stamped on the sides. Tossing my purse onto the table, I try to toe out of my boots, but it isn't as easy as my flats. Once I'm finally free, I pounce on the bed and drag over a box.

Yanking and tearing, I pull out a white one-piece snowsuit with gold around the stitching.

"It looks like an Elvis costume," I murmur.

This is totally Bridget.

I move to the next box and find a retro snowsuit with color stripes that reminds me of the eighties doll, Rainbow Bright. It pulls a smile from me.

By the time I finish, there are three snowsuits, all ugly and bright. Long underwear, gloves, hats, scarfs, thermal socks, and even a face protector that looks as if I'm going to rob a bank.

It's all spread out on the bed, and I pull out my phone.

Me: *You didn't have to.*

Bridget: *I wanted to make sure if you go missing it was easy to find you.*

I smile and hug my phone as though she's right in front of me.

Me: *You're the best sister.*

Bridget: *Nah, you are.*

Me: *Thanks so much.*

Bridget: *Save the one with the stripes for me. I think I'll rock it.*

Me: *You got it. Love you.*

Bridget: *Love you.*

Putting the phone down, I look at the new clothes that probably cost her thousands of dollars. I hope I can be there for her one day the way she's been here for me through this.

After snapping a picture with my phone, I send it to Denver, and he replies instantly.

Denver: *Man, who is your Santa? And where do they shop because I'll never go there.*

Me: *I guess I'll keep it all for myself.*

Denver: *Can't say we'll lose you in that outfit.*

Me: *You better not lose me.*

Denver: *I always have one eye on you, Cleo.*

My heart flips and flops as I fall into the softness of my mattress. I'm in so much trouble. I'm headed into the Alaskan wilderness, and I'm more afraid I'll sleep with Denver than be attacked by a bear.

FIFTEEN

Denver

Days later, at six in the morning in the darkness, a white goddess walks into Lifetime Adventures. Cleo is all decked out in a white snowsuit with metallic gold trim.

"All you need are some blue suede boots," I say.

She takes off her hat. "Funny. But it's the best of the three." Stopping, she looks at me and frowns. "Where's yours?"

"In my bag. You're not going to want to wear that in the plane. We'll be cozy in there as it is."

"Oh, okay."

I shake my head. "Strip, baby." My eyes fall over her body. I'm kind of hoping she wore nothing under that snowsuit.

"I have clothes on underneath," she says as if she can read my mind.

"Damn." I laugh and finalize the paperwork since Nancy is off for the weekend. Straightening it, I put it inside the folder and turn to her. She hasn't taken off the snowsuit yet. "Do you want help?"

"No."

"I'm always here to lend a hand or a finger or... whatever you need." I laugh, walking into our office. It's quiet in here this morning, so I hear the torturous sound of her lowering her zipper. Expectations to prepare for takeoff hit my lower region.

Sorry, fella, not today.

"Where's Griffin?" she calls.

"He and the camera crew are meeting us this afternoon."

"Why didn't I know that? It would've saved me from waking up at four in the morning to do my hair and makeup."

I turn my head toward the door. "You do look good. I meant to compliment you, but we're not filming until tonight. They're letting me set up camp first, mostly because they care more about how I'm going to teach you and Griffin to get your dinner."

"So it's just us?" she asks.

I smile when I hear the hesitation in her question. Maybe I'm not the only one thinking about the other one naked. This'll be interesting.

I come out of the office, and she's stepping out of her boots to get her snowsuit off. I see that she is indeed wearing pants and a T-shirt. Not nearly enough clothing to keep her warm when we get up in the air. I snag my sweatshirt off the desk and toss it at her.

"What's this?" she asks.

"You'll need it on the plane."

"Then why am I getting out of my snowsuit?"

"Because I don't want to crash land when an eagle flies into us, thinking God is calling him home."

She doesn't laugh at my joke but distorts her face into a look that reads, 'That the best you've got?'

I go back into the office and grab the sweatshirt I wore yesterday and forgot here and stuff it into my backpack. "You ready?"

She inhales. "Yeah."

"Have you flown in a bush plane before?"

"With my dad when I was, like, fifteen."

"Then you know what to expect."

"I do."

She follows me out into the hangar, and I open the door. We get the plane out. It's perfect timing because the sun is just coming up over the horizon.

Twenty minutes later, her white snowsuit is shoved in the back with our bags, she's sitting right behind me, and we each have our headphones on. She's definitely more familiar with this routine than I thought she would be.

"Tell me you aren't afraid of flying?"

"No." Her voice has that hitch I've realized she gets when she's not admitting to something. Getting on a bush plane isn't an easy thing for some people.

"Then let's get going." I start the plane and strap myself in. Within minutes, we takeoff after taxiing down the plowed path made just for the bush planes. "You okay?"

"Yep."

We're still climbing, but steadily enough not to scare her too much. I maneuver the plane and all my anxiety about this trip disappears with our view of the landscape below. When I fly, I tend to forget that I'm with people unless I'm on a tour.

I must've zoned out because when Cleo speaks through the headphones, I startle.

"It's so beautiful. The land. The snow. The blue water."

I glance over my shoulder and see her face is plastered to the window. "I kind of thought you'd put your head between your legs and pray until we're back on the ground."

She giggles. "I told you I've flown in one before."

"Yeah, but you're trusting *me* to get you where you're going."

There's silence. I hate that I can't look at her while we're talking. "So?"

"So trusting your dad and trusting me are two different things. Especially since you hate me." I slowly turn us to head south.

"You wanna know a secret?" she says, her voice lowering as if she shouldn't tell me.

"Who doesn't love secrets?"

Another pause. "I don't hate you. I kind of admire you."

"Admire me?" We head over a glacier and I take us lower to give her the million-dollar view. And to show off a little, if I'm honest.

"You're doing what you love. So many people dream of that and never find it. To wake up every day and do what you love."

I think for a moment, allowing her to 'ooh' and 'aah' over the glacier. "That's why I was unsure about taking on Life-time Adventures. It takes away from my freedom of being able to get in my plane and go. I tend to use it to escape."

Her hand touches the back of my neck in a gentle manner. "Everyone needs an escape sometimes."

I nod but think back to how many times I disappeared for days in order to avoid family shit. I recognize how it was for them now only because Kingston is doing the same thing. Using the excuse of his job to dodge his problems.

"If we keep Lifetime Adventures, it will change that for me," I say.

"It doesn't have to. If we're still partners, we'll schedule you time to escape." I laugh, and she joins me. "Maybe I should learn to fly so I can take over the trips when you want to escape."

"You're really thinking long term, huh?" I never asked her straight out, so she wouldn't ask me.

"I'm not sure, but if I could do this every day? Maybe."

I increase our altitude and move away from the glacier, heading over a large lake in the middle of a mountain range. "I can teach you."

She's silent again.

We have a half hour to go since I didn't want to go too far with Griffin after what happened last time. We're going to a place I've been numerous times so the other plane can get in, but when I fly Chip's ashes up north in a month or so, I'll be winging it. I've yet to tell Cleo what was in his letter to me. Today isn't the day to tell her that though. I won't be responsible for stripping that smile off her face.

"Hey, Cleo," I say.

"Yeah," she says, her hand landing on my shoulder.

"I don't hate you either."

She squeezes my shoulder, and I want to land this plane on the edge of the Earth and lay her down on a blanket. Too bad that's not one of my options. Sooner or later, I'm going to have to decide if I want it to be.

SIXTEEN

Cleo

You know what not to do when you're already attracted to someone you shouldn't be?

Don't allow him to fly you in a small plane over the most beautiful terrain you've ever seen. Don't allow him to say sweet things through the microphone. Don't witness him doing, with the skill and precision of a master, something not many can.

And don't allow him to show you all his talents over the course of one day. I've witnessed him put up two tents, set up a camp, and build a fire, which he started on his first try. All of this with a gun strapped to his chest in his holster vest. I'm starting to think he could fight off a grizzly bear with his bare hands.

None of this is good for me and my already thriving libido for this man.

My only chance is the distraction of the camera guy and Griffin, who finally appear late in the day. The other plane lands and taxis over next to Denver's.

"Don't cry, princess. Your alone time with me is over." He walks away as I sit on the log he found for me. He stops before he's too far away. "Until tonight. We're sharing a tent."

My head whips around. "There are two!"

"Yeah, we're the smaller one. Griffin and the camera guy get the other one because it's bigger."

"That looks like a one-person tent."

"Well, you shouldn't mind. We *are* a couple." He smiles and heads toward the plane.

Griffin climbs out, looking oddly in his element. His clothes look warm and dark and subdued. The cameraman, a red-haired man with a short-trimmed beard and a lanky body, join him. The pilot and Denver talk, and five minutes later, he's taking back off.

How did I not realize it was just going to be me and three men?

"Cleo!" Griffin hugs me and kisses my cheek. "It's so fucking cold."

I shiver in his arms because I stepped away from the fire. "I know. We couldn't have done this in the summer?"

"Right? This is our camera guy, Heath."

I politely shake his hand.

"So you and Denver own Lifetime Adventures?" he says.

I wonder if he's going to interview me, but after I answer, he busies himself next to the fire with his camera. He's all business.

"So what's the protocol here? Like, we just act normal?" I say.

He smiles at me as though I'm not the first one to ask that question. "Yeah, you two are a couple, right?"

Denver shuts the door of his plane and heads over, so I lie. "We are."

"Then I wouldn't worry, we'll get good footage. We always do."

"Wait." Griffin puts his finger out toward me then Denver. "I thought you two weren't a couple?"

I look at Denver. He's a better liar than me.

Denver smiles easily and comes to my side. "It's kind of new, so sorry ahead of time if you think you hear bears in the middle of the night. Cleo can get a little loud."

My mouth drops open as I stare at him in disbelief. "I think he's mistaken. It's usually him who causes the police to come for a noise disturbance. He can't handle a little bit of pain from nipple clamps."

But of course my comment isn't payback because Denver never gets embarrassed about anything.

"Oh, I see dollar figures in your future." Heath laughs, burying his head back in his camera.

"Interesting," Griffin says and gets into his tent. "Thanks for fixing this up for me. What are we doing first?"

Denver rubs his gloved hands together. "You're catching our dinner."

"I can stay here and keep the camp going," I say.

All three men stare at me.

"You have to be everywhere we are unless I'm interviewing you," Heath informs me.

I groan. I mean, I wasn't going to put my feet up and read a book but staying by the fire sounds like a better option.

"Give me two minutes and I'm ready," Heath says.

"Do you film in Alaska a lot? You're so prepared," I say.

"Yeah. I do the crab boat fishing show and the pioneer family. They called me here for this since I was close and familiar with the elements. Just be happy you didn't get Roman. He'd probably stay in his tent the entire time."

I'm not sure that's a bad thing.

"And then you'd never get a show out of it."

True. Mental note to listen to Heath. He knows what the hell he's doing.

WE WALK to the lake which isn't too far. Denver really did pick a good location. He holds my hand because we're supposed to be a couple. He's got a backpack on, and he's given Griffin one. Heath follows us. I inhale a deep breath right before we get to the lakefront. I'm going to have to touch a fish.

Denver leans in close. "Just relax." He kisses my neck. Obviously for the show. "We gotta talk about perfume, babe," he says loud enough for the others to hear.

"You said you liked this scent," I say louder.

Griffin looks over then at Heath.

"Yeah, but not when we're around grizzly bears who'll want to eat you as much as I do."

I smack on my fake smile and push him back. "Oh, babe, you're so jealous." I look at the camera. "He's so jealous all the time." Ugh. I'm terrible at this on camera stuff.

"Watch out, he'll be pissing all around you soon," Griffin says, kneeling at the lake's edge.

I laugh, but it's too obviously fake. Denver shakes his head. So far, we're not exactly rocking this acting thing.

While Denver and Griffin talk about the last time they were together, Heath lowers his camera and signals for me to come near him.

"Cleo, you should just be yourself. Act like I'm not even here or that I'm your best friend filming our trip. I promise, our editors will do wonders for you." He rests the camera back on his shoulder.

Denver's teaching Griffin how to fish with a net, as though they found one in the woods. Griffin is wearing water boots, so he steps into the lake and casts the net. The two work well together, while I sit there admiring them as if I'm a viewer at home and not an active participant in the show.

Denver glances back at me right before he says, "Now we wait."

Heath lowers the camera, and we all shoot the shit about our plans for the next two days. Griffin talks about his divorce and how he's happy to be away from that situation for the time being.

What seems like forever later, the net bobs and Heath picks up the camera. "Let's have Cleo do it. She needs to get involved."

Did I say listen to Heath earlier? Heath should really shut the hell up.

"Perfect idea." Denver waves me over.

Griffin helps me, and Heath ends up filming in the water to get the best view. The fish is not happy to be trapped and I'm trying to use the skills my dad taught me over a decade ago, but as soon as I get him off the net, he clamps his mouth around my hand and I screech.

"Relax," Denver says, picking up the fish and handing it to Griffin to hold with the mouth open.

Tears are pricking my eyes as Denver leads me out of the water.

He pulls an antiseptic wipe from his backpack and sits me down and bandages me. "Are you okay?"

"Other than being humiliated? I'm going to blow this entire thing."

He lowers to his knees, puts his hands on my cheeks, and stares into my eyes. "No, you're not. The audience is going to love you." Sliding his finger over my cheek, he tucks a loose strand of my hair behind my ear and fixes my hat.

"If we make it out of here, can you please be an asshole again?"

He laughs, and my forehead falls into his chest. "You sure you're okay? I think you caught something. Sounds like maybe you don't hate me so much anymore," he whispers.

His voice is so soft I want to ask him to repeat it, but I glance up and Heath's camera is focused on us.

"I'm going to be the next one with an injury if you don't hurry up over here," Griffin says.

Heath swings the camera around as Denver leaves me to go to Griffin. I sit on the wet snow and watch Denver be a hero again. Yeah, I caught something. It's called the feels.

SEVENTEEN

Denver

Nighttime falls, and as we sit around the campfire, Cleo relaxes. We've jabbed at one another a few times, which Griffin and Heath seem to love. We argued about who would clean the fish and how she gagged when I taught Griffin how to filet it. She definitely hasn't taken on the role of master survivalist, but she's a funny sidekick who comes up with better one-liners than me.

"We should tell ghost stories," she says, wrapping the blanket tighter around her legs.

"I think we should talk about wild animals attacking. Make it more real," I offer, sitting back down and handing her a hot chocolate.

Instead of either suggestion, Cleo starts up a conversation with Griffin which is good thinking since this is probably the kinda stuff the viewership would be hoping for when they watch.

"Where did you grow up?" Cleo asks Griffin.

"Georgia," he answers.

"And why do you love this survivalist thing?"

Griffin's face lights up and he talks about how different it is up here. The pressures of the business and success in LA are long gone. When he comes to Alaska, no one really recognizes him and he actually feels like Griffin Thorne, not Griffin Thorne, Music Producer.

"Are you okay talking about the accident with Denver?"

Heath has the camera, and he's right, you do forget he's there sometimes. Griffin's eyes meet mine, and I nod.

"It was hell," Griffin says.

"But you came back for more," Cleo says.

They laugh, but my eyes are focused on Cleo. Her cheeks rosy from the cold, her lips pink from layers of Chapstick. She's found where she fits, and this is it. She can interview the guests.

"I owe Denver my life. What he did for me? I could never repay him. Plus I never turn down an opportunity to sleep under the stars." Griffin looks at the sky.

They continue their conversation about his past, his first break. Griffin touches briefly on his divorce and mentions little about Maverick. The three of us have an honest conversation, and I mentally note to thank Griffin for being so forthcoming.

"And remarriage?" Cleo asks.

Griffin groans. "I'm not sure I'm the marrying type. Sometimes you have to fail at something to realize you kind of suck at it."

They laugh and Cleo glances at me. I wonder what she's thinking.

"What's with men not wanting to commit?"

Guess I don't have to wonder anymore.

"There're lots of women who don't either," I say.

"Far more men," she counters.

"Okay, guys, you can continue fighting this one out. I'm going to bed." Griffin stands.

Heath does too. "We can shut down for the night. That was a great honest conversation. Did you have those questions written out, Cleo?"

She looks at me and back at him. "I was just making conversation."

"Well, you did a great job. Griffin's fans will love getting an in-depth look into his life."

They climb into their tent and I put another log on the fire, hoping it will keep us warm all night.

"You ready to get some sleep?" I ask Cleo, and she nods.

We climb into our tent. I'd already put out the sleeping bags. She takes off her boots and snowsuit before sliding into the bag with her hat on. I do the same.

It's weird to be so close to her, but at the same time exciting. The perfume I said something about earlier lingers in our small space. I wish we had an excuse to strip naked for body warmth.

"Denver?" she says, her voice low. I'm guessing so the guys don't hear us.

"Yeah?"

"Are you a guy who never wants to commit? I mean, I know you like your variety and never have anyone serious, but do you think you'll be like that forever?"

Huh, she's a straight-shooter. I'm not blind to what's happening between us. She probably wants to know right now if she'd be wasting her time. She wants me to shut her down and say, "Yeah, I will be like this forever. I'm never going to settle down with anyone." But I don't think I can.

"That's a hard one. I'm kind of fucked up," I answer.

"I'm not against commitment. I'm just not sure I can do it, as much as I might want to."

"Oh... okay." She nuzzles into her sleeping bag some more.

Although she probably thinks I'm giving her a bullshit answer, I was more truthful with her than I've ever been with anyone. As I wait to hear her slow, even breaths, I listen to the noises of wildlife around us, but I'm more scared of the woman lying next to me than the animals who could kill me.

WE'VE BEEN LIVING OUTDOORS for two days now and I'm smelly and disgusting, but we're done shooting. The other pilot took Griffin and Heath back to Anchorage, and I'll fly us into Lake Starlight. Cleo sleeps the entire flight. If I had to give us a score, I say we got a B. We each have our talents and I think that we complemented each other's personalities.

Before he left, Griffin pulled me aside and told me I was an idiot if I didn't lock Cleo down soon. I saw the way he looked at her, but when I asked him about it, he said he's more of a brunette kinda guy.

By the time we land and get the plane and equipment all put away, it's late on Monday night.

"Where are you going tonight?" I ask Cleo.

I've purposely not pried, knowing that she has nowhere to go other than her dad's place. Wyatt called me before we left and gave me the scoop that she wouldn't stay at Glacier Point even though he was willing to offer her a free room.

Usually the gossip within a big family works against

you, but there are those rare occasions where it works for you.

"I'm going to my dad's."

We're in the office with the lights on, so I can see how nervous she is—her trembling hands, her eyes darting anywhere but on me.

"You're welcome to come to my house. We have an extra room and Phoenix loves you so..."

"I need to go," she says.

"Okay. I can drive you."

"I have my rental."

"It's been a long few days and you're tired. Let me drive you."

She hesitates for a moment but then nods.

"You should really just return the thing. I can take you into the office every day." I'm happy to be her chauffeur.

"Hmm, maybe. Let me grab my suitcase, I left it in the office." She slides by me.

In the past weeks, I've noticed that Cleo Dawson put up a front when she came into this town, all hell-bent on putting me on the stake. Right now, that same mask is on. The woman who couldn't walk into her dad's house two weeks ago has summoned the courage to spend the night there?

I call bullshit.

And I would've called her out on this bullshit already, but we have a lot in common. We hide our vulnerabilities so no one can see them. She deflects by being mean, and I deflect with humor.

Wheeling out her suitcase, she smiles tightly and walks past me. "I'm exhausted. Can we hurry this up, please?"

"Coming, princess."

After locking up the office and double-checking everything, I follow her to my truck. She's already seated, her suitcase in the back.

"I could've gotten that for you."

"No need. I know you don't realize it, but I'm stronger than you think."

I start the truck, repeating to myself that I should keep my mouth shut and drive. But before we turn off the gravel path onto the paved roads of Lake Starlight, I find my silence too hard to hold. "I'm going to throw out the offer one more time."

"And I said thank you, but I'm fine. It's time to be a big girl now." She stares out the window.

I drive with the radio volume on low, the sounds of Van Halen softly filling the cab.

She holds her purse tighter to her chest when I have to stop on the street, my turn signal indicating that I'll be driving down Chip's road any second. My tires hit the gravel-and-dirt road, and I hear her inhale deeply. Is spending the night with me really the lesser of the two options?

"You good?" I ask.

This time I don't get an answer other than a low noise from the back of her throat.

My lights shine, as they did two weeks ago, on Chip's house that is in desperate need of repairs. Cleo opens the truck door, shuts it, opens the back door, and drags her suitcase out before I have a chance to do it for her. We end up meeting at the side of the truck.

"Want me to walk you in?"

It's dark and hard to see her expression, but I'm guessing from her silence that's a resounding no.

"Could you pick me up tomorrow?" she asks.

"Yeah, for sure."

"Thanks."

Her suitcase rolls on the gravel until it hits the wooden planks of the porch. She stops at the front door. I was completely wrong. She's fine with going to her dad's. Huh. Did I do something wrong to make that bitchy side come back out then?

"Bye, Denver," she says and waves.

"I'll just make sure you get in."

It's so quiet outside, I hear her put the key in the lock and turn the knob before disappearing inside. Turning on the light, she waves one more time. "See. I'm good. Goodnight."

The door shuts, and I stand there attempting to wrap my brain around what's happening. A girl who couldn't go in there weeks ago just did so without hesitation.

I climb into my truck and turn it around when she doesn't run out the door in tears. As I head down the driveway and imagine her in there, my stomach sinks. Memories of when I walked up to the cemetery where my parents' headstone is. How heavy every limb felt, like my body was trying to convince me not to go through with it.

Then I remember the relief I felt when Rome was there, waiting for me. As if he knew I was coming and knew I had never been. Twin telepathy maybe. We sat on the bench and retold stories of Dad coaching us in Little League or Mom's ability to always know when we were about to do something stupid. We were honest with one another about how much we missed them.

I reach the main road and do a U-turn, speed back down Chip's road, and slam on my brakes at the edge of the house. Running to the door, I stop short at the porch when I find her seated on the wooden planks, her knees bent up and her head down, sobbing.

I should've listened to my gut.

"Shhh, I've got you." I pick her up without any argument from her, deposit her into my truck, and strap her in.

After retrieving her suitcase and making sure the house is locked up, I drive her to where I should have the first time—my house.

EIGHTEEN

Cleo

Once I'm in the cab of Denver's truck, I wipe my eyes, thankful it's dark outside. "I'm really okay," I say right before another hiccup escapes.

"You're not, and you're going to come home with me tonight. We'll go back together when you're ready."

The drive to his place is silent until he pulls into his driveway and parks. A dim light illuminates one window, but otherwise it's black. I'm guessing that means Phoenix is awake.

"I'm twenty-seven. I should be able to go into his house and sleep."

Denver undoes his buckle and releases mine. He climbs down, opens the back door, and pulls out my suitcase. Before I have time to really think, he's opening my door and holding out his hand.

"Maybe just take me back to the hotel?" I'm sure I can afford one night at Glacier Point.

"I'm putting my foot down. You're staying here," he

says, putting his hand farther into the cab. "Come on. I promise to keep my hands to myself."

I blow out a breath. Before I can respond, Phoenix opens the front door.

"How was Griffin? I'm assuming he still knows nothing about me?" She's wearing a cute pajama set. Somehow, Phoenix seemed like a boxers-and-T-shirt kind of girl for nighttime attire, but apparently not.

Denver holds up his hand. "Not now. We're in the middle of something."

Phoenix peers into the truck and waves.

"Hey, Phoenix. Please go ahead and give your brother the interrogation, but if you don't mind, I'm going to stay the night."

"Oh." Her gaze shoots to Denver, and they have a silent sibling conversation I'm not privy to. I can feel the rawness around my eyes from my tears, so I'm sure she doesn't miss the fact that I've been crying. "Definitely. I'll go make sure the spare room is good to go."

She disappears inside, and I step out of the truck, not accepting Denver's hand. I'm taking way too much of his help lately. He doesn't appear to take offense and follows me up the walkway to their house. Phoenix left the screen door unlocked and the inside door hangs open. When I enter, I see her pass by the top of the stairway with a blanket and a pillow.

"I'll run this up to the spare room," Denver says, motioning to my suitcase. "You hungry?"

I hate to admit it, but I'm starving. Eating fish all weekend has left me craving some greasy junk food. "Yeah, but I should just go to bed."

"I'm sure we have something. I'm hungry too." He

walks up the stairs and heads in the same direction Phoenix did.

I hear their murmurs and decide to go to the kitchen so I don't have to hear what Denver must be divulging to Phoenix—that I'm a complete basket case who can't control her emotions.

I hear Denver coming down the steps before I see him.

He ignores me and heads to the fridge. "Honestly, we don't have much, and nowhere is open for delivery or take-out this late. How about cereal?"

He opens the cabinets, pulls out five boxes of cereal, and brings them to the counter. All of them are sugar-filled children's cereals, but I'm not complaining right now. Within minutes, we both have a bowl—his Fruit Loops and mine Lucky Charms—and the only noise in the kitchen is chomping. Phoenix doesn't join us, and though I really like her company, I'm thankful for the peace right now.

"You know when my parents died, it took me five years to visit their grave after the funeral." He rinses his bowl in the sink. "Chip just died. It's going to take time. Maybe you're rushing yourself."

When he sits back down across from me, I finish my bowl. I'm happy for the distraction of rinsing my dish, so I don't have to look at him. He's trying, and I get what he's doing. I'm just not sure that out of all the people in my life, Denver is the one I should divulge my deepest regrets and fears to. If he can somehow make it better, that'll only stamp savior on his chest. And then I'm nowhere closer to keeping things uncomplicated between us. But at the same time, it might feel good to talk to someone about what's rattling around inside my brain.

I sit back down at the table and pick at the placemat. "You want to know why I didn't like you?"

"Since you say didn't, does that mean you like me now?" His arrogance shines through his smirk.

I smile back. "It's like fifty-fifty."

"Oh, I think it's a little more than that." His tongue slides out of his mouth, swiping along his bottom lip, and my stomach somersaults.

Yeah, it's more than that.

"Chip was a part-time dad at best." I feel guilty saying the words now that my dad's gone, but I can't change the past.

Denver doesn't say anything. I'm not sure how much is known around Lake Starlight about Chip and me, but he never once left Alaska to come visit me.

"I came up here every summer for two weeks until I turned eighteen, and every time I talked to him, all I heard about was you."

"Me?" He points at himself.

"He taught you how to fly, didn't he?"

He nods.

"And survival skills?"

He nods again, and I see the moment realization dawns on him. He grabs my hand. "He loved you."

I don't move out of his grip. "He loved me because I was his daughter, his flesh and blood. But I always felt like he wished you were his son."

His fingers tighten on mine, and when I don't look up, he tightens them again. "When I was with him, he'd brag about his daughter in college. How smart and beautiful you were. That you were going to make something big of yourself."

A soft smile graces my lips. At my college graduation ceremony, I knew he was proud, but he didn't attend.

"Then he left you half the company, and I was so mad

because he assumed I'd need you. I took offense, and it brought up all these feelings. The truth is, you were closer to him than I was."

"That's not true."

It's nice that he's trying to be polite, but we both know the truth. "You were. And now that he's gone, it feels worse because I can't ever change that."

"I never saw it as a competition."

"Because you're..." My next words might cause an argument. We've been getting along so well lately that I'm not sure I want to risk it.

"What? Just say it."

"You're the winner. You had his sole attention. I had his obligatory attention. He felt like he had to give it to me because we shared DNA."

Denver frowns. "I'm sorry you felt that way, and I get that your feelings are your feelings. Nothing I can say will change those. But for what it's worth, you were all he talked about when we were camping. How you were out there seeing things and doing more than he ever did."

His phone dings and I take the opportunity to stand. It's surreal that the man I was jealous of is the same man I'm telling all this to.

"Can I ask you a question?" Denver says, pocketing his phone and heading to the freezer.

Venturing into the family room, I watch him grab some ice cream.

He lifts the container. "Phoenix must like you. She's offering up her mint chocolate chip ice cream."

"She's sweet."

The sound of a drawer opening, and the clank of silverware comes next. "You might be the first person to ever say that."

I chuckle. He joins me in the family room and motions with his head for me to sit on the sofa and I do as he suggests. With each of us armed with a spoon, he offers me the first scoop.

"I never would've thought you were such a gentleman."

"Didn't you ever think that's the reason why women gravitate toward me?"

"I always thought you gravitated toward them."

He mocks offense and moves the ice cream container away from me just as my spoon is about to dig into the creamy goodness.

"I'm irresistible," he says, bringing the ice cream back between us.

I agree. He is, and it took me a long time to see it.

"Why did you decide to stay and take over half the company when you had no interest in it all these years?" I must make a weird face because he adds, "This has nothing to do with us owning it together and all the buyout talk we had. I'm just curious because you never seemed to care before, and now you're an eager beaver."

I raise an eyebrow at his choice of words. But he's right. What is a girl who grew up in high society doing running a tourist company in Alaska? The answer is so easy but goes so much deeper than I've gone with Denver.

I take a heaping spoonful. When I look up, he's staring at me with such reverence, the words fall from my mouth. "I have nothing else."

If he's surprised by my words, he doesn't show it. Instead, he digs into the ice cream. "Can I ask one more question?" His voice lowers this time as if he knows he might be crossing a line.

"Yeah."

"Do you think you could be happy here?" Now his eyes seem to be searching for something in mine.

"I think maybe I could."

His lips tip into a smile I've never before seen on his face. Almost as if he'd been holding his breath, waiting for my answer.

NINETEEN

Denver

Cleo sits in the dimly lit family room, sharing a carton of ice cream with me. I realize now that we have a lot in common, though my issues have been in existence more than a decade longer than hers. Which makes me a veteran and the more knowledgeable one.

I should probably say goodnight and go upstairs—to our separate bedrooms—but I keep asking questions instead, needing to know more about what makes this woman tick. "So you'd like to stay and run Lifetime Adventures?"

Her shoulders rise and fall. "I guess. I mean, I am kind of enjoying building it from the ground up again. And eventually I'm going to win the debate with you about incorporating a family dynamic."

I shake my head, and she laughs. It's been an ongoing conversation since day one. I think she did inherit Chip's stubborn side, which means at some point she probably will win.

"What about you?" She pokes me in the chest and steals the ice cream container.

"What about me?"

"What are you looking for?"

I think of a way to answer this question. I'm enjoying running Lifetime Adventures too, and I loved filming the show this weekend. It was like the best of both worlds, allowing me to explore but also get paid well.

"I've never looked for anything in my life." It's the most honest answer I can give her. Although I've bullshitted a lot of women in my time, I try not to do that with Cleo.

"Nothing?"

I shake my head. "Not since my parents died. I like living my life one day at a time. What's the point in making plans when you may not get to see them come to fruition?"

Her lips tip down and she hands me back the ice cream, staring at me as if we're having a staring contest. I blink first.

She stands and licks her spoon clean. "I should probably go to bed."

When she slides through the space between my legs and the coffee table, I stop her, taking her wrist. "Did I say something to upset you?"

She wears a smile, but it's fake. Like the one she used in the lawyer's office. "No, I'm just tired."

I release her and listen while she puts the spoon in the dishwasher.

"Goodnight," she murmurs.

Does she really want to do this now? Because it has the potential to ruin everything we've developed these past weeks.

"Do you want to ask me a more direct question?"

She says nothing, but from the lack of movement

behind me, it's clear that she's stopped moving toward the stairs. "No."

"Are you sure?"

"I think you've given me enough clues to figure out the answer for myself."

"Maybe I'm dodging," I say, standing and turning to face her.

"Are you?"

I run a hand through my hair and look down. "I want you. I can't deny that. I want you in a way I've never wanted another woman."

A flush rises up her neck into her cheeks. "But?"

"But we're building this company together and I tend to fuck things up. If I sleep with you, it'll ruin the fragile friendship we've developed, and I think both of us need this to be successful. So for the first time in my life, I'm not going to listen to my dick but my brain."

Our gazes lock and neither of us looks away.

"Then maybe we need to set some rules because I can't lie either… I want you in the worst possible way."

Fuck. I've heard women tell me they want me. Cleo isn't the first. But she is the first woman who I think I might want more than she wants me. I know this yearning inside me will only be satisfied when she's screaming my name and I'm deep inside her.

"Then let's make some ground rules," I say.

She steps forward, but she sits on the chair and I sit back down on the couch.

"First of all, I can't live here," she says.

"Once we get the rules set, you'll be able to live here."

I have willpower when I choose to. I quit drinking for an entire six months for a bet. I was even celibate for three months—thankfully my hand didn't count. I squirm just thinking about how chaffed I was after that stint.

"Okay. Rule number one, no more sexual innuendos or jokes." She stares at me because I am the king of that.

"One a day?"

She blows out a breath. "One a week?"

"That'll never work. We need to set parameters I can actually manage. And if I have to be around you all day, one isn't gonna cut it."

Her face lights up. Maybe I don't have the willpower for this, because I'd do just about anything to kiss her right now.

"Fine," she says.

"No walking around in towels," I blurt.

"I don't really do that," she says.

"So you take your clothes into the bathroom when you shower and dress in there?"

She laughs. "Okay. Then no walking around barefoot."

I quirk an eyebrow. "Barefoot?" Then I think of her cute pink toes and grin, realizing she finds my feet as attractive as I find hers. "Deal."

"No being nice," she says, pointing a finger at me.

"Nice?"

"You've been almost sweet lately, and when you mix it with your skills in the wild, it's unrealistic to think that I won't jump you one day."

An image of her toppling me over and the two of us falling to the ground in a frantic kiss that turns into clothing being ripped off one another assaults my mind. I shift to keep my semi covered up.

"And no masturbating to thoughts of each other," she says.

Talk about intriguing. "You've masturbated to me?"

That pink in her cheeks turns apple red. I should probably admit defeat on this because all the rules she's putting in place are rules I've broken.

"Yeah," she says quietly. "Not like every night or anything. Keep your ego in check."

I inch forward, my hardening cock pressing against my pants. "Tell me what I do."

She leans forward and pushes my shoulder. "That's against the rules and now I'll be turning to porn."

"*Ugh,* that's so unfair." I put the heels of my hands to my eyes and groan.

"What?"

"You gave me a visual of your hand down your pants, watching porn."

"Sorry."

I try to erase the image, but when my eyes pop open and see her, it all magically appears again. "Did you imagine me chopping wood without a shirt on?"

She looks at the ceiling and purses her lips. "Nope."

But she crosses her legs, which I know she's doing to release some pressure that's building. After this conversation, if we don't fall into bed with one another, it'll be a miracle.

"Do you think if we did it once... I mean, just one time to get it out of our system?" I throw the idea out there.

"Shut up. That works for no one. We're better off setting these rules. Eventually it'll feel platonic between us." She smiles. I think she might actually believe what she's spewing. I hope she really is smarter than me.

"It was just a suggestion." I shrug.

"A bad one."

"So... we have no sexual jokes, dressing in the bathroom, no masturbating to the other one, and I can't be nice because that turns you on?"

"Especially when we're on the excursions."

I nod. "So on excursions, I'm an asshole to you."

"Yep."

"That should make for great television. The audience will hate me."

"But we won't sleep together, so mission accomplished."

I laugh. "Anything else?"

She thinks for a moment, and all I notice is the length of her neck. I'd do just about anything to have my lips there to feel her pulse.

"We can add as need be." She puts her hand out between us. "Here's to building a friendship with you, Denver Bailey."

I shake her hand. "I've never been friends with a girl before."

"Well, I'm honored to be your first."

So many jokes hit my mind, but I shove them down. "Well, friend, do you want to watch a movie?" It's worth a shot. I know we both said we wanted to shower and go to sleep but now I find myself wanting to spend more time with her.

She stands. "In a dark room with you? I'm not ready for that yet."

"I am hard to resist."

She laughs. "It's going to take some time for us to get to a normal state." She pats my shoulder. "Goodnight."

I sit in the dark with only the glow of the kitchen light on behind me. I'm not sure I'll be in a normal state ever again. "Goodnight. Remember, no sliding your hand anywhere it doesn't belong."

"Technically," she says from behind me, "I can slide my hand. I just can't think the hand is yours."

I whirl around, but she's giggling down the hallway. "Just remember if you play dirty, I'll play dirtier."

Her laughing stops. I'm sure she's envisioning me getting really dirty with her right now. Truth is, this deal is bullshit. If we keep this up, she'll be under me in a week.

TWENTY

Cleo

One whole week has passed, and Denver and I haven't abided by half the rules we set forth. Jokes about the other one naked or us sleeping together are on constant repeat. We openly talk about how we might have masturbated the night before, saying it was to someone else when we both know it was the other person teasing our thoughts.

Selma called. We won't know anything concrete for four to six weeks because of the editing required before they can show the first episode to the pilot group. But they did give us a nice sum for our time thus far, which allowed us to pay Nancy.

"The weather is supposed to break next week. I'm thinking we might be super busy after we hear back from Selma, so maybe we should plan to spread Chip's ashes sooner than later." Denver leans back in his office chair, weaving his fingers across his flat stomach.

"Oh." In my mind, we still had some time before that would happen.

"If you'd rather, we can wait."

"No. Let's do it. Where does he want them scattered?" It hurts a little that Denver knows, and I don't, but he does know where Chip's favorite places were.

He sighs. I've become familiar with this habit of his. He sighs like that when he's hesitant about sharing information. "Remember the letters your dad wrote us?"

I glance at my purse where mine still is. "Yeah."

"He told me that he wants me to take you up in his bush plane and…"

I loathe how slow he is to tell me anything that might upset me—because it means he cares, and if he cares, then there's something more than lust between us. "What?"

"He wants you to pick the spot."

"Me!" I screech, sliding back in the chair and bringing up my knees.

Denver stands and sits on the edge of the desk in front of me. "He wants me to fly you around and have you pick the place you think is the most beautiful. But the instructions were clear—you're to choose his final resting place."

My chin dips to my knees. "Why? I feel like I barely knew him."

Denver's hand lands on my knee. "You did know him. But I think this was more his way of feeling connected to you."

"It feels like a lot of pressure."

He chuckles and slides closer, lifting my chin to make me meet his gaze. "I'll be right there with you. I promise you'll know it when you see it. All you have to do is choose the most beautiful place to you."

"Okay," I say in a small voice.

He smiles and takes his finger away. "We'll leave Wednesday and come home Sunday." Rounding the desk, he sits down and slides in his chair, his eyes back on his computer.

"Why on Earth do we have to be gone for so long?"

He looks up, seeming surprised. I thought it would be at most a two-day trip. "We're heading farther north, which means some stops along the way. Relax, it's gonna be fun." He winks and buries his head back into his computer.

Four nights. Four nights with Denver. Alone.

"I want my own tent," I spit out.

He laughs. "No worries, I'll have us in cabins. I didn't want you to rough it since it'll be so hard anyway."

"I told you no being nice."

His smile says he loves pulling a reaction out of me. "I can't seem to help it with you. Sorry not sorry."

He acts as if he doesn't notice me staring at him, which is good. If he acknowledged it, I'd probably be straddling him right about now. I need to talk to someone. Someone who can give me the advice I need about him, because I'm about to lose my damn mind.

Bridget is still in Dallas. She's doing the weather now. I could call her, but I think she'd tell me to sleep with him and forget it. I'd hate to involve one of his sisters, so I decide to reach out to the women the Bailey men have won over.

Phoenix put me in a family group chat that I've tried to get off of but keep getting added back in. Colton is in it as well and he's not with a Bailey, so I figured what's the harm. I use that to text Harley and Holly, asking them to meet for lunch this week. We agree on Tuesday and that we'll meet in the neighboring town of Greywall. There are too many eyes in Lake Starlight.

I WALK into the cafe that Harley chose. She's tucked into a corner booth by herself.

"Holly should be here soon," she says, getting up and hugging me hello.

"Great."

"Rome and I found this place a few months ago. Great sandwiches and they have cookies Calista loves. Rome tried to replicate them because he loves a challenge, but Calista keeps saying, 'Nope, not it, Daddy.'" She laughs.

A ping of jealousy hits me right in the heart. Her life is so full, so happy, so peaceful. Well, not peaceful. Maybe consistent is a better word. "That's very cute."

She sips her tea. "Yeah, they have cute tea parties for kids too. I think when Calista is older, we'll all come here."

"All?"

She laughs again. "You'll soon find out, when it comes to the Baileys it's *all*, not *some*." She looks at the door. "Oh, there's Hols." Her hand goes up, and I turn to find Holly looking behind her and rushing over to our table.

"I'm sorry. She followed me, and Sheriff Miller didn't see her leave the city limits." She slides into the booth.

"Who?" I ask.

Holly and Harley look at one another. "Dori," they say in unison.

"But I didn't—"

Holly laughs. "You don't have to. I should've known. She's been popping up wherever I am lately. The other day at the doctor's office, she said she sees the doctor there too. Is she trying to get pregnant, you think?" She rolls her eyes. Harley doesn't laugh and Holly's shoulders fall. "Stop feeling guilty."

"But—"

They have no time to talk about it because Dori walks in with another woman as though she's not looking for us.

"Look at her acting all sly," Harley whispers.

As she says it, Dori circles around and she points at us. "Girls!" When she nudges her friend, they come over to our booth. "Cleo, hi, sweetie. This is Ethel, my friend."

The red-haired woman smiles and puts out her hand. "I recognize you from Buzz Wheel."

"Thanks." I grace her with a small smile. "I always seem to be in distress and Denver's my knight in shining armor in those pictures."

Harley and Holly laugh.

"Oh, we can tell you some stories," Harley says.

"Should we get a table for five?" Dori asks, disregarding the entire Buzz Wheel conversation.

I wonder if she was ever on there. Something tells me they'd steer clear of her for fear for their lives. Dori has one of those personalities that you look to for safety, but she's also like a mama dog and if you go for her puppies, she's going to bite you—hard.

"Well, Cleo wanted to—"

Holly gets cut off by Dori waving to the waitress. "We need a table for five."

The waitress looks at us.

"Sorry," Harley says quietly.

"I'm sure this man wouldn't mind moving."

The guy at the table beside us looks up from his cup of soup. After a stare-down from the two older ladies, he wipes his mouth and stands. "By all means."

"Perfect. What a gentleman." Dori beams and she and Ethel move the poor man's table to join our table of four. "Come on, girls."

The waitress gives us a disapproving look and places some menus down, takes our drink order, and flees—to complain about us in the back, I'm sure.

"So why are you girls meeting? And meeting in Greywall?" Dori asks.

"Why are you and Ethel in Greywall?" Harley asks.

"Rome told me about this place, and we wanted something different. Right, Ethel?"

Amazing how believable her story is.

"Yes." Ethel leans closer to me. "You're more beautiful in person."

That was a nice compliment, and I feel my cheeks heating up. "Thank you."

"I see why Denver's so enamored," she continues.

"Can I kiss you?" I say, and Harley laughs.

"Oh, sweetie, I'm not a lesbian." Her face is straight, so I bite back my laughter so I don't embarrass her.

"Back to why you're all here." Dori isn't going to let this go.

"We were just getting to know Cleo," Holly says.

Harley sips her iced tea in silence.

I appreciate the girls trying to mask the real reason we're all here, but I'll take the bait Dori's throwing. She'll answer honestly. "I asked them to meet me because I'm having issues with Denver."

Dori sighs and the corners of her mouth turn down.

Ethel looks at the table. "Why is everyone so quiet? We all know Denver has issues."

"Ethel, zip it," Dori says.

"What am I missing?" I ask.

Dori looks at the girls. "What exactly was your plan? What were you going to tell her?"

Holly shrugs. "I didn't spell out why I asked them here

but they're smart women, I'm sure they had an idea. "We were going to tell her our experiences, that's all."

"Yeah, just that sometimes it's hard to fall in love with a Bailey," Harley says.

Luckily our waitress arrives, and we're distracted by ordering our food.

But as soon as she leaves, Dori sets her focus solely on me. "Do you like Denver?"

Nausea rolls my stomach as if a wall of waves is hitting me over and over.

"Excuse me for a moment." I bolt down the hallway toward the bathroom..

TWENTY-ONE

Cleo

A knock hits the bathroom stall door.

"Cleo?" Holly says. "It's just me. Harley is taking one for the team and talking about Calista and Dion, so we have some time."

I open the stall door. I didn't throw up. I'm not even sure where the urge came from.

Holly touches my forehead. "Are you pregnant?"

"Unless it's a miraculous conception, no."

"So you and Denver haven't…?"

I shake my head.

I'm sure Holly doesn't mean to look relieved, but her emotions are transparent. "I'm sorry. It's none of my business. I'm so happy for Rome and Harley, but I'm not sure I could take the news right now."

I put my hand on her shoulder. "I completely understand. No worries on my front."

We head to the sink so I can wash my hands.

"Dori is protective of them, as you can understand."

Holly leans against the wall. "They were affected in different ways when their parents died. I think what Dori tries to hide is how much Denver fears the unknown now."

I nod. I know that about him by now.

"What you guys are doing with Lifetime Adventures—I mean, the family is in awe that he's stayed committed for this long." She must realize what she's said because she puts her hand in the air like "disregard that." "Not that I don't think he's incapable of it. He's just never tried anything like this before. I'm not saying he can't change. I don't want you to take that away from what I'm saying."

I shake my head, although I think I know where this is going.

"When Austin mentioned your shared ownership, and I saw you at the funeral, I honestly thought one of you would've called uncle by now. But the fact that he's working side by side with you and the two of you haven't slept together is shocking."

"Why?"

Her face softens. "Why what?"

"Why did you think we couldn't work?"

Holly smiles in a tender way. But I don't fill the silence, so she eventually continues. "Because you both grieve in similar ways."

I say nothing because I'm not sure what I can say.

"You both ignore things instead of addressing them. Denver's been ignoring his parents' deaths for years. And maybe it's because I have my own dad issues, maybe it takes one to recognize one. You hid your emotions well at the funeral. You never cried. When Austin told me a little more about what you'd experienced, I realized we have a lot in common."

"I think you just answered the question I came here to

have answered."

She tilts her head. "What was that?"

"When it comes to Denver, I should steer clear."

She shifts forward then backs up a step. "I would never say that. Never. You're only hearing the negative. What I was originally saying was he's different around you. He's... I've never seen him like this. Ever."

"I have no idea what to do at this point."

"Do you like him?" She puts her hand on my shoulder as the bathroom door swings open.

A middle-aged woman makes her way in, and we slide out of the way. I nod in answer to her question.

Holly wraps me in a big hug. "Why are you upset about that?"

I mumble into her chest the one big fear I have. "He's going to break my heart."

We stand there hugging, and for the first time, I feel as if someone gets me. She doesn't try to tell me no or change my mind. She just holds me tightly, letting the silence rest between us.

The door springs open again. "You have about ten seconds. Dori just told me I talk too much about the kids." Harley rushes into one of the stalls. "I have to pee. One of you needs to tag in."

She doesn't even seem to notice we're hugging. We break apart, giggling to one another. Holly looks at me with a question in her eye, asking if I'm okay, and I nod.

"We'll go out, take your time," Holly says to Harley.

All we hear is a sigh of relief followed by a stream of pee in the toilet. "Come and get me after the lunch. Just have the waitress deliver my meal in here."

The other woman who came in stares at Harley's door like "What is her problem?"

"She's pregnant," Holly says, and the woman nods with a smile now.

We walk back out into the restaurant. Our food is on the table. Thank goodness, this lunch will be over quickly.

"Are you okay?" Ethel asks.

I stare at my turkey club and chips. "Yeah. Thank you for asking."

"I'm going to lay this out there for you and you can do with the information what you want," Dori says. "Ethel and I will eat our soup and you can continue talking to Holly and Harley. I understand I'm just an old lady to you all."

"That's not true," Holly says. "I just think Cleo wanted to get a non-Bailey perspective."

"You and Harley are Baileys," she says as though she takes offense to Holly saying they aren't.

She loves them. Clearly anyone her grandchildren marry she includes in her security blanket of protection. It's actually very sweet.

Holly puts her hand on Dori's. "I know. I didn't mean that—"

Dori cuts her off. "Denver is my wild grandchild. He never ran away from Lake Starlight though. I thought as soon as he turned eighteen, he'd be gone."

Harley slides into her chair, not interrupting the conversation.

"Rome did though." Dori's eyes go to Harley. "He ran. I think that hurt Denver too and made yet another lasting impression."

"What do you mean?" I ask then take a sip of my drink.

"When Denver was five or six, he begged for a pet. His

parents got him a fish because they didn't want any animals, what with their house already being full of kids." She spoons her soup and sips her drink while we all wait patiently. "He fed it so much and changed the water so many times as an excuse to touch it, the fish died in three days."

Holly's lips tip down while I picture a disappointed little boy with a mop of brown hair.

"The next time, they got him a cat. He almost smothered the thing. He kept it on a collar and leash. He wanted that thing with him all the time. He'd squeeze it so hard, I thought its eyes would pop out. As soon as it got old enough, it would hide from Denver."

"Denver and pets aren't compatible," Ethel agrees.

I wonder how long they've been friends?

"Worst was Glacier." Dori shakes her head. "It wasn't Denver's fault, but everyone kind of made fun with him and told him it was."

Ethel joins the conversation. "They got a shelter dog, and of course the dog couldn't pee without Denver standing guard over him. He ran away after a month and no one ever saw him again."

I take the meaning of each story and add on his parents dying and finally figure out what Denver's so scared of. He doesn't want to love anyone or commit to anything because he doesn't want his heart broken either. We have the same fear. That's what Holly meant in the bathroom.

"My Denver loves hard and fierce, or at least he used to. But he acts like it's a deadly disease now. So when I asked you if you liked him, I meant do you like him enough to fight for him. I see the way he looks at you," Dori says. "The way he's been caring for you just like that goldfish, the cat, and Glacier the dog. But he's probably not going to admit it without a little help."

I push away my club sandwich. This is not what I came here looking for. I wanted to know if I should sleep with him. Some conversation with other women who, at one time, had to have felt torn. I know Harley and Rome's story is different and with a lot more baggage, but at some point, she had to decide to trust him. And Austin and Holly had to learn how to mesh a personal and professional relationship.

I definitely didn't want to know that Denver is like a wounded shelter dog who's been returned time and time again so that he no longer trusts or believes that people won't disappoint him. That does nothing to stop me from sleeping with him. If anything, I want to hug and kiss him and tell him what a great guy he is.

"Is this why you've stayed out of it with them?" Holly asks Dori.

Holly's partially right. Since the family dinner, Dori has disappeared. From the stories Phoenix tells, it sounds as though Dori has a hand in every Bailey couple. I kind of figured she saw something between Denver and me and backed off because I wasn't the right fit for her grandchild.

She sets her spoon down beside her bowl. "Every couple needs something different." Dori touches Holly's hand. "So I'm going to ask you again, Cleo, do you like Denver?"

I swallow, and all their eyes land on me. "I think I do."

"Think?" Ethel says.

"Do. I do," I correct, and Holly and Harley laugh.

Harley reaches across the table. "I know it wasn't what you were looking for when you came here, but I think it still answers your question."

Lucky for us, Dori stops the waitress to ask about dessert.

Harley lowers her voice. "The whole 'sleep with him now and figure it out later' thing isn't really an option with Denver. At least not where you're concerned."

That's a gut check. If I'm so wounded, how could I ever hope to heal someone else's pain?

TWENTY-TWO

Denver

I'm in the office when Cleo barrels in with a brown box. "I brought you lunch."

I look up from the new logos the graphic designer sent over. We won't be able to change all the signage at once, but the advance from *Uncovering America's Beauty* will help. "Thanks."

"And I want to go to my dad's. Will you come with me?" She must see my surprised expression because she adds. "If not, I can do it by myself. I shouldn't ask you, it's just—"

I stand and round the desk. "How many cups of coffee did you have?"

"None, I had iced tea."

"If you want to drive, I'll eat on the way and we can go now." I grab my jacket from the back of the door, and she smiles at me.

"You're going to let me drive your truck?"

"Yeah. Why?"

She shakes her head. "No reason. Has anyone told you you're a good guy?"

Now I crinkle my forehead. "What's going on?"

She's trying really hard to act as if everything's normal, but she's practically bouncing from one foot to the other. "I want to heal. I'm sick of it weighing me down. I need to feel him again instead of just the loss of him."

"Okay." I pick up the brown take-out box and toss her the keys. We lock up the office. Nancy's at lunch, so I'll text her on the ride. "I forgot to tell you, Nancy made us cold brew this morning."

"She did?"

"Well, she poured coffee over ice." I shake my head.

Cleo laughs. "She's really trying."

"Yeah. I think she misses her role. I never really knew what it was."

We climb into the truck and sitting in the driver's seat makes Cleo look like a child. "You want a book or something to sit on?"

"Haha." She starts the truck, puts it in reverse, and I almost choke on my sandwich when she accelerates back. "You have touchy gas."

I raise my eyebrows like "Whatever you say."

Fifteen minutes later, my truck is parked in front of Chip's house for the third time with Cleo next to me, but she seems determined this time. We climb out, and I follow her to the door of his cabin-style house.

I put my hand on her back, and she stills with the key in the lock. "Are you sure?"

She looks at me, and I want so desperately to kiss her and assure her that I'm here to catch her if she falls. "I'm sure."

Covering her hand with mine, we turn the key together.

The doorknob turns, and the door opens. The scent of stale cigarette smoke accosts us first, but Cleo doesn't seem to notice.

She stands in the entryway that's pretty much the family room. The green-and-red plaid couch-and-chair matching combo sits in front of a television. His paper and a pair of his reading glasses are next to the chair on a TV tray. A kitchen table has a bouquet of fake flowers in a vase. The small kitchen is neat and organized. In all the times I was here this place was never this clean or organized.

"Do you think someone else has been here?" I ask.

Cleo looks at me. "Did you come back after he went to hospice?"

I shake my head.

"I came once to clean the kitchen when he was still in hospice care, but the table was overflowing with books on Alaska and planes." She walks in farther, her curiosity now overriding her fear of being here in the first place. Opening up the fridge, she finds a small cake and half gallon of milk. She sticks her hand in. "It's cold." When she shuts the fridge and opens the freezer on top, she pulls out an ice cube tray. "These aren't even completely frozen yet. This is weird."

She heads to the back where his bedroom and bathroom are. "The bed is made, and I know I didn't do that. I'd been thinking I had to clean the sheets but couldn't do it."

I stare at two bins stacked on the kitchen table. A label in Chip's handwriting on the top box says, "Important papers box number one." What must it be like to know you're leaving this earth?

I've imagined what my parents' thoughts might have been right before their snowmobile hit the tree. Did they cling to one another? Think of all of us? Did they think that this might hurt or know that they were going to die? Or did it come out of nowhere and they were laughing and then all of a sudden there was nothing?

To be able to plan things out as Chip was able to… I'm not sure which way is better. Especially because as much as I admire Chip, his daughter is still searching for her place in this world. She never found peace with their relationship, and now she has to do it by looking through his things. Isn't a death bed made to seek forgiveness from the ones you've wronged so that the person you've wronged can accept and forgive you because they want you to go in peace?

Cleo comes out of the back room. "Someone else has been here. The bathmat is new and so are the towels."

"These are clearly labeled." I point at the boxes.

Her shoulders fall. "I don't understand. I mean, did he hire a cleaning crew? I'm so confused." She almost looks disappointed that she can't do it herself.

"Do you want to go through the boxes?"

"I want to find out who else has a key to this house. Was he dating anyone?" she asks, then spies something on the mantel of the fireplace and she moves over to it.

I've seen the picture before, but it was always in his office. It's of a young Cleo standing at the side of a local river and holding a fish up that she caught.

Her fingers run along the frame and she picks it up. "I remember this day. It was the first time I'd caught a big fish and my dad tried to teach me how to clean it. I was so grossed out." A sad smile tilts her lips. She shakes her head, clutching the photo to her chest.

"Do you wanna sit down?" I wrap my arm around her waist because the longer she stands, the paler she becomes.

She places the picture back on the mantel. "Denver?"

"Yeah?" I crowd her, wanting to be here for her in whatever way she needs.

"I want to leave," she says softly.

"Okay."

We climb back into my truck, but this time, I'm driving.

"I think that was a success," I say.

"I think I choked," she says, staring out the window as I drive through Lake Starlight.

"You went all the way to the bedroom."

"Only because I felt like we were the three bears looking to find out who ate our porridge."

"It is odd," I say. "Maybe we should ask Luther Lloyd." Her eyes bulge out as I turn down the next road to take a back way to his office. "He should know, right?"

"I imagine so."

Her mood improves with the idea that she'll at least get the answer and a piece of the Chip puzzle will be solved. Cleo doesn't like the unknown, and Chip's life is a lot of unknowns.

TWENTY MINUTES LATER, we're back outside of Luther Lloyd's office with no answers.

According to Luther, Cleo was given the only key. No one should be occupying the house without consent from her. He asked her a bunch of questions about whether she was sure it was different than after he went to hospice. As if she was delusional and maybe she was grieving and forgot she'd made the bed and cleaned up.

"He thinks I'm crazy," she says as we descend the stairs.

"I know you're not."

"Do you think he has another... child?"

"No!" But I question whether I would know. He talked about Cleo, but for the most part, he was quiet about his personal affairs.

"A wife?"

"No."

I open my truck door, and she slides in. "Do we call the police?"

I shut the door to have time to think about what to do. I round the front of the truck. It's all so odd. Our police department isn't huge, and maybe we're jumping to conclusions. Maybe he did have a girlfriend who cleaned up but then stopped coming.

I've already made our reservations for the trip to spread Chip's ashes. We're scheduled to leave tomorrow. I hope this new development won't jeopardize that.

I climb into the truck and start the engine, but Cleo's still deep in thought. "We'll still leave tomorrow. When we return, if we find something out of place, then we'll alert the police that something is going on."

She nods. "Okay, that sounds like a plan. I hope it was someone he shared his life with. That would make me happy, because I was such a shitty daughter."

My hand touches her thigh, but I move it because we're crossing those boundaries we've been doing so well with. Well, doing so okay with. I wouldn't give us an A, but a solid C for sure.

She yanks my hand back and covers mine with hers. "I need this right now."

I pull the truck to the side of the road and get out before walking around to her side. I yank open her door as she looks at me as if I'm crazed. Opening my arms, I wave her to me.

She doesn't wait, she unclips her seatbelt, and almost falls into my arms. I hold her as tightly as I can.

"We'll figure this out, I promise," I whisper into her ear.

She doesn't cry or sob, but her body sinks into mine. I could hold her like this for days. After a few minutes, she steps back, and my arms feel empty.

"There you go being nice again." She laughs and climbs back into the truck, shutting the door.

Realization dawns on me. My need to fix everything in her life, to put her above myself... I need to give her some space before I smother her, and she runs away forever.

TWENTY-THREE

Cleo

The next morning we're back at Lifetime Adventures, except this time Denver is packing my dad's plane. The only good thing about taking Dad's plane is that we'll be able to sit side by side.

"I'm bringing a tent just in case, but we can play it by ear," he says.

"Okay, but the cabins... are we..."

He turns around from having his ass in front of my face, which wasn't a problem for me. "Sharing, yeah. Sorry, but I'll sleep on the floor or in the bathtub. We just don't have the money for two—"

I put up my hand to stop him. "No, of course not. We'll figure out a few new rules."

Truth is, I'm done with the rules. After what Dori said, I decided to admit that I do like Denver and I'm done denying it. But there's still the problem of how he feels about me. Attraction is one thing. Commitment is another.

I've been taking his nurturing me to mean he cares

about more than how good my ass looks in jeans, but what if he's doing it because he likes to take care of others? Then I remember Dori's words. Is it because he likes me too that he wants to make sure I'm okay? Ugh, maybe my life was better in Dallas when I was a loser who'd ruined my step-dad's cattle farm, and everyone looked at me as though I wasn't quite good enough.

"Make sure to give me some notice, because I'll need to mentally prepare to adhere to our rules." His eyes light up with mischief, and my stomach ripples with warmth.

"Hey, you two." Nancy strolls into the hangar. "I made you guys a jug of cold brew to take with you." She holds it out to me. It's in a thermos, and not one that looks as though it can go hot and cold.

I take it and hand it to Denver to pack. "Thank you so much."

"You're the best," he says.

"Can I talk to you for a second?" I whisper to her as Denver goes into the plane to arrange all the gear.

Nancy looks at me skeptically but steps away.

"We'll be right back," I say.

Denver nods and waves.

When we're a safe distance away, I stop her. "I want to redo the office. Nothing major, but at least get us two desks. I'm done with sitting criss-cross applesauce in the chair because there's nowhere for my legs."

Nancy laughs.

"So could you... and if I'm overstepping, please let me know." I put my hands up in front of me in a placating gesture.

"Cleo, I'm literally dying of boredom. Please, whatever it is, I'm happy to do it."

I chuckle. "Thanks. I was hoping it wouldn't be a problem. So I have two desks being delivered. They should fit in the office. The biggest thing I need is my dad's stuff gone. Don't throw anything away. Maybe just box it up and we can go through it later?"

"Sure." She touches my upper arm. "It'll all be handled when you come back."

"Thanks."

"What you and Denver are doing with Lifetime Adventures is awesome. You two deserve to make this your own. I'm really proud of you."

I can't remember the last time a person said that to me. "That means a lot to me."

She hugs me. "I hope you stay."

I haven't made a final decision on what I'm going to do. Right now I'm taking it as it comes. Besides, a lot will depend on what happens with the show. Everything in Lake Starlight feels right. My eyes linger on Denver, who's getting out of the plane. Everything really feels right with him too.

"I like it here," I say to her.

Nancy pulls back, her hands clasped on my upper arms. "You're so much like your dad." She points at my heart. "Always guarding that gentle muscle." Her gaze wavers to Denver and back to me. "I wish everyone could just love. No game playing."

"In a perfect world." I act as if I have no idea she's referring to Denver and me.

"Ready, Cleo?" Denver says, brushing something off his jeans.

"Yeah."

"How many ugly retro snowsuits did you pack? Your luggage was heavy." He laughs, and Nancy does as well.

I hug her one more time. "See you Monday."

"Have a safe trip, you two."

Denver walks by Nancy and kisses her temple. "Thanks, Nance, but you know I'm an expert."

"Don't jinx us," I say.

He stops at the door before pushing it open. "There's no jinxing when you're in my hands."

Nancy purses her lips and widens her eyes like, 'How can you not fall for this man?'

Ten minutes later, we're side by side in the airplane, and I get to witness Denver do what he loves without peeking over his shoulder. There go my ovaries again, putting the man beside me at the top of their to-do list.

WE TRAVEL NORTH, according to what Denver says over the radio. He's much more vocal this trip, as if he's giving a tour. I'm still awestruck over the ease with which he maneuvers the plane. He flies lower over the valley between two mountain ranges then comes back up as though he's moving with the mountains and the terrain. Everything is flawless and makes me feel as if I could be sitting on a big comfy cloud gliding through the air.

"We're going to land here for the first night." His voice soothes me like honey down a sore throat.

I see cabins in the distance and a blue lake below us. "That's where we're staying?"

"Yeah, I figured we'll see the ice cave then grab dinner."

"Perfect."

He lands, and we taxi over to where the other planes are parked and check-in. Our cabin is small but quaint. If he isn't going to sleep on the bed with me, the bathtub is his only other option because there's hardly any room on either side of the bed.

"It's small," I say.

"Yeah, I don't quite remember it being this small." He laughs, putting his bags in the closet and flopping onto the bed. "So lay out the rules for me."

My heart and my girly parts contract at seeing his large body sprawled across the bed. "Um."

"Are you as tired as me?" He changes the subject right when I was going to go for broke. His shirt rests a couple of inches above the waistband of his jeans with his hands behind his head like that.

"Not really, but I didn't fly. I got to enjoy the ride." I open my suitcase and grab my toiletry bag to take to the bathroom in order to distract myself from the view of his happy trail.

"Let's take a nap," he murmurs, and I figure he's already half asleep.

Come on, Cleo. You've literally thought about every way this can go. You're prepared for whatever happens. Just talk to him.

"I was thinking about something..." I walk back into the room.

His eyes pop open, and he smiles. "You're always thinking about something."

"Yeah, probably."

He pats the bed and I sit down. "What's up? You want me to sleep in the plane?"

I shake my head. "I'm not sure I want to live with the rules anymore."

He sits up, and if I thought he was tired, I was wrong. His eyes are alert and focused solely on me. "Meaning?"

"Well, I'm not going to just sleep with you without it meaning anything."

He nods.

"Oh, forget it. This is so stupid. What are we, thirteen and I'm asking you to go steady with me?" I stand, but he leans over the bed and grabs my hand, pulling me back down.

"Don't do that," he says.

"Do what?"

"Don't discount your feelings and what you want."

His hand hasn't left mine. My stomach feels is a pinball machine right now, the silver ball bouncing all over the place and never landing. "I just—"

He puts his finger over my lips. "Don't water it down. Tell me what you want."

I say nothing and he removes his finger, waiting. It's now or never. "I want you. But not just for tonight. I know we own this company together and it's stupid to get involved, but at this point, it feels more stupid that we've been dodging this... *thing* between us."

"And by this *thing*, you mean...?"

I bite my lip. "Are you really going to make me do this?"

"Let me hear it." He grins.

I huff. "I want to date you." I fall forward so my face hits the bed. He's so going to pay for this.

He pushes me onto my back so he's half lying on top of me. "Is that a question?"

He laughs as I push him off me. "I can't believe you just made me do that!"

"Don't you want to hear my answer?" He rolls onto his back and pulls me in to lie on top of him. It's difficult not to be distracted by the feel of his hard body under mine.

"I don't think I do." I wiggle, but he grips me tighter.

Eventually I give up the fight and his hands land on either side of my face. "Yes, Cleo Dawson, I'd love to date you."

I'm shaking my head at the complete ridiculousness this situation has come to. I feel like a moron. But then he rolls us back over and his fingers brush my hair away from my face. He stares into my eyes with so much pent-up desire that I forget all about my embarrassment.

"I really like you," he says before dipping his lips to meet mine. He brushes them lightly along mine, barely touching. His teasing makes my body respond like a wildfire spreading through me from barely a kiss. "I've wanted you for a long time." He places his lips on mine, a little harder this time. "And not just your body." His fingers slide down my ribcage. "You. I want you. I want you to be mine."

Where did this side of him come from? I shouldn't care or think twice about it, just enjoy it, but he wasn't a steady relationship guy when we met. But I can see, feel, and hear the sincerity in his words, so I allow myself to sink into our kiss. He drags his lips off of mine before it becomes a full-on make-out session.

"I'm not going to have sex with you right now," he whispers in my ear and his lips continue to venture, his tongue teasing. "No matter how much I'm kicking my brain right now."

"Why not?" I choke out. I'm in flames and he's decided not to use the hose? What the hell?

I want to scream that I gave him the green light. All the flirting. All the sexual innuendos. All the touching. All the heartfelt conversations. And he's putting on the brakes?

He sits up on his knees and straightens my shirt so it lands at the top of my jeans. "Because I'm taking you on a date."

"A date?" I groan.

He laughs. "Yes, ice cave, dinner, then we'll come back here for dessert."

I sit up. "You're enjoying this, aren't you?"

He crawls on his knees to reach me and again tucks a strand of hair behind my ear before kissing my lips briefly. "I've withheld doing what I want to do to you for months. I want a night with you that doesn't include rules. And I'll show you what it'll be like dating me."

How can a girl say no to that? Denver Bailey is a romantic? Not even Buzz Wheel had the scoop on that one.

TWENTY-FOUR

Cleo

Denver has taken this date thing so far that he dressed then waited outside our cabin for me to get ready. Of course, we're going into an ice cave, so it's not like I'm wearing a dress and heels. I'll be completely covered up.

But I put on my tightest pair of jeans and the short sweater I'm pretty sure he's fond of, with a cami underneath. I top it with my parka and the boots Denver bought me. I grab my hat, scarf, and gloves to take with me. I triple-check my reflection in the mirror before I go outside. I managed to put on a little extra makeup, heavy on the eyeliner and mascara.

When I step out of our cabin, Denver's talking with a tall man who's years older than him. He spots me and waves as though I would've missed him. Then he shakes the man's hand and heads my way.

When he reaches me, he kisses my cheek. "You should've planned your coming-out party at a better time. Although I will have fun stripping those layers off later."

A rapid spread of heat hits me from head to toe. If this is what I have to look forward to when it comes to dating Denver, I'm kicking myself for waiting so long.

I cock my hip out to the side. "You could've stripped them off already."

He takes my hat and puts it on my head, wraps my scarf around my neck, and holds out my gloves for me to push my hands into.

"This is so romantic," I say sarcastically, but it kind of is because I never would've imagined he'd be so attentive.

"Wait until I kiss you in an ice cave." He waggles his eyebrows.

"Promises, promises," I tease, and he offers me his arm. I slide my hand through the crook of his elbow. "You're too much."

"You do tend to fall a lot in my presence."

I roll my eyes but allow him to guide me wherever he wants.

Turns out the cabin rental place owns a shuttle that takes us to the ice cave. So a half hour later, we're outside of it. I have to admit, the cave is slightly terrifying. The blue ice is a feast for the eyes, but I'm walking into an abyss of ice to earn that kiss Denver promised.

Once we're farther inside and away from the group, we look up and around. While I was scared coming in here, now that we're in the depths, it feels peaceful and quiet. As if the world outside doesn't really exist and we're cocooned inside this place that is ours alone.

I really hope I'm not one of many girls he's kissed here. I'm annoyed by that thought.

Denver tucks me into a spot where there aren't many witnesses and unties my scarf from around my mouth. "It's beautiful, right?" His voice is low, and his hands are on my hips, but there're too many layers to really feel him.

"It is," I say.

"Not nearly as beautiful as you though." He lowers his head.

I raise mine while my heartbeat skyrockets. His lips touch mine like a soft embrace, his knuckles trailing down my cheek. How is he this perfect? I admit I want to date him, he agrees, holds off on sex, and gives me a kiss in an ice cave that I'll remember the rest of my life.

His tongue slides into my mouth, and all my limbs relax. With all the men I've kissed—and it's not as though there have been a ton—I've never felt my legs get heavy and want to give out. But with Denver, my entire body melts and tingles. His hands cup my face as if I'm the most precious thing in the world. A low groan sounds from his throat right before we pull apart, and I'm a goner. He's ruined me for any man who comes after him.

As he rests his forehead on mine, our eyes lock and a small smile lights up his entire face.

"Am I the first?" I blurt. Damn it. How stupid am I to ask that?

Denver steps back, the smile wiped off his face so well it looks as though it was never there in the first place. "I can't change my past. You understand that, right?"

I'm so stupid. Why am I allowed to talk during moments like this? "I do, and I'd never want your past not to exist. You are who you are from all those experiences. It was a stupid thing to ask, I'm sorry."

Denver nods.

But then a new bravado hits me. I owe it to myself to ask, and I'm not going to imagine this great, special kiss only to find out later that he brings everyone here. I need to know what this is.

"You know what? I do have to know. I'm sorry if that upsets you, but what I know of you, I like a lot. Fact is, you have a reputation. I need to know why you're being so different with me and so easily accepting of this dating thing. Maybe it's because it's not a big deal and you've brought a million girls here?"

He blows out a breath and takes off his hat, scratching the back of his neck. "Maybe I moved us too fast."

"Too fast? Are you crazy? I threw myself at you and you screeched us to a halt."

Denver looks around because my voice got a little loud for a moment. He moves us farther away from the group. "What can I say? I have enjoyed women with no strings. They all knew the score, though some acted like they didn't. I've never told a woman I wanted to date her. I've never brought a woman to an ice cave because the majority of the time, I only brought them to my bed. But Cleo... I didn't want to have sex with you right after you told me you were into me because you're different. You deserve to have a date where I kiss you in an ice cave and get to know you over dinner. Where I take you back to a bed without drinking too much. You deserve the sweet kisses, the gentle touches, the tease of fabric falling from your skin. You deserve all of it, and I want to give it to you." He takes a breath, and I push back tears. "You deserve everything I have and probably a helluva a lot more. But I'm giving you my all, and I can only hope it's enough for you."

I suck in a breath because at some point during his speech, I forgot to breathe. "I'm sorry."

He shakes his head, looks at our feet, then back up at me. "Don't ever be sorry for sticking up for yourself. I should've told you all that this afternoon when you were so open with me. But words are one thing, and I was trying to prove with my actions that I'm not the guy you think I am."

I giggle, and his eyes meet mine. "You have no idea."

"What?" Annoyance grates in his tone.

"I think you're wonderful just the way you are. The way you've navigated my issues with my dad? You've been my rock the entire time. All while my issues are reminding you of losing your parents. What you've done with Lifetime Adventures... for a guy who didn't want all the added responsibility in the beginning, you're the first one there in the morning. I see you researching at night. And now you want to date me. Denver, whatever happened to change you, I see it and I love it."

He steps closer to me and his hands cover my cheeks. "It's you. You're what's changed me."

"Denver?"

He presses his lips to mine. "Yeah?"

"Can you romance me tomorrow?" I murmur against his lips and feel his smile.

"Why do you ask that?"

I pull away and look him straight in the eyes so he can see how much I mean it. "Because I need you. Just me and you with nothing between us."

"As always, princess, you get what you want."

We rush to the shuttle and can't keep our lips off one another the entire ride back.

DENVER PUTS the key into the lock, and we fumble into the small cabin. We each take off our hats, scarves, gloves.

I unzip my jacket, but he stops my hands. "Let me undress you."

He sits on the bed, slowing our pace. He stares at me as his fingers slide the zipper of my coat down until it opens.

"My favorite outfit," he says when he sees my sweater and pushes my coat to the floor.

"You were extra flirty with me when I wore this."

He presses his head to my stomach and wraps his arms around me. After unbuttoning my pants and pushing them down my legs, he signals for me to lift my leg. He unties and takes off each of my boots.

"I think you need to catch up," I say, looking at him still fully dressed and sitting on the bed. I undress him the same way he did me.

Once we're both nude, we each take the other in. I couldn't have dreamed up a more perfect body than the one Denver's rocking. Long corded muscles, six-pack abs with the V that make up the perfect groin cleavage, and a treasure trail of hair that leads to his large and erect manhood straining toward his belly button.

Oddly enough, I don't feel self-conscious standing in front of him. The way he's looking at me makes me feel like the most desirable woman in the world. His brown eyes are darker than usual, and the heat pouring from them is scorching.

Denver flips me onto the bed on my back, pressing his lips to mine. And it's then I discover that Denver messes around the same way he banters. He teases, ramping up the sexual tension with each movement. He's definitely a breast man, because though he might not stay in one place long, he visits my chest over and over. Licking, biting, and tugging on my nipples until I'm desperate for more of his attention. My fingers thread through his hair and my body strains upward under his expert tongue and hands.

He's vocal, as I assumed he'd be. Dictating, seeking guidance, and needing confirmation that what he's doing is sending me toward the edge. For some reason, our bodies resting along one another's feels familiar even though I know nothing about his body.

What I love the most is the push and pull between fast and slow. Two extremes with no middle ground, but that's true of Denver in all things. It's groping and tugging or grazing and gliding. There's a struggle inside him, and the fact he's having a hard time controlling himself only turns me on more.

"I have to get a condom." He lifts off my body.

It already feels foreign not to have him there. I watch him dig through his suitcase. "Did you think we were going to sleep together?"

He arms himself with the condom and slides back over me. "Hoped. I hoped. Things between us have been more intense, and I wasn't going to be the jackass who wasn't prepared."

I kiss his neck, the small amount of stubble tickling my skin.

"Thank God you're a survivalist," I say as the tip of him pierces my opening. "Always prepared."

"You can thank me later." He slowly pushes inside me, inch by inch until he's fully seated.

I wrap my limbs around him. I feel fuller than I've ever been, and I want to commit this feeling to memory.

Earlier, Denver treated me like a precious jewel, but there's nothing slow and gentle about him now. His head is buried in my neck, whispering praises about me and my body while he surges in and out of me. My legs tighten around his waist as I'm barely able to hold my orgasm at bay. It all happens so fast—sweat coating our bodies, my hands gripping his shoulders, and him anchoring me to his body as if we're one.

He rears back when a strangled sound comes out of me. He must see that I'm nearly there, because he thrusts harder and changes his angle a bit, hitting my G-spot. My body clenches and tenses until the relief mixed with ecstasy comes. I explode into a million particles, like stardust floating through space, and I cry out.

He watches me come apart underneath him. "So fucking beautiful."

He gets up on his elbows and kisses me as he picks up the pace and follows me with his own release, my name slipping from his lips. The weight of him over me after he's come is something that will stay with me forever, because it feels as though this is how it was always supposed to be. He kisses me until he has no choice but to get rid of the condom.

Denver Bailey owns me now, and I should be more scared than I am, but I've never felt like I belonged to someone before and I can't help but wonder what it's like.

TWENTY-FIVE

Denver

Cleo is everything I imagined when I fisted my dick late at night when the ache of not having her was too strong.

"I should probably admit that I broke the rule about not masturbating to you." I slide closer to her under the sheets, and she forks a piece of steak and places it in front of my mouth.

"That's okay. I did too," she says, a grin on her face.

We both chew. After two rounds, our stomachs decided that without any food, we might not be able to go at it with one another again. So I put on some clothes and paid a teenager working here to drive to the nearest restaurant and bring us back some food.

When I returned, Cleo greeted me naked in bed in a sexy pose, the fake flower from the small vase on the bathroom counter between her teeth. So cliché, but I dropped the food and jumped on her. She cried out and tried to wiggle away because of how cold I was.

Now we're both warm and eating naked in bed. With no television and sketchy cell service, I have her to myself. Does life get any better?

"So basically, we should've been doing this weeks ago," I say.

After cutting the roasted potatoes, she positions the fork in front of my mouth again, and I take a bite. "Probably, but I think the build-up was worth it."

"You say that now, but I could've just as easily been sleeping in the tub right now."

She smiles over her chewing. "I'll admit, having you here with me is nicer than you in the tub."

"For me too. I wanted to be a gentleman, but damn, by the end of the trip, I wouldn't have been able to stand."

She laughs, and her head falls against my chest. I take the opportunity to kiss the soft skin on her shoulder. I'm a little surprised by how easy it was to admit what I was feeling for her. I have no idea how Cleo changed me so fast. She's the only one who could've done it. One thing is true though—I'm going to do everything in my power to keep her. Something about the two of us together feels right.

"So this worked out well for you then," she says.

I pick up the tray and move it to the small side table. "You're reaping a lot of rewards in the form of orgasms."

I lower her upper body to the bed, my undying need to have her under me too much to resist. We stare into one another's eyes, and she holds a smirk that says she's enjoying what's happening. It is pretty spectacular, I have to say. I can't get enough of her. I don't want to stop touching her or listening to what's going to come out of her mouth next. It feels euphoric, and I can't stomach thinking about it coming to an end.

"Let's forget this trip and just stay here until Sunday," she says.

I kiss her forehead, her nose, then her mouth. "I have some amazing places to show you."

"Okay, but I think we're going to be spending a lot of time inside the cabins."

I chuckle and widen her legs with my thighs, and she opens them willingly. "Fine with me. We could camp out one night and see if you can be louder than the wolves." She hits me in the chest, and I chuckle again. "You're loud, but I love it."

My dick finds its spot between her thighs, but I have to disappoint the dude because I need to do one thing I haven't so far. I slide down her body, taking the time to suck her nipples—she has amazing tits and I'm not missing an opportunity to have them in my mouth. Her fingers weave through my hair and it feels like a caress. Kissing down her stomach, past her navel, I situate myself between her thighs.

She sighs my name, as if I needed any other incentive to show her that this mouth of mine isn't just good for banter. I have a pretty talented tongue too.

IT'S dark outside when we finally finish our cold meal. Her head lays on my chest and my finger runs up and down her spine.

"What's your favorite color?" she asks.

We've been playing this game as if we're prepping for an immigration interview after marrying for a green card.

"Blue." She nods against my chest, and I ask, "Favorite movie?"

She takes her time to think about it. "*Wizard of Oz.*"

"Ah, there's no place like home."

She squeezes me tighter. "Yeah, I think I always felt like I was searching for something. I could relate to Dorothy."

I run my hand over her silky hair. It's as soft as it always looked. I tilt her head up to look me in the eye. "And now?"

She shrugs. "I like Lake Starlight. A lot."

"So much that you think you fit there?" It'd be hard for me to move to Dallas—there's no need for bush pilots there for one—but I would if she wanted me to.

Even I'm shocked by that thought, but I don't feel any sort of panic.

"I feel more at home there than I have anywhere but is it because of you?" she asks.

"I kind of hope so. Sometimes it's not where you fit but who."

She seems to think over that then crawls on top of me. "Well, you definitely fit me," she jokes, and I recognize the move for what it is—a defense mechanism. "Favorite position?"

Yep, she definitely wants to change the subject. Since this is all so new, I'll let her, but we have three more nights together. By Sunday, she'll know where she fits—with me.

I slide my hands down her sides and rest them on her hips where she's rocking over my hard cock. "I'd love your tits in my face while you ride me."

She dips down and I capture a nipple with my teeth, latching on. She moans and lowers herself, allowing my entire mouth to suck her tit. Bringing my other hand up, I squeeze her free one. She reaches across to the nightstand to grab another condom.

I'm going to have to stop at a store to get a bigger supply. Not a bad problem to have.

———

A FEW DAYS LATER, I thank Gene, our latest host, for having us and we hop onto the plane. This time we travel between the mountains, watching the thawing snow cascade down to the rivers below. Hearing her 'oohs' and 'aahs' through the headset, I have to work to keep my dick at half-mast.

It's my last night with her, and after going through two boxes of condoms, I still have a hard time looking at her without wanting her. I think she feels the same way because she can't stop touching me either.

I really don't want to go back to reality. Tonight we're going to spend the night in the tent, and I'm excited to really show off my outdoor skills. She liked that last time.

We land and set up camp. I build the fire, and when I look over to check on her, she's holding Chip's urn, staring at it. With everything we've done on this trip, we haven't spread his ashes yet.

I poke the fire to position a log the way I need it. "Have you decided where you want to spread them?"

"I'm thinking somewhere high."

"If you want, we could open a window as we're flying."

She still holds the urn. Not tight or protective, just kind of there. "I still feel like I barely knew him."

Sitting on the log next to her, I wrap my arm around her waist and kiss her temple. "I think you're putting a lot of pressure on yourself."

"Because this is leaving him somewhere."

"Do you really believe that's him?"

She stares at the urn as if she's waiting for him to pop up like those jack-in-the-boxes. "No, but why did he put me in charge of it?"

I wish I had some insight to offer her. "We don't have to do it this trip. We can come back."

Her shoulders sag. "That's a waste of a trip."

"I think it's been a pretty great trip, so I'm not opposed to having to do a repeat."

She smiles. "Maybe I can fly you next time." She hits me in the rib with her elbow.

I roll my eyes. She wants to learn to fly, and she wants me to be the one to teach her. I'm all for it, but Rome asked me to teach him and we almost got into a fistfight at ten thousand feet. Sometimes you shouldn't teach the ones you're close to.

"Maybe," I say.

"So we can wait?" she asks.

"We can wait." I squeeze her knee and stand. "Ready to go to bed?"

"When haven't I been ready to go to bed with you?" She rises and places the urn back in its box. "Where should we put this?"

"I'm sorry, he's not coming in the tent," I say.

"So you believe he's in here?" She throws my words back at me.

"I'm not going to screw his daughter while his ashes are in a tent with us."

She laughs and I'm glad that the serious moment is over. "Plane?"

"Plane." I pick up the box and head toward the plane. "I'm sorry, Chip, but I think in a way, you wanted me to be with Cleo. At least that's what I got from your letter. If I was wrong and you're up there pissed off that I'm with Cleo, I'm sorry, but I'm not giving her up."

After locking the urn in the plane, I head back to the

tent in a rush to get back to Cleo. I strip before I get in, and she's already laughing.

"You better be naked in that sleeping bag." I zip us into the tent and crawl into the sleeping bag she's in.

"You've taught me to always be prepared."

Later that night, she's in my arms when she starts another round of questions. I think I know all her favorites by now. She loves Three Musketeers, which I told her it isn't a real candy bar. She likes plain chocolate ice cream with nothing on it, which seems like a travesty when you have things like caramel nut fudge available. Her favorite pasta is lasagna, which I'm down with. I could probably answer a questionnaire about her at this point, and I find that I like knowing all these things about her.

"What are you most afraid of?" she asks.

I lift my eyelids since I was almost asleep. Obviously, we're delving into the serious questions tonight. I take a minute to consider whether I want to be open with her or not and find that I do. "Honestly? I'm afraid of being devastated like I was when my parents died. I'm afraid of someone I love leaving me."

She picks up her head as her hand cradles my cheek. My beard is fuller than it usually is since I haven't shaved on this trip. "I can't imagine you being so young when you lost them. But you have your whole family."

I nod, sleep taking over. Drifting in and out of consciousness, I kiss her forehead. "Falling asleep, princess."

"Go to sleep." She kisses my chest, and I pull her closer. I'm not sure if I dream it or not, but I swear, she whispers, "I'll never leave you, Denver Bailey. Not willingly anyway."

TWENTY-SIX

Cleo

We were in town for five minutes before the news about Denver and me was out. Somehow while we were miles away from Lake Starlight, the rumor mill started that we'd gone on a romantic trip together, when in reality we'd gone to spread my father's ashes. It's beside the point that we didn't end up doing it.

"It's the first time they've got it wrong." Phoenix pushes the iPad over to me. "In all my years, what's in there has always been true but a secret no one wanted out."

I bite my lip and stand. Denver and I didn't discuss whether we were coming out as a couple or planning to hide it.

"Hey, me and Juno are going out in Sunrise Bay this weekend. Come and have a girls' weekend with us." Phoenix spoons her mint chocolate chip ice cream into her mouth. Once again, she's wearing a matching pajama set at only six in the evening.

"Okay, let me think about it."

"And don't worry about Denver joining us. The guys are going out too."

"Denver is going out with the guys this weekend?"

"Yeah, Kingston and his asshole buddy Owen planned the entire thing. Denver's probably invited to keep those two from fighting."

I shake my head. "I'm sorry, what?"

She nods like 'Yeah you don't know?' "Kingston and Owen have this ultra-competitive relationship. They're best friends, but everything has always been a competition ever since they were young."

"Sounds immature," I say.

"Well, yeah, it's Kingston."

Kingston is the only brother I've yet to spend any time with. He seems nice but more reserved, at least in front of me.

"Anyway, you're totally coming with us," she says before taking another big bite of ice cream.

"Coming where?" Denver walks in, puts down his computer bag, and eyes the iPad. "I see you read that they figured out what we did this weekend."

As he grabs a water out of the fridge, I freeze, but Phoenix laughs. "Yeah, *you* plan a romantic weekend? I told Cleo it's the first time Buzz Wheel got it wrong."

The water bottle stays tipped to his mouth, and he eyes me over the bottle. I try to convey that I'm not sure how he wants to handle this.

"Yeah, I'm not romantic at all, right, Cleo? I made her sleep outside while I stayed in the cabin?" He stares me down as I shift in my seat.

Phoenix must hear his change of tone because her head swivels back and forth between the two of us. "Shut up!"

I blow out a breath. "I didn't know if you wanted people to know," I say to Denver.

He shakes his head, puts the water on the counter, and wraps his arm around my waist, kissing my neck. "I do."

"You guys are together?" Phoenix's eyes are wide, and her mouth is agape.

I laugh at her disbelief.

"Why is that so hard to believe?" Denver's lips travel to my lips, and he kisses me. "I'm a catch."

"Cleo's the catch," Phoenix deadpans. "What on Earth do you see in him?"

Denver picks up the water bottle and tips it so water splashes all over her. She laughs, and I can't help but think that watching their sibling interaction is fun.

"Better hope she doesn't find someone better this weekend when I take her to Sunrise Bay," Phoenix says.

"I heard you're going out with the guys this weekend," I say. Not bothered about it. Nope not at all.

He stares at me as if he doesn't remember. "Shit, yeah. I agreed to it before you jumped my bones this week."

I hit him in the stomach and roll my eyes.

"Cleo, how much for you to hold out on sex until he introduces me to Griffin?" Phoenix asks.

I laugh. She's always working an angle, this girl. Denver wraps his arms around my waist so my back is plastered to his chest. He kisses my neck, trailing those delicious lips up to my jaw. "Sorry, she's the nympho, not me."

Heat spreads from my head to my toes. Is this what being with Denver is going to be like? 'Cause I like it.

Phoenix snaps a picture. "I'm sending it to Buzz Wheel."

"What?" I turn to Denver. This is getting out of control.

Denver doesn't shift away from me. "Go ahead. Then

every guy will keep their hands and eyes off Cleo because they'll know I'll kick their ass."

I like that he's owning this relationship. It makes all those pesky bad thoughts dim in the back of my head.

"That reminds me, we have to go to my dad's," I say. I need to deal with his place, and after the time away with Denver, I finally feel better equipped to do so. Plus, we need to see if his "guest" came back.

He nods. "Let's go and we'll pick up some food, too."

"Hello?" Phoenix closes up her ice cream. "I'm bored. I'm coming."

Denver grabs my hand, and I quickly snatch up my purse. I'm fairly sure he wants to do more than just kiss when we get in the truck.

"You're in your pajamas." He glances at the microwave clock. "At six o'clock. Maybe you should live with G'Ma D at the Northern Lights."

"I'm unemployed. Give me a break." She follows us in her pajamas, slipping on a pair of Uggs and a big jacket.

"You're totally ruining my game here," he says to her while opening the door for me.

Phoenix gets in the back of the truck. "Cleo's my friend too, and now she'll be family soon."

Denver shuts the door. I have no idea if what she said made him skittish or not, because when he gets in the truck, he turns the ignition and we head out.

"The sooner we leave, the sooner she's out of our hair," he says.

I smile, but Phoenix huffs in the backseat. "I'm not sure I can live here if you two are banging every minute of every day."

"Not every minute. I promise," I tell her.

"But maybe close your eyes and call out before you

enter a room." Denver winks at me, grabs my hand, and squeezes.

Damn, the butterflies are alive and kicking in my stomach.

Fifteen minutes later, we pull up at my dad's, and I notice a set of decorative metal stars hanging on the outside of the house that were not there last time we were here.

"Um..." I point at them, a sourness drowning the butterflies from moments ago.

"I know."

Phoenix follows us toward the house. "So what's the deal? You think Chip had a chicky on the side?"

I hand the keys to Denver because I'm freaked out now.

"I'm starting to wonder." Denver unlocks the house and opens the door, flicking on the light.

"There are fresh flowers now," I say to Denver with wide eyes after I see the vase on the kitchen table.

He nods and goes to the back of the house, returning five seconds later. "We're alone."

I pick up the afghan on the couch. "This is new too!"

Phoenix squirms around as if she saw a spider. "This is creepy. Why did I come?"

I mostly ignore her because Denver tells her to go wait in the truck. Phoenix says she's not going anywhere by herself.

On the table by the chair, I spot another addition. I point over and over.

Denver rolls his eyes as if my reaction is unwarranted. Whatever. He picks up the book—a bestseller that came out *after* my dad died.

"We need to call the police," I say.

"And say what? Goldilocks has come and read in my

chair and left flowers and a blanket?" Denver's sarcastic tone is not appreciated.

"No! To tell them that someone is trespassing on private property." I pick up my cell phone and dial the police station.

Denver groans. "I'm starving."

"We'll eat after they get here. We need to figure this out."

He plops down on the couch.

"Denver, get up. Fingerprints!" I say.

He doesn't move. "This isn't *CSI*, babe, they aren't going to fingerprint anything. Even if they did, I'm pretty sure criminals with fingerprints in the database don't spruce up the home while robbing it."

Phoenix is pacing. "Maybe it's not *CSI* but *Paranormal Activity*. We need to go." A shiver runs through her entire body.

"Everyone, calm down," Denver says.

Someone at the police station finally answers, and I'm told that Sheriff Miller will stop by on his way home for the evening. Only in a small town, I swear. If it were Dallas, there would've been five cop cars here already.

SHERIFF MILLER TAKES his sweet-ass time showing up at the house. Denver is about to gnaw off his arm because I won't let him eat anything in the house. Phoenix won't sit down and keeps swatting at imaginary things, saying she felt a cold breeze.

I open the door, and Sheriff Miller saunters in. "Cleo Dawson, correct?"

"Yes sir. This is my dad's place."

He holds out his hand, and I take it. "Ah, Denver Bailey."

Denver gets up but not in any type of rush. "Sheriff." He pretends to tip a hat that he's not wearing. "Stop for dinner on the way over?"

I shoot him a look like 'What the hell are you doing?'

"Hi, Sheriff. Do you guys have a paranormal division?" Phoenix asks.

"Hello, Phoenix, and no."

He seems like a no-nonsense guy. His thumbs rest in his belt, and he rocks back as though it weighs a hundred pounds.

"I'm the one who called. Denver and I came here last week and noticed things had been moved around. When we got here tonight, it was the same thing. This afghan and that book were here." I point at both of them. "We talked to Luther Lloyd, and he said I have the only key."

The sheriff appears to listen to me but then he sets his narrowed gaze on Denver. "You two are an item, I hear."

Denver shakes his head in disbelief. I'm clearly missing the bad blood between these two. "We are."

Sheriff Miller looks back at me then at Denver. "Are you pulling a prank on your girlfriend?"

I rear my head back. "He's not fifteen."

Phoenix laughs after jumping a foot to the right and staring in the direction she jumped from.

"Oh, Denver likes pranks. It was only two years ago he, Rome, and Liam decided to cover a car with Post-it notes and post a sign on Lard Have Mercy about no pants day."

Phoenix laughs harder. "Oh, I missed that one."

I look at Denver. He shrugs, but his smirk makes it clear that the sheriff is right.

"I have nothing to do with this," Denver says.

"Rome?"

"He's pretty busy raising his kids. They have another on the way, you know."

The sheriff smiles. "Offer them my congratulations."

"Sure thing."

"Liam?"

"You think Savannah would let him stray that far?"

They go back and forth as if it's a game they play often.

The sheriff appears to think about the Savannah thing and nods. "Well, all I can really do is drive by a few times a day and see if we catch anyone. You could install cameras if you'd like. Have you found anything missing?"

"Just the fake flowers they replaced with real ones," Denver says and shoots me a look to say, 'I told you so.'

The sheriff looks over the door again. "There's no forced entry, so my guess is the person has a key. Denver, you should stake the place out. You, Rome, and Liam used to enjoy waiting around until it was late enough to cause trouble. Those skills will come in handy." He says this as though he's serious.

Denver chuckles. "Those days are over. I have a lot better things to do at night now."

Phoenix stops doing kung fu moves in the air to laugh.

I widen my eyes at Denver again to say, 'What is wrong with you?' He doesn't even look at me.

The sheriff just rolls his eyes. "I better get going. I'll have an officer drive by a few times. But think about those cameras. If there's ever anything missing or forced entry, give me another call."

"Thanks, Sheriff," I say, walking him toward the door though I'm not sure what I'm thanking him for considering he just blew me off.

"Nice to meet you, Cleo. Denver, Phoenix."

"Sheriff." Denver nods.

I shut the door and watch through the window as he gets into his car and leaves.

"Can we go now?" Phoenix karate chops the air again, heading toward the door.

"I'm starved." Denver's hand slides into mine, making me feel warm and safe.

"I take it you and the sheriff aren't on the best terms?" I ask while Denver locks up.

"You take that right. To be honest, I did some stupid shit when I was younger." He shrugs as we walk to the truck that Phoenix is already in.

"So you're like a bad boy?"

He opens my door for me. "I can be whatever turns you on, but yeah, I was a very bad boy. I probably deserve to be punished."

I push him away and he laughs until he gets in the truck. I can't remember the last time my cheeks hurt from laughing so hard, but this is a feeling I could get used to.

TWENTY-SEVEN

Denver

Saturday night, I'm sitting in Juno and Kingston's apartment, waiting to head out for the night. This blows. I could've screwed Cleo five times already. Okay, maybe a slight exaggeration.

"Owen will be here in, like, ten and then we're leaving," Kingston says, coming out of the bathroom looking as though he tried entirely too hard to get ready.

"Just so you know, I'm not breaking any fights up tonight. You guys can't play darts, you can't play pool, and you definitely can't bet on who gets the girl," I warn Kingston, because I'm not winding up in jail tonight over their usual antics.

Kingston looks at Colton on the couch. Kingston knows that it's going to happen. They'll find *something* insane to compete about.

"Hell no. Don't look at me," Colton says. Colton looks like me, not putting forth his best effort to look good tonight.

"How's veterinary life?" I ask him.

"Same old. Lifetime Adventures?"

Colton and I went to school together. With us only being a year apart and him being Juno's best friend, he's practically another brother to me.

"Any women in your life?" I ask.

He shrugs. "Nah, it's hard with the schedule."

"Must be hard with your Juno schedule too. You spend all your free time with her." Kingston raises his eyebrows, bringing us all a beer.

I decline since I'm the DD tonight—and because I'm not having whiskey dick when I crawl into Cleo's bed in—I lift my watch—four hours tops.

"We're friends," Colton says, but he sounds defensive.

"Man, you've been permanently friend-zoned, you understand that, right?" Kingston takes a pull of his beer.

"I'm fine with being friend-zoned."

"Denver, do you stare at your friends the way Colton stares at Juno?" Kingston has this dry humor that always cracks up a room.

Colton is laughing now, shaking his head.

"I did, and now I'm dating her so..." I glance at my watch. Three hours and fifty-eight minutes.

"Exactly." Kingston eyes Colton like 'Come on, dude, admit you want my sister.'

Colton circles his beer in his hand and looks relieved when there's a loud bang on the door.

"Owen," we say in unison.

Colton gives me the same look I'm sure I have on my face. "'This sucks, and I'd rather be doing anything other than this." *I hear you, buddy.*

Owen bursts in, telling the "best story ever" about what happened to him on the way over. It's probably so exaggerated, the truth is marginal at best. I pull out my phone.

Me: *Take a titty picture and send it over.*

Three dots appear, and I hope the quick response means she's missing me like I'm missing her.

Cleo: *Dick pic first.*
Me: *Is that a challenge?*
Cleo: *I know better than to challenge you.*

I stand and head to the bathroom.

Me: *If you send me your nudie first, I'll be able to show you him in all his glory.*

A second later, a picture shows up on my phone—it's her tits tucked into a bra.

I take out my dick, pump him up a little to make him look as regal as can be, and snap a picture before sending it to her.

Cleo: *Not sure what to say to a dick pic.*
Me: *Don't worry babe, swallow the drool first and then respond.*
Cleo: *I miss you and him a lot.*
Me: *I miss you and yours a lot. Meet me at one in my bed?*
Cleo: *I'll race you there.*

A pounding on the door from Owen has me stuffing myself back into my pants.

Cleo: *The girls are calling me. See you later.*
Me: *I'll see you first.*

I open the door, and Owen smiles that goofy grin I hate. I have no idea why Kingston likes this guy.

"Owen." I put out my hand. He shakes it too hard, as if he's trying to break my bones.

I'll be breaking up a fight tonight, I just know it.

"Let's go. I'm dying to get out. It's been months."

"What do you do now?" I ask, following him into the family room.

Colton is already rolling his eyes.

"I was doing some salmon fishing, but now I'm running the plant." He sits next to me on the couch. Owen's bigger and taller than Kingston or any of us Baileys, but he's not nearly as gorgeous.

"I thought Jed Lear was in charge of the plant?" Colton asks.

Right about now, I love that Colton knows everyone and is willing to call people out on their shit. Well, everyone but Juno and himself.

"Well yeah, Jed's still there, but I'm taking over when he retires," Owen says.

"Isn't he, like, forty-five?"

I fucking love Colton.

Owen fumbles with a few answers that turn into a stuttering, "Whatever, Stone, you finally fucked Juno yet?"

Colton gets to his feet.

Kingston steps in front of him and holds his hand against Colton's chest. "Whoa. Whoa! No talking about any of my sisters fucking anyone."

"I'm in agreement. We got through Liam dating Savannah without ever having to hear any of that shit." I shoot Owen a get-in-check look.

Owen laughs, but Colton is the one who's about to go ballistic.

"So not worth it," I say, and Colton stands down. "Let's get the hell out of here."

"Good idea," Colton mutters.

The sooner we're out of here, the sooner I'm home.

After they all down their beers and throw the bottles away, Owen puts his hand on my shoulder. "I heard you're settling down? You used to whip the pussy and now you're pussy whipped? Can't wait to meet her. She must be killer in bed to keep you tied down, huh?"

I look at Kingston and he shrugs. Truth is, they're not as close as they once were. I'm not sure they'll ever be where they were before high school when they fought over Stella.

"None of your fucking business," I say. "And if I find out you've talked to her, I'll put you on your ass a lot faster than Kingston ever has."

We file out of Kingston's apartment in downtown Lake Starlight.

Owen holds up his hands. "Jesus, you're protective over this one."

I say nothing because Owen likes nothing more than to get people fired up. He might still get under Kingston's skin, but fuck if I'll give him the pleasure.

WE END up at a bar in Sunrise Bay, a new one called The Merry Moose. It's a lot like Lucky's except twice the size. Which means more pool tables and dartboards I need to keep Kingston and Owen away from.

Colton and I sit at a table. I kind of want to guide him to someone else. I mean, I'm actively dating, but he's not. He should be with Kingston and Owen, trying to pick up women. But it's not my place, and if Juno really does like him, that's a dick move by her own brother.

"So how's it going at Lifetime Adventures?" he asks.

I nod. "It's really coming together. We're waiting for the show deal to go through. They have the episode we filmed with Griffin Thorne with a focus group right now. If they like it, then we have the green light for five more. They'll air those as filler between the end of one season of some show and the beginning of another, and we go from there."

Cleo and I have been as discreet as we've been able to about the company's financial issues and the fact that we're only doing the show for the money. We don't want to tarnish Chip's reputation in this town.

"That's awesome. I think I need to book something with you. I'm getting antsy here."

I should tell him to find someone he can fuck on the regular and then his life would be a lot more interesting, but again with the Juno thing. "Are you taking over the office from Dr. Murray?"

"Most likely. He's going to let me buy it over time on a payment plan. It's the smart thing to do." He lifts his beer to his lips.

"I hear a but?"

He shrugs, sipping his beer. "Like I said, I'm antsy."

"Like maybe you want to leave Lake Starlight?"

He's quiet for a moment. "Don't say anything to Juno, but I've thought about it."

It's easy to think he won't leave because Juno would never leave her business, but who knows? She'd be stupid to move her matchmaker business. I mean, she'd have to completely start over. Plus, Juno loves being with family, and with Rome having another baby and Austin and Holly not far behind, she's not going to be cool missing out on that.

"I won't say anything."

The waitress brings over a drink and sets it in front of Colton. "This is from the brunette at the bar."

Colton looks up to see who she's talking about. The girl is cute, and I'm surprised she'd send a drink. She looks more like the girl next door than one who would be forward.

Colton smiles and nods, picking up the drink. "I should thank her." He slides off the bar stool.

"Yeah." I watch him approach her. If Juno wants him, she'd better snatch him up soon because he won't wait around forever.

I scan the room and find Kingston and Owen at a table full of girls out for a bachelorette party. Owen's all over the bride-to-be, who has penises all over her veil and tiara, and Kingston's with another girl off to the side. He catches my eye and nods me over, but I'm not into spending my night with drunken girls with fake penises all over them. The days of me sucking a Life Saver off a shirt are over—unless it's Cleo's.

I sip my club soda and lime, debating on texting her again, but I don't want to be the boyfriend who never leaves her alone.

"Denver Bailey." The voice that holds accusation in its tone says I probably screwed this girl and never called her.

I turn to find that yes, this is a girl I screwed, and I screwed her multiple times off and on over a two year period. "Polly McAlister."

She doesn't wait for me to invite her to sit down, sliding a bar stool closer and joining me at my table. She sets her girly drink complete with umbrella on the table. She's from Greywall, and I run into her every now and then. We've hooked up on occasion. From the way she's eyeing me as if

I'm the buffet and she just smoked a blunt, I think that she thinks tonight might be a repeat.

Sadly for her, it will not.

"Isn't that your younger brother?" She points at Kingston.

I nod. It's sad really, but some people have a thing for the Baileys. We get attention because of the company and the fact that our parents died. Shitty reasons. Our actions get excused sometimes because people pity us. She's probably thinking of moving on to my younger version.

"He's a hottie. What does he do again?"

This is where Kingston puts me being a bush pilot to shame. "He's a firefighter in the fall and winter, and a smokejumper in the spring and summer."

Her eyes light up and she looks him up and down, practically licking her lips. She places her hand on my thigh and leans forward. "He's nice and all, but I do prefer a pilot. They know how to steer well."

Sad, sad pickup line.

I move her hand off my thigh and place it back on hers just as someone puts their hands over my eyes. Instead of saying anything, the hands drop, and I hear a gasp.

I close my eyes because I know exactly who that is.

TWENTY-EIGHT

Cleo

My hands drop from Denver's eyes when I notice his hand on her thigh.

"Who's this?" the woman says in a voice that insinuates I'm the interloper here.

Denver swivels on the stool, stands, and puts his arm around me. "This is my girlfriend, Cleo." He leans in to kiss my neck, but I pull back. He groans.

I don't really give a shit what he thinks right now. I'd like to see how he'd feel if I had my hand on someone else's thigh.

"Girlfriend? Since when?" she asks with a look of disgust.

"Listen, Polly," he says, his hand not leaving my hipbone. "I was about to tell you before Cleo surprised me. We've been dating…"

I do the math in my head. For what? For nine days. Is that what he's going to tell her?

"For a while, and I'm with her now."

Polly looks me up and down, slurps the rest of her sugar-filled beverage, and slides off the stool. "You know where to find me whenever this ends." She wags her finger between the two of us.

Denver tightens his grip on me. I don't know if he's doing it because he likes to be right and Polly is doubting that he can remain faithful or what. "This isn't going to end."

His sweet talk isn't going to work this time. Polly gives him the same look I do, that he's crazy.

"Excuse me," I say before she has a chance to leave first.

I search for Juno or Phoenix to tell them I'll be calling an Uber and going home. I find Juno at a table by herself and circle around to follow her line of vision. There's Colton chatting and laughing with a brunette at the bar. My guess is that he doesn't even know Juno's here.

"Cleo." Denver approaches us. "It was nothing. I was just about to text you."

"That's convenient."

"What's going on?" Juno tips back her drink and finishes it off with her gaze still glued on Colton.

"Looks like Denver and Colton found some women tonight," I say bitterly.

"Jesus." Denver groans. "That's not even close to the truth."

"I'm heading back to Lake Starlight. You wanna come?" I ask Juno.

"I'm taking you home," Denver practically growls.

"No, I think I'm gonna stick around." She slides off her stool, puts her fingers through her hair, and saunters over to a group of guys playing darts.

"This isn't going to end well." Denver sits down and pulls me into his lap. "Listen."

I stubbornly look around.

His hands cup my cheeks and tilt my face toward him. "I don't want Polly or any other woman in this bar. I'd been counting down the minutes until I could see you. If you don't trust me, this is never going to work."

I know he's right, and I told myself when I saw him talking to her that it was nothing. He knows a lot of people. She could be a friend from high school. That's why I approached them. But then his hand on her thigh threw me.

"She put her hand on me and I removed it. You happened to come over at the worst possible moment."

"But—"

He shakes his head. "There's no but. I'm crazy about you. This is strange new ground for me, but the last thing I would ever do is risk what we have for some bar chick. I couldn't even get it up for anyone but you."

I quirk my eyebrow, and he laughs.

"I'm dead serious, he was saggy until you arrived." He takes my hand and puts it between his legs. Typical Denver. "Give him some time. He's a little scared to come out right now for fear of his life."

I can't hold back my chuckle. "How come when we have a conversation, he's always involved in it?"

"He and them"—he eyes my boobs—"are key members in this relationship."

I nod. He puts up a convincing argument. "If you ever cheat on me, you do know there won't be a 'he' anymore, right?"

"Duly noted." He stands and towers over me. "Let's go home and fuck and make up."

I wind my arms around his neck and press my body to his.

"You have no idea how much I missed you and it's only been two hours," he says.

I laugh into his neck. I felt the same way when I was with the girls earlier. When they said they wanted to go check out The Merry Moose, I purposely didn't tell them the guys were going there because I missed Denver and wanted to run into him.

"Come on. I have to tell the guys." His hand slides down my arm, linking our hands, and we step away from the vacant table.

As we reach the back of the bar, the clear sound of arguing can be heard.

"You didn't win," Kingston says from beside the pool table in the corner.

"Fuck." Denver sighs and lets go of my hand, venturing toward his brother.

"I did too." Owen is right up in Kingston's face now.

"You scratched on the eight ball," Kingston says.

"I scratched on the four ball. How much have you drank tonight?"

Both of them are half drunk and arguing about who won a damn pool game. From what I understand, it comes from something so much more than that, but no one seems to want to address it.

"Come on." Denver puts his hand on Kingston, and he pushes Denver off. "This isn't worth it."

Kingston sips his beer then sprays it all over Owen. "You're a fucking asshole. Always have been."

"Kingston Bailey, the jealous prick who couldn't get the one thing he really wanted in Lake Starlight. You'll never get over the fact that she wanted me." Owen points at himself as though someone should slap a ribbon on him. Unless it says World's Biggest Jackass, he doesn't deserve it.

Colton appears out of nowhere, pulling Kingston away.

Kingston strains against Colton holding him back. "She dumped your ass. Don't forget that fact."

Denver pushes Owen back as he says, "I couldn't give two shits about her. The fact is she picked me over you and that's been eating away at you for years. How could she not want the fucking prince of Lake Starlight, right? The star shortstop. The Bailey brother."

Owen pushes forward, and pretty soon Colton and Denver's backs are pressed to one another.

"You think I'm jealous? You've been jealous of me our entire lives. You only went after her so I couldn't have her. What kind of best friend are you?"

"She came to me, Bailey. Remember that."

Colton gives one last push, and Phoenix and Juno help by each taking an arm.

"We're leaving, let's go." Denver pushes Owen toward the door. "I'll take Owen, you take Kingston, Juno."

"Sounds good."

Looks like The Merry Moose isn't that merry for everyone.

"I DON'T UNDERSTAND why we drove him home if we don't like him," I say from the front seat after we dropped off Owen.

"Because he's like family," Phoenix says. "Tomorrow he and Kingston will apologize and make up. It's a messed-up cycle between those two."

"Who's the girl they were talking about?" I ask.

Denver glances in the rearview mirror at Phoenix.

"I don't think you've met her yet," Phoenix says. "Her

mom, Selene, owns the Cozy Cottage B & B. Stella, her daughter, doesn't live here anymore though. She went away to school and hasn't returned. Most of us think it's because she couldn't handle the situation between the three of them. It's the classic story of two best friends being in love with the same girl."

"They're pretty aggressive with each other for something that happened so long ago."

"Alcohol and egos don't mix. It's better when Kingston's smokejumping in the spring and summer and he's not around Owen," Denver says.

"I find that sad."

Neither of them says anything. It seems like at the time, things were pretty bad, so I let the topic go for now. Minutes later we're home and taking our shoes and coats off in the foyer.

"Goodnight, Phoenix, I have some groveling to do," Denver says, taking my hands.

"Ew! TMI, bro."

"Put your earplugs in tonight." He laughs, dragging me up the stairs. When he gets me into his room, he presses my back to the door. "I think no more girls' and guys' nights out until we're good and sick of one another."

I duck under his arm and step into the room. "You're gonna get sick of me, huh?"

He comes up behind me, and his hands slide under my shirt. "No, you're gonna get sick of me."

His lips scatter kisses on the back of my neck and I circle in his arms. "Did you say something about groveling?"

He raises my shirt over my head and tosses it on the floor. His mouth lands on mine, and his tongue slides inside at the same time his hands reach behind me and unclasp my bra.

"I'll never get sick of these," he says into our kiss, his hands grabbing my breasts.

We finish undressing and I lightly push him onto the mattress. By the look on his face, he knows what's coming as I fall to my knees next to the bed.

He groans. "Not tonight, I want to bury myself inside you."

"You can do that later."

I hold his hard length and swirl my tongue around the mushroom tip, then I swallow him all the way down and drag my mouth back up, my hand steady at his base.

His hands slide into my hair, and he makes noises at the back of his throat that only stirs my arousal. I want him to masturbate to this memory next time. The live version of me sucking his cock. Not what he thinks I would do. Not what he imagines. But the reality of me getting him off.

I pump him as I suck and lick all over, deep throating him once more, I look up at him when he bucks into my mouth, a look of pure desperation in his eyes.

"Shit, baby." He tucks a strand of hair behind my ear.

Of all the moves I thought he'd do when I was giving him a blowjob, I never imagined something as intimate as that. I feel slightly foolish for not trusting him tonight. He's done nothing to make me second-guess him. It's only his reputation that scares me, but people change.

"I'm going to come," he says, struggling to get the words out.

I continue swirling and pushing him deeper down my throat while pumping him. He grips my hair firmer and forces his hips up, his body tensing right before his cum spills into my mouth. I swallow, and he unleashes a long, satisfied groan.

Once he's recovered, he grabs me by my arms and brings me to him on the bed. "Now it's your turn."

He kisses down my body, and I widen my legs, making room for his wide shoulders until I'm the one moaning and tensing and coming. I'm falling way too hard and too fast. As we slide into bed naked as we have every night since we started dating, I'm quick to realize, there's no falling—I've already fallen.

TWENTY-NINE

Denver

I walk into the office on Monday morning and lean on the doorframe, studying the changes. Cleo laughs.

"His and hers desks, huh?" I ask.

When we returned from our trip north, she'd already had Nancy clean out all of Chip's stuff. Nancy, being Nancy, had taken it upon herself to do more cleaning than asked. She somehow even got out the smell of stale cigarettes.

But this is different. Now there are two desks facing one another. Hers white to my dark gray. A vase with flowers sits on the corner of hers and a clock on mine. The walls have been painted a light gray, and Chip's old map of the Denali National Park is framed and hung on one wall. The new logo is on proud display on the back wall.

"Here's your muffin, you schemer." I bend down and kiss her.

"I heard there was a big rush on muffins this morning," she says to my pressed lips.

"When Sweet Suga is doing a buy one get one, I'd say so."

She laughs and puts her arms around my neck. "I did as much as I could. Thank Nancy, because she painted and got the pictures framed. Phoenix recruited Kingston, and they came by and put the desks together yesterday. So all I had to do was decorate a bit this morning."

"And was it worth not having your morning orgasm?" I kiss her again, which is worth the strain in my back from bending over.

She looks around me at the clock. "It's still morning."

I kick the door shut and pick her up, placing her on the desk. "Let's hope Kingston put your desk together, not Phoenix."

Her legs part to make room for me. My lips descend on her neck, my hands crawling up her shirt. I can't wait for the warmer weather to come so she'll wear less for me to take off. My fingers are on the clasp of her bra when the phone rings.

Nancy must pick it up, so I continue my quest to christen the new office. Our office. All the pieces are coming together. Decorating the office must mean she's staying for good, that Dallas is no longer an option on the table.

The phone on Cleo's desk buzzes, and she presses the button. "Hey, Nancy."

My chin hits my chest in disappointment.

"Cleo, Selma is on the phone."

I lean back, and Cleo looks at me as if we're about to find out the result of a pregnancy test. This is it. The moment we find out whether we can save this company.

I sit in her chair and pull her into my lap.

"Send her through," Cleo says, and she kisses my cheek. "If not, we'll find another way."

I nod. I'm glad she's optimistic, but I'm not sure we have the option of staying open if this doesn't come through. We need this money to run some ads and upgrade some equipment, offer new services.

Having her this close will make it easier to take this bullet.

"Selma?" I answer on speakerphone. "How are you this morning?"

"Hey, guys, we're good. I have Tommy and Glen on with me. You both there?"

"Hi, guys," Cleo says.

They say hi in return.

"Well, let me start by saying we were surprised by the news that you're now a couple. Although it usually makes for better television, you guys are a new couple, which means you're pretty amicable on the camera. You're in that sweet phase and the camera shows it. How attentive Denver is to you, Cleo, and how you look to him for guidance before doing anything. That's great and all, but it doesn't usually make for good television in the long run."

Cleo's lips dip and she leans her head on my shoulder.

If it's the show or Cleo, I'll take Cleo, hands down.

"We showed the focus group though, and they had the opposite thinking we did. They thought you two were adorable and loved the interview portion with Griffin. You did an amazing job, Cleo." Selma inhales and exhales. She must be smoking.

"So did we get it or not?" I ask.

Cleo bites her lip.

Silence falls over the receiver for a moment. "You got it."

Cleo and I whoop and hug each other.

"Five more episodes?" Cleo asks, her body practically buzzing.

"Actually, Zeke set you up for thirteen. A full season."

I think Cleo's eyes are as wide as mine, and our mouths hang open.

"You do accept, right?" Selma clarifies when we say nothing. "We want to start filming immediately, because most guests are going to want to do it in the nicer weather. We're going to try to get some more people who are on the public's radar to go on these excursions with you. Kinda like we did with Griffin."

I look at Cleo. We aren't just agreeing on the show— we're agreeing to be part of each other's lives for the foreseeable future. She nods.

"Of course we accept. We'd never say no," I say.

Cleo straddles me in the chair and presses her tits into my face, a huge grin on her lips.

"Great. I'll email you the details and the contract. Have your lawyer look them over. We'll be in touch with the recording schedule once we firm up some details on our end."

"Thanks, Selma, bye," Cleo says, leaning back and ending the call.

Cleo screams and I pick her up, circling us around.

"Congratulations," I whisper before capturing her lips.

Her moan and firm thighs wrap around me. When I lay her across our desks, she wiggles and pulls a stapler from under her waist.

I press the button on the phone. "Nancy, take an early lunch."

"But it's only—"

"Lunch, Nancy." I click it off and my hands slide up Cleo's shirt.

She gets up on her elbows and unbuckles my pants. We not only got the money to keep Lifetime Adventures going, we're christening our office with what I'm positive will be the first of many early lunches for Nancy.

WE WALK into Terra and Mare that evening. Since Monday is one of the days the restaurant is closed, it's family only for our impromptu celebration of Cleo and my good news about the show.

Cleo kisses my cheek but heads toward Harley and picks up Dion. She spins him around and nuzzles her face into his. He blows saliva bubbles as he smiles at her. Can't blame the kid. His thighs are massive, but Harley took great offense when I mentioned it before, so that topic is off-limits. I mean, I was only complimenting him, like he'd be an awesome wrestler or something.

"Beer?" Kingston hands me a bottle.

I quirk an eyebrow because I haven't talked to him since The Merry Moose.

"Sorry," he mumbles.

"You and Owen should really just part ways. You aren't healthy together."

He's already shaking his head. I hate being the one to give Kingston advice. He and Austin are so far apart in age that they've always had a more father/son dynamic, but I've remained faithful to the big brother role.

"He's my best friend," he says.

"Is he really?" I ask.

He shrugs and downs more beer. "This is why I like spring and summer. I like not being here."

I nod. That's a conversation he should have with Rome, because he wanted to get out too. I never did. Even if I drove five minutes out of my way to avoid passing the cemetery, I never contemplated leaving Lake Starlight. This is where our memories exist, some of them as painful as they are. The problem with Kingston is his tortured memories aren't only of our parents. They're of Stella. He thinks no one knows, but I do. I've just kept my mouth shut because it's none of my business.

"Why don't you get a place in Anchorage for the winter?"

"What about Juno?"

I scour the room, finding her in the corner with Colton. She's laughing and his eyes are on her as if he'd give up his life for just one kiss. How is my matchmaker sister so blind? "She'll land on her feet eventually."

After taking a pull of his beer, Kingston says, "You know that night of the fight, Colton slept on the couch instead of going back to his place."

"Why?"

Kingston eyes me like 'You know why.' "He said Owen could come back, and he didn't want to chance anything happening to Juno."

"But you were there."

Kingston nods. "Exactly."

I shake my head, but then I hear Cleo's laugh from across the room. She's with Brooklyn now, and they're looking at her phone. Dori walks over and kisses Cleo's cheek before heading toward Calista. Rome walks in from the kitchen and places some food on the table, nodding hello to me.

Phoenix calls everyone to attention and stands on a chair.

"Phoenix, you know how expensive those chairs are?" Rome says.

"I'll buy you a new one." She has her phone held up and pointing at us all. The screen is so small, everyone is squinting and leaning in to see what's on it.

"With what? You don't have a job." Rome's a minute away from blowing up.

Harley comes to his side and kisses his cheek, whispering something that seems to calm him.

"It's Sedona," Phoenix says. "She FaceTimed me."

"Hi, guys!" Sedona waves. "I have Jamison with me."

Phoenix rolls her eyes.

"Hi!" everyone screams.

"Jamison is back in the picture?" I ask Kingston. He's the closest in age to the twins, so I figure he'd know.

"I guess he's playing soccer in New York and they hooked back up."

I don't have an opinion on it, but the fact that Phoenix does raises an alarm in my brain. Sedona and Jamison dated in high school when he was a foreign exchange student from Scotland. I never thought anything about the kid, but Rome told me he walked in on them once and he was pretty sure they were having sex. Jamison was respectful and apologized later. Rome gave him a sleeve of condoms and said if she gets pregnant, they'll be talking.

Everyone shoots them some questions about school, the weather, and Jamison's soccer career, but Phoenix wraps up the call pretty quickly and steps down from the chair.

"Phoenix really isn't happy they're back together, huh?" I say to Kingston.

"I think it's the twin thing. Maybe Phoenix is in a funk and a little jealous that Sedona is figuring out her life while she's in a holding pattern." He pats my shoulder. "I knew a twin like that once when his twin found a wife and purpose and had a couple kids." He winks and walks away. He sits down next to Phoenix and gets her to smile with what's probably a joke about one of us.

"Hey, you." Cleo comes up alongside me. "What are you thinking about?"

"What an idiot I was once upon a time." I was a complete dick to Rome and Harley when they started out. I look at Cleo as all the dots connect. Rome didn't want to go out back then. The restaurant and his family were important because he loved them so much.

"Well, all that matters is that you're not an idiot now."

"So you agree? I was an idiot?"

She shrugs. "You said it. I didn't."

Bringing her in front of me, I bend to kiss her, but right before my lips touch hers, I murmur, "Are you happy, Cleo Dawson?"

A wide, sparkling, earth-shattering smile spreads on her face. "Happiest I've ever been."

I press my lips to hers. When the whistles start from my family, I break apart in an effort not to embarrass her too much.

Rome announces that the meal is ready, and we all sit, passing dishes and talking about our jobs and the news in Lake Starlight. At the end of our meal, Rome presents a cake with a bush plane and "Congratulations, Cleo and Denver" written on top.

I catch Cleo's eyes soaking in my family. Yeah, they can be a bit much at times, intrusive to an unfathomable degree, but they already love her. If I'm honest, I think I love her too.

THIRTY

Cleo

I'm on cloud nine, walking on air, tickled pink, over the moon, and every other idiom that can be used to describe how happy I am in this moment, walking out of Terra and Mare with Denver's hand in mine.

"Let's stop by Chip's and check on the place," he says.

"Sure." I'd almost forgotten about the strange things going on over there. I've just been in this happy bubble with Denver, and I don't want anyone or anything to burst it.

He stops me at his truck, pressing my back to the door. "My family loves you."

"I love them."

I've never had this feeling before. So casual and nothing forced. Just being myself with a group of people who accept me for who I am. It's like winning the lottery. I've been searching for this for so long, and to think my dad is the one who made this all happen. I wasted my time with my mom. I should've lived with my dad.

Denver's knuckles run down my cheek, and his eyes say

what his mouth doesn't. I know because it's the same thing I feel. But we've only been dating for a little over two weeks. It'd be absurd to admit it, right?

We drive the fifteen minutes to my dad's with our hands interlinked, his thumb lazily grazing mine. The anxious feeling that used to make me nauseated when we'd pull onto my dad's gravel driveway isn't there this time.

Until Denver stops the truck at the house. There's a car parked in front. A car we're both familiar with. A car we see every day.

"Stay here," Denver says, keeping the truck on. "If anything happens, just drive away."

I roll my eyes at his dramatics. Grabbing the keys, I turn off the ignition and get out.

"Cleo, I said stay in the car."

"It's Nancy," I say, storming past him.

He catches up and takes my arm. "At least let me go first."

I hold up my hands. "Okay, bodyguard. She might actually bake you a cake or something."

Denver knocks, which goes to show how ridiculous this is. Nancy opens the door with a book in her hand and reading glasses on the tip of her nose. She doesn't smile but cringes with an 'I'm sorry' expression. Denver and I file in, and he heads straight to the back of the house to check things out.

"Hey, Nancy," I say. Her line of vision is on Denver, and I wave him off. "Don't mind him."

He returns with nothing. Of course he does. I feel pretty stupid that I didn't suspect it was Nancy coming here in the first place.

"Hi, guys." She puts her bookmark in the book, sets it down next to the chair, and places her reading glasses on top. Then she folds the afghan and places it on the back of the couch.

"So you have a key?" I ask.

She nods.

"And you never mentioned it."

Denver is still on high alert, almost sliding along the wall to reach me as if Nancy's going to sneak attack him.

"I heard you say you haven't been able to come here, so I figured I'd keep it nice for when you thought you could. Plus..." She falls onto the couch and her head drops into her hands. Her back racks from her sobs and hiccups. "I miss him."

I step forward to approach her, but Denver stops me, shaking his head. Disregarding him, I sit at her side and he blows out a breath like now I've done it.

This is Nancy. Sweet Nancy who is grieving. I knew my intuition was right. I should've never listened to Denver. Men are blind.

"Nancy, were you and my dad... involved?"

She nods.

"I'm sorry," I say and put a comforting arm around her shoulders. "Why didn't you say anything?"

"You... know... Chip."

Actually, I'm not sure I did. A fact I've had to make peace with.

"He... just... didn't like the... goss—ip."

Denver sits in the chair, probably thinking he should be close in case she pulls out a spatula or something.

"So you guys remained a secret all these years?" I ask.

She shrugs.

"How did you dodge Buzz Wheel?" Denver asks. "You might have a bestseller on your hands there, Nance."

She laughs although it's short-lived. Denver does

manage to get her to pick up her head and look at us though. "We stayed in a lot. You know no one really bothered Chip much. They were afraid of him."

I look at Denver, and he nods.

"We went on a lot of trips and stayed away from Lake Starlight." Denver passes her the box of tissues on the table, and Nancy grabs four at once. "I'm sorry."

"You have nothing to apologize for," I say.

She sits in the corner of the couch, and I tuck my hands into my lap. Even though I suspected, I didn't see this coming.

"I should have just told you. The first time, I said it was the last time. I just sat here for an hour to feel him, you know?"

I don't unfortunately.

"Then you guys went on the trip with Griffin Thorne and I knew I didn't have to worry about you guys coming here. I just wanted to make it nice, like it would have been had we ever…" She doesn't finish her sentence because a new rush of tears cascades down her cheeks. Obviously, it was Chip who didn't want to make their relationship public or permanent. "One thing kind of led to another, and I never saw a sign that you'd been here, so I just kept coming and reading. And now…"

I look at Denver, and he shrugs as though he has no idea what to do.

"I talked with Sheriff Miller," I say.

She nods. "He came by while you guys were up north. He can be discreet when he wants to."

That worries me a little. It's his responsibility to tell me. I'm the owner of the property. But then I see Nancy, who's grieving for a man I've yet to shed a tear for. Maybe the sheriff is a good guy who saw a woman hurting and did what he could to help.

"I told him I wouldn't return, but I knew you were at dinner tonight," Nancy says.

"You don't have tracker devices on us, do you?" Denver asks, and I balk. "What? It's a legit question. She's had access to our phones."

Nancy looks hurt, which she should.

"Forget him. He's still absorbing all this." I stand and dig inside my purse. When I sit back down, I open her hand. "This place is yours. It obviously means a lot more to you than me." I tuck my key into her hand.

"No. Chip was clear. He wanted you to have it."

I look at Denver. I could never start a life here with him. If we move in together on our own, I want a fresh place. "He was wrong. This place is meant for you."

"No. No. I'll at least pay you rent. You need the money."

I shake my head. "No, we have the show coming. We're going to be fine, and I didn't think I was ever going to sell this place anyway. I really want you to have it."

Nancy stares at the key. Although she must have another on her keychain, it's a gesture on my part to show her that I'm serious. "He loved you, Cleo. I know you doubt that, and I never wanted to break his trust, but he wished he'd done it differently with you. Things with your mother were difficult. He told me so many times he wished he had fought harder."

I nod. Her words do hold weight. They were obviously close. I lean into the couch. "I think I understand him a little better now. And I know my mom is hard to deal with. Can you tell me the story of how you got together?"

Her face lights up as if I just gave her an unexpected

birthday present. Denver stares at me like 'We're going to sit here and listen to their love story? Really?' But when I nod, he leans back in the chair and nods.

I'm sure he's going to say no to me one of these days.

Nancy talks about how when she interviewed for the job at Lifetime Adventures, there was this sizzle between them. She started the next week, and things progressed slowly from there.

At some point, she switches to talking about my relationship with my dad. How he took a two-week vacation every year when I came up so he could spend time with me. How she wishes she would have pushed him to be more open with about what had gone on over the years behind the scenes, but that wasn't Chip's way. All the conversations she overheard between my parents. How one summer, my mom said she wasn't sending me up, and he put his foot down. How he'd come out of the office sometimes after getting off the phone with me and tell her all about what I was doing.

Her words make me examine my relationship with my dad with fresh eyes and without the resentment that's weighed on me for years. I realize that he never went too long without calling, and he did text me once I got my first cell phone. I almost chuckle, remembering how he had a flip phone and how long it must've taken him to write some of those messages.

"Do you think he really loved me?" I ask, tears threatening.

Denver rushes to my side.

Nancy sits up straighter. "Listen, Chip Dawson had a lot of flaws. I loved every one of them, but I don't excuse them. One thing I know more than anything in this world is that your daddy loved you. He was just never good at showing it. He thought he was doing the right thing by letting your mom take you to all these different cities with the privilege of money."

Denver squeezes me into his side as my tears soak his shirt. We sit for a few moments, no one talking before Nancy finally stands.

She picks up a set of storage containers I noticed the first time we were here and places them at my feet. "I don't want to pressure you, honey, but I think what you're looking for is in these boxes. Chip never threw anything away, so if you want to know about his life, these papers might give you the closure you're looking for."

I stare at the labeled bins.

"Denver and I are going to get some ice cream and give you some time alone. Is that okay?" she asks.

I panic. Stay here by myself?

"If you're not up for it…" Denver doesn't stand to meet Nancy at the door.

I suck in a breath, and with as much courage as I can muster, I say, "She's right, I need to do this." I grab his hand. "For myself and for us."

He smiles and squeezes my hand. "I'm only a phone call away and I'll race back here. I'm not scared of Sheriff Miller." He winks. My stomach still flip flops every time he does that.

A minute later, after reassuring Denver I'm not going to run into the woods and freak out, they leave. I wait to hear his tires crunch over the gravel before I lift the lid of the first box, and dig into Chip Dawson's life.

THIRTY-ONE

Cleo

I'm halfway through the first box when I figure out this might be a two-day job. I've found paperwork from when he bought his first bush plane, which he's sold since. He really has kept everything. But then I find a file folder labeled "University of Indiana." Why would he have a file on my college?

Opening it on my lap, I find invoices and bills. My dormitory and my tuition. Even a bill for my apartment my junior year. There are copies of checks written to my mom. I thought Phil paid for my college tuition, but according to this, my dad paid it. Why did he never tell me?

Leaning into the warmth of the couch, I absorb the fact that Chip would do that. Surely my mom didn't make him do it. When Bridget and I started taking our ACTs in junior year and applying to colleges our senior year, Phil said he would take care of my tuition. I'd thought I might be able to get financial aid, but he said he'd think of it as an honor to pay for my college.

Chip had his own organizational system, so I dig for folders labeled with things familiar to me.

After box one, I move on to box two, where he has files for every year of my childhood.

Cleo (one year), Cleo (two years), Cleo (three years).

I pick up the stack and put them on the coffee table, pushing all the other papers aside. My stomach clenches when I see pictures and paid bills. My dance classes at three, paid by Chip Dawson. My karate classes at six, paid by Chip Dawson. My thirteenth birthday, two plane tickets to Hawaii with a cancellation number and refund written on them. I have to assume my mother interfered somehow in that. Pictures of him and me that year when I came up for the summer. Hair saved in my year seven folder from when I took it upon myself to cut bangs. A tooth in my five-year-old folder and a picture of me with my front tooth missing, holding up a dollar bill from the tooth fairy.

"He did love me," I say.

My prom dress receipt with a copy of a check to my mom. My hands shake as I go through everything he kept. All the keepsakes from my two weeks of every year spent in Lake Starlight, Alaska.

Year fourteen is thicker than the rest, and it's packed with legal papers. His application for permanent placement of me. The court records and an interview schedule. A ticket to come to Dallas, canceled and a refund code scribbled in his writing. A letter from my mom, stapled as if it was the final closure of the case. She writes that I'm doing so well, thriving. That she's dating a man who can give me whatever I want. Begging him to let her keep me and she promises him more time. Holidays and longer summer trips.

He must have agreed. But I never spent a Christmas with Chip, so she lied.

After I turned eighteen, the file folders stop. But there's one last one, labeled with my name and this year. Sensing this will be more sentimental, my heart grows heavy as I open the manila folder.

His will. His account numbers. Pretty much everything the lawyer gave to me. An envelope tucked under it all, with my name on it. How did he even know I'd go through all this stuff?

Before I read this new letter, I pull out the one Luther Lloyd gave me and read it again. I've carried it in my purse since I read it the first time, unable to put it somewhere for safekeeping.

Cleo,

Don't be mad. Listen to me first. I know you might not understand me leaving half the company to Denver Bailey. You get everything else of mine, because it's always been what's mine is yours. But Denver will help you keep Lifetime Adventures running. His knowledge is too great to throw away, and I think if you give him a chance, you'll see that the two of you could have a great partnership.

I'm not sure why you've always disliked him, but I ask you to try to put that aside for the time being. You don't see it now, but you're a perfect business pair. I know I've shot down your marketing ideas before, but I'm an old cranky man and set in my ways. Invent a new Lifetime Adventures. There's no limit to what you can do. Get your flying license. Have Denver take you on excursions. I know with hard work and dedication, you're going to succeed.

I've seen you struggling from afar. I'm probably to blame for that. You're trying to find a spot where you fit in this world. Give Lake Starlight a try, honey. I promise the people are kind and caring and won't disappoint you like the people closest to you have throughout your life. Don't fly back to Dallas. Stay a while. Give Lifetime Adventures a chance, and who knows, maybe it will be the adventure of a lifetime for you.

Always know, no matter what I love you.

Love,

Dad

SOMEHOW, he knew. He knew I belonged here. And rereading his letter now and knowing what's developed between Denver and myself, I have to wonder if this was part of his plan all along.

I set the letter on the table and pick up the sealed envelope containing the unread letter. My finger glides under the seam of the envelope. I slowly take out the paper as if it might fall apart if I move too quickly.

It's another handwritten letter from my dad.

Cleo,

If I know you at all, you've waited some time before digging into this and probably needed some encouragement from Denver. I could've thrown this all away. I could have died and remained silent. But

I needed—no, that's not right—I wanted you to know that I did take care of you. I paid every bill included there. And I don't tell you this to brag, but I fear after I'm gone from this earth, your mother will tell you something different and I can't bear the thought of you thinking things were anything other than the way they were. I pray that this letter doesn't end up unread in a bonfire. Shit, now I'm thinking I should tell you this in person. But I don't want you to go through my funeral and the reading of the will knowing what I'm about to tell you because I fear it'll change you and you'll never give life in Lake Starlight a chance.

Enclosed in the envelope is your birth certificate. You're going to see that the father's name is blank.

I PUT down the paper and open the envelope. There on my birth certificate is my mom's name, but no father listed, like he said. I've never seen this birth certificate. The one I have has both my parents' names on it. I drop that on the coffee table and pick up the letter again.

It's blank because your mom never put down the father's name. There's one more Cleo folder, and it's at Lifetime Adventures in Nancy's desk. It has your adoption papers. I met your mother soon after she became pregnant with you, and I adopted you as soon as you were born.

The paper slips from my hands and falls to my lap. I sit

there in stunned silence for I don't know how long, unable to make sense of the words. But I have to read what else he wrote.

I am your father, Cleo. Believe that. Your mother never told me who your biological father was, and I never asked because I selfishly wanted you to myself. When your mother and I divorced, watching you get on that airplane to the lower forty-eight, a piece of me died because although I'd adopted you, the courts didn't understand that biology means nothing when you love a child. I put up a good fight, but so did your mother. She had resources through marriage that I couldn't match. I never wanted you to end up in the middle of a war between us, so I backed down. I've questioned whether or not that was the right thing to do every day since.

I never once thought of you as not mine. If you get anything from this letter, please take away that. You are my daughter in all the ways that count.

Love you,

Dad

Headlights cast a glow in the window, and I come to from my shocked stupor. I bolt up from the couch, needing air, needing out, needing to be anywhere but here.

I tuck his letter and my birth certificate into my purse, ready to get the hell out of here. But when the door opens and Nancy sees me, she instantly knows. She must. The files are in her drawer.

"You knew," I say through choked sobs. "You never told me."

Denver takes one look at me and panic morphs his features. "What? What does she know? Babe?" Denver drops the ice cream on the counter and comes to my side.

Nancy stands there, saying nothing.

She allowed me to act like I'm someone I'm not. To feel like I belong here. I don't belong here. I have no ties here. Anger fills me, and I welcome it with relief. Because I found out before I was in too deep.

Then Denver's hand lands on my back and I look up at him. "The company is yours," I say.

"Cleo, don't decide that now. Don't be rash." Nancy's hand reaches out as I try to pass her, but I back up.

I hiccup through sobs that won't stop.

"Please tell me what the hell is going on?" Denver raises his voice.

"Let her tell you. Oh, never mind, she likes to keep secrets too much." I turn from her to Denver. "Chip Dawson wasn't my father."

Denver shakes his head. "Yes, he was."

I look at Nancy.

"Your dad wanted you to go through all this stuff so that you *knew* you were his daughter. He planned for this discovery because he was worried your mom would tell you in haste just to be spiteful. He wanted you to know exactly how he felt about it." Nancy says.

"I need to leave."

"Let's go," Denver says, urging me outside. "I'll call you, Nancy."

I have no idea what she says because I'm halfway to the truck.

Denver drives us to Savannah's house. Another temporary port in my life. A place I thought I belonged, but I only belong here because of Denver. Because my fake father left me half a company that I have no right to own. Denver's family has wrapped their arms around me, grounding me to this town, but this isn't where my dad lived and died. It's where a stranger I hardly knew paid my bills.

"Can we talk?" Denver asks.

"There's nothing to talk about. I don't want the company. It's yours."

I climb out of the truck and run to the house. The door is unlocked and I head up the stairs, but Denver's footsteps follow right behind me.

"Cleo?"

I grab my suitcase and fill it.

"What are you doing?" he asks from the doorway of his room.

"I'm packing."

"For what?"

I glance over my shoulder to look at him. All the stories Dori told me about the dog, the cat, the fish… I hate seeing him upset, but I can't be here right now. I can't. I sit down on the bed. "I have to leave. I need to clear my head."

He falls to his knees in front of me, his hands on either side of my thighs. "We'll figure this out together. It changes nothing. This is where you belong."

"I need to get out of this town." Fresh tears trail down my cheeks.

He sits back on his heels, stripping his hands off me. "Where are you going?"

"Dallas? I don't know. Just away from here."

"Okay. I'll take you. We'll fly out tomorrow, stay away as long as you need."

I shake my head. "Denver, you *are* Lake Starlight."

His face drains of color, and he stands. "So what you're really saying is that you need to get away from me?"

"You know what I mean."

I continue to pack because he has the power to convince me to stay. He's the person who could anchor me to this town. But why? So I can remember that behind every bend in the road was a man who *pretended* to be my father? No, he lied and my mother along with him. Her, I would expect it from. As long as he was paying the bills, what did she care? But him? Granted, we weren't the closest father and daughter, but I'd never known him to be anything other than truthful.

"I'm not sure I do." He leans on the doorframe and crosses his arms. "So by leaving Lake Starlight, you're leaving me?"

"No. I mean for a week or something." I grab the entire contents of my underwear drawer and shove it into the suitcase. "I can't have this conversation right now."

"You can't?"

"Do you not understand what just happened? Chip isn't my dad! I have no ties to Lifetime or his bank accounts or even my last name."

"What I understand is that you're running away," he grinds out.

"I'm not running."

He steps into the room and puts his hands over mine. "If you leave here without me, we're over."

He's so calm, it's eerie.

A fresh dose of anger washes through me. He thinks he's going to tell me how to deal with the fact that the man I thought was my dad was not? "Then we're over, I guess."

He backs up as if I slapped him.

I pick up my suitcase, forgetting anything else I left, and trudge past him.

"There are no flights right now. You're being ridiculous," he says from behind me.

I fumble down the stairs with my suitcase, and it bounces down each step with a thud. When I get to the bottom, I realize I have no car to get to the airport.

Denver must realize it too, but he puts up his hands. "Hey, we're over. Boyfriend obligation to be your chauffeur is over."

"I'll take you." Phoenix walks down the hall in another matching pajama set. She slips into her Uggs and grabs her jacket.

"Phoenix," Denver warns.

She opens the front door for me but probably figures I need some time, because she sneaks out before me, putting her hand on my shoulder and squeezing as she goes. I turn around. Denver's halfway down the stairs with his hands shoved into his pockets. How did we get here so fast? One minute I was so high I thought I'd made it through all the bullshit to my happily ever after, and now I'm neck deep in crap.

"I'm sorry it ended like this," I say.

He jogs down the steps. I'm desperate for him to understand and come to me. Take my head in his hands and tell me to take the time I want. That he'll be waiting for me. But when he reaches the bottom of the stairs, he just glances in my direction and heads to the kitchen.

My heart hollows. Spinning around, I close the door quietly and head to Phoenix's car.

THIRTY-TWO

Denver

I bang on Kingston and Juno's door, a twelve-pack in hand. No way I'm staying at my house. I can't go to Rome's because of the kids and Harley doesn't need me on their couch when she's pregnant. Liam is screwing my sister, and Austin and Holly? No way. That leaves them.

Kingston opens the door in his boxer briefs, running his hand through his messy hair. "What the hell?"

Juno comes out of her bedroom, her hair wild and not in an I-just-woke-up way. She shuts her door quietly. "Denver?"

I don't even wanna know what that's about right now. "Both of you, stay single." I head straight to the couch. "You can go back to bed. I'm going to drink until I pass out." I crack open a beer and put my feet up on their coffee table.

"I'll be right back." Kingston heads into his room before reappearing in a pair of pajama pants and his threadbare smokejumper shirt.

"What's going on? Did something happen with Cleo?" Juno asks.

I balk. "Why do you say that? I couldn't give two shits about Cleo."

Juno looks at Kingston, and they both blow out a breath.

"I'm sure you all knew it was going to end. I mean, me in a serious relationship? Please." I down half my beer. "That's not for me. She did me a favor by leaving."

"Maybe we should call Rome," Kingston says.

I finish one beer and crack open the second one. "Why do we need Rome? I just need your couch because I can't spend the night in my bed."

"Why?" Kingston asks.

"Because I have to wash the sheets and go through the house to get any memory of her out of my life."

Juno moves to the couch and puts her hand on my knee. "Let's talk about this."

"I'm not saying it's a bad thing, it's just an inconvenience." I click on their television and sip my beer.

"You guys seemed happy," Juno says.

Kingston is quiet. This isn't his thing. Feelings and emotions. He gave up on those a long time ago.

"She was a great lay, but now it's over. Oh well. I'll have to figure out the company. She had too many girly ideas anyway. Now I can run it like Chip did." I look Juno in the eye, so she knows I'm not just a half-drunk, pissed-off Denver. "It's a blessing."

She inhales deeply as though she's annoyed with me but now isn't the time. "I think you're wrong. You two were great together, and you're acting like a complete asshole saying the things you're saying." She stands. "Man up and go after her if you're so upset about it. But this whole 'I don't care' attitude is bullshit and we all see through it."

She storms out of the room and slams her door, locking it.

"She's so touchy," I say to Kingston. "Is she on her period?"

He stares at me.

"It's cool, bro, we don't need to talk about it." I pick up a beer. "Want one?"

He takes it, unscrews the top, and puts up his feet to watch ESPN with me. Kingston is the perfect person to go to when you're down. He's not going to call me names and tell me I'm stupid. I love my brother.

I put my second empty in the case and take another one. I've missed this since Cleo entered my life.

Cleo

Thanks to Bridget, who put a last-minute flight to Dallas on her credit card, I land at nine the next morning. On the way to the airport, I called Luther Lloyd and left a message to get the paperwork ready for me to sign over my half of the company to Denver. I'm painfully aware it's only six back home. *Ugh*. Not home, Lake Starlight. My mind wanders to what Denver could be doing.

By the time I've collected my bag, Bridget is there with open arms. I figured she'd be in her pajamas, but she's fully dressed, with makeup and hair done.

"You look so good," I say, feeling a little self-conscious over my eyes that are raw, red, and puffy.

"It's the whole television gig. People are starting to recognize me, so I don't want to look grungy in public."

She puts her arm through mine, and it's as though we were never apart. Walking to the car, she asks me nothing. Talks about her weather job and how she's moving out of Phil's house and into her own condo in the city. On the escalator, I really look at her. She's glowing. She's happy and thriving. I thought I was happy and thriving too.

We put my suitcase in her car and leave the airport. She drives for a few minutes before she brings up the proverbial elephant in the car.

"I know you don't want to talk about it, but you're going to have to." She merges onto the highway.

"Chip isn't my dad," I say.

She doesn't say anything.

"Did you hear me? Chip isn't my dad. Not biologically."

She glances at me. "I know."

"You knew!" I screech. "How did you know?"

"Are you hungry? Let's get breakfast first."

I sigh. "I'm not hungry, Bridge."

"Breakfast burritos and a walk around White Rock Lake?"

"Just tell me how long you've known?"

"Almost since the beginning."

The swift kick of deceit knocks me over. I want to open the door and jump out, not caring if a car runs me over because I already feel as if life has bulldozed me. I can't catch a break. Just when I thought I'd found where I fit, I found out about Chip. Thinking about Chip makes me think about Lifetime Adventures, which in turn leads to Denver. I dig my phone out of my bag. No missed calls.

"What happened with Denver?" Bridget asks.

"We broke up."

She looks at me, apparently self-shocked. "You didn't!"

I nod with a self-satisfied gleam. I knew he wasn't meant for a relationship, that he wasn't some prince wrapped in a bachelor reputation. I was right all along. That chick from the bar was probably his piece on the side.

"Don't you do that to yourself," she says, changing lanes.

"I'm not doing anything."

"You're convincing yourself that Denver isn't the one. That you didn't fall in love with him."

"I didn't."

"Really?"

I shake my head and cross my arms. "I was simply reminding myself to trust my gut."

"I talked to you up there. You were happy. I saw your Instagram. You both wore love well."

"You're wrong. If you'd been there in person, you'd know that I found him with another girl at the bar." Even I'm knocking on my head, wondering if anyone is home right now. I'm going off the deep end. I quickly change the subject because I know he wasn't doing anything with that girl. I'm just searching for anything that will make me feel better about our breakup. "This isn't about him anyway."

"It is if you broke up over this new revelation," she says and pulls into the small drive-thru. She orders four breakfast burritos, one cold brew and a latte for herself.

I check my phone again because I thought it vibrated. Nope.

We end up on the path by the lake, eating our burritos and sipping our drinks.

"I missed this," I say.

"Me too." She knocks her shoulder into mine. "But you know you don't belong here, right?"

I sigh. "I'm not sure where I belong."

She knocks me again.

If I'm not careful, I'm going to end up in the lake. "Can you stop doing that?"

"Maybe you need a cold dunk to get your brain back in working order."

"Why didn't you ever tell me about my dad?" I ask.

She crumples up her wrapper and digs in the bag for number two. One thing we've had in common from day one is that we're stress eaters. "At first I thought you knew. I overheard my dad and your mom talking one day. When I asked him about it, he swore me to secrecy. Said it would upset you if you found out from me, and I never wanted to hurt you. After that, I didn't think much of it. In my world, there are all different kinds of families. Even now, I don't see the big deal."

"You don't see the big deal?" I whine. "I have a mom who skipped around husbands and a dead dad who really wasn't my dad. I have no roots. You belong here with Phil. He's your blood."

She sips her drink and eyes me from the side. "I'm not sure blood means anything."

"That's because you have it," I fight back, and she doesn't say anything.

We walk a few paces, finishing our burritos.

"So you're just going to move back into the ranch?"

I sigh. "I don't know. I don't want to live with my mom after this. Maybe I'll get a job somewhere."

"You could always head back to Lake Starlight and run the company your father left you."

"Have you even been listening?"

She sips her latte and throws it out after finishing only half. "I'm listening. I love you, Cleo, you're my sister, but guess what?"

"What?" I groan, waiting for her next pearl of wisdom.

"We're not blood."

I stop walking and she continues. She slowly turns around when she realizes her point was so easily made.

"That's different. We knew from the get-go." I catch up

to her, but I have to say my "argument" hangs in front of me like an annoying neon sign.

"If you say so." She slides her arm through mine.

We walk the entire path around the lake. Then she drives me to the ranch so I can confront my mother.

Denver

Someone pulled a prank on me. That's the only explanation for why my mouth feels as if it's filled with cotton balls. Seconds later, I hear faint voices.

"You're not going to pour water on him. It'll ruin my couch."

Juno.

"He's going to get his ass up and stop acting like a child."

Austin.

"Let's write 'You're a jackass' in permanent ink on him."

Phoenix.

"Come on, guys. We've all been here."

Holly.

"I've never been where he is. I fought for my fiancée."

Rome.

"We had our problems. This is a bump in the road for them."

Harley.

"Wyatt ran."

Brooklyn.

"I didn't run."

Wyatt.

"You went to New York."

Brooklyn.

"I was back in a day."

Wyatt.

"Mommy and Daddy, stop fighting."

Kingston.

"He's not going to talk to any of you."

Liam.

"We have to try. Should we call Dori?"

Savannah.

"What's wrong with Uncle Denver?"

Calista.

My eyes pop open. My niece's head is tilted over mine, staring at me. I pick her up and sit up, feeling as if my brain is jiggling around. She squeals, and a happiness I haven't felt since before the shitstorm of last night warms me. Until I look at all my siblings and their significant others staring at me.

"Time to talk," Austin says.

I glance at the clock on the wall. Shit. It's only seven in the morning. I release Calista and lie back down. "Not now."

Austin grabs the pillow from under my head and it hits the arm of the couch.

"Damn it," I whine.

"Maybe that will make you think clearly. We all have jobs to get to. We can't babysit you all day."

I sit up again.

"Calista, go into Aunt Juno's room and watch television." Harley nudges her that way.

Juno runs to the door before Calista can get there. "Go to Uncle Kingston's room. Mine's messy."

Everyone stares blankly at her. Calista doesn't give a shit if a room is messy. But Calista, being easygoing about everything, skips to Kingston's room. A second later, we hear "Baby Shark" playing.

"Damn it, I left my phone in there." Kingston pats his pajama pants.

"Denver,"—Rome slides the beer bottles over and sits on the coffee table—"what happened?"

It's not my news to share. I don't know if Phoenix opened her mouth, but I'm not telling anyone about Cleo's situation with her dad without talking to Cleo myself.

"It doesn't really matter. We broke up and my kid sister over there drove her to the airport." I roll my eyes at Phoenix.

"Yes, because she was hurting, and all you were doing was giving her ultimatums. She was clearly freaking out, and I thought she needed space. I planned to try to convince her not to go on the way to the airport, which I did try, but damn that girl can be stubborn."

All the women in the room give me a death glare. I raise my hand because I don't need some "come to Jesus" moment from them.

"You're acting like one of our students," Holly says. "Sometimes people need space to figure things out. It doesn't mean they don't care about you."

I stand from the couch. "I have to go to work. My partner just left me high and dry. Hey, any of you want to do a reality show with me?" I circle my pointer finger around. "No? Figures."

"Denver, can we please be real for a moment?" Austin says.

I open the front door. "No." Then I slam it so they know the conversation is over.

I'm almost to my truck when the apartment window opens.

"Might want to check Buzz Wheel!" The window slams shut again.

Sitting in my car, I take the bait Phoenix threw out, pulling up Buzz Wheel on my phone. The picture of the Welcome to Dallas sign is a sure tip-off that it's about Cleo.

I HAVE sad news for our Lake Starlight residents. We thought after losing Chip Dawson that we wouldn't have to change our population size because his daughter, Cleo, would take his spot, but rumors have it that she hopped on a plane back to Texas late last night. Apparently, she and Denver Bailey are on the outs and she's given him her half of Lifetime Adventures. I'm hoping this rumor isn't true, but the Baileys were seen congregating at Kingston and Juno's place early this morning. Add on the fact that Denver's truck was there all night, and someone saw Phoenix pull into her driveway at one this morning, and it would seem the timelines meet up. I'm sad that we might have lost her and lost the new-and-improved Denver Bailey right along with her. I have confidence that these two can find a way to figure things out if they decide to do it together. If you're in Texas, Cleo, come back home to Lake Starlight.

· · ·

I THROW my phone onto the passenger seat. All I can see is Cleo sitting there, her legs crossed, and her flirty smile aimed my way.

Damn, my heart hurts. I rub my chest. How many times will it suffer like this before it just shuts down completely? I'm sick of going through this shit.

A HALF HOUR LATER, I walk into Lifetime Adventures.

Nancy's smiling in front of the coffee maker. "I made you a cold brew."

"Thanks." I look at her, then at the door with Manager in a nice script. "I'll be working in the hangar today."

I walk out and shut the door. Today is going to be a reorganization day. I'll bury myself in the storage locker.

"Denver Bailey!"

Fuck. G'ma D. Can I not catch even a small break today? She thinks the siblings don't talk about her incessant need lately to fix us all up.

I say, "Go away. I don't need any stories."

"Oh, I'm not going to tell you any stories." She follows me into the supply closet. "I'm going to say this once, and you're going to get down from that ladder and listen to me."

I climb down the ladder because this woman will probably grab me down by my belt loop if I don't. "What?"

"Do you have any idea how hard it was to put all the pieces in place to get you and Cleo together while making it look like I had nothing to do with it?"

"Sorry for wasting your time." I turn, but she grabs my arm and flings me around. I'm not sure I've ever seen her this mad.

"Oh, you're not going to have to apologize to me—

because you're going to get on that plane and fly to Dallas and grovel."

I laugh. "Uh. No."

"Stop destroying your future with your own hands. So you've been hurt. We've all been hurt. I lost your grandfather. I lost my son and my daughter-in-law Your eight siblings all lost their parents too." She puts her hand on my heart. "I know it hurts and you don't want to go through it again, but it's life, honey. Life and death go hand-in-hand. Cleo lost her father only to lose him all over again by finding out he's not her biological father. Put yourself in her shoes."

"She left me." I sit on a box. "Her first reaction was to run." I look up at her. "Run from me."

G'ma D sits on a rung of the ladder. "I know, and she'll have to apologize for that and work it out, but are you really going to sit here and not go after her? Where is the Denver Bailey who fights until he's got nothing left? You're accepting defeat."

"Who knows where we were going anyway?"

She hits me on the back of the head. "That shit might work with someone else but not me. You love the girl."

I don't argue—because she's right. Somewhere in this crazy situation, I fell so hard for her and what hurts so badly is that maybe she doesn't love me like I love her. Otherwise her first reaction wouldn't have been to leave me. "I don't think she loves me."

"I think she does, but there's only one way to find out." When I look at her, she seems exasperated. "Go get her."

"She probably won't take me back."

G'ma D picks up my phone from the shelf and hands it to me. "There's an easy way to find out."

Phoenix comes out of nowhere. "No. He needs to go to her." She turns to me. "You need to go to her."

G'ma D nods.

"Shit." I look down at myself. "I smell like a brewery. I can't go now."

G'ma D pushes me out of the storage room. "It'll mean more that you couldn't wait one second."

I nod. "I gotta get a flight."

Phoenix bites her lip and grins.

"What?" I ask.

"I saw on Instagram that Griffin Thorne flew in on his private jet yesterday."

I don't know why he's here, but it doesn't matter. I'm not too proud to beg. I can't let Cleo slip away from me without at least trying to drag her back to Lake Starlight. I dial him up, and he answers right away. After I explain the situation, he says to meet him at the regional airport, and he'll arrange everything.

"I'm going too," Phoenix says.

"You're not going."

"I got you the information! Come on, just an introduction." She follows me out of the hangar, and I hop in my truck and lock the doors before she can climb into the passenger seat. "*Denver!*"

I'll fix that later, but right now I'm only on a mission to apologize to Cleo and win her back.

***

FORTY-FIVE MINUTES LATER, I'm at the airport. Maverick is running circles around Griffin in the small lobby. I throw the truck into park and get out.

Griffin meets me at the door. "Plane's ready and it'll park at the airport overnight, but tomorrow morning, it has to return here because Maggie will have a coronary if I don't get him back to LA on time."

I shake his hand. "I owe you so much."

"I owe you my life. This is nothing." He tucks his hair behind his ear.

"Hey, Maverick." I hold out my fist to bump him.

He does it then jumps from chair to chair.

"There's an expiration date on that owing-me-your-life thing," I call and run through the set of doors.

I board the plane. When he said ready, he meant ready. The stairs come up, the pilot starts the engine, and I barely have my seatbelt on before we're speeding down the runway.

THIRTY-FIVE

Cleo

B ridget drives me to Phil's house. For some reason, I've referred to it as solely his since the day I moved in. I came to this house every day after school for three years, but it was never home. It should've been, because my mother lives here, but Phil made me feel more welcome here than my mother ever did. Talk about a mother who treats you like a stepchild and a stepdad who treats you like a real daughter.

"Are you sure about this?" Bridget asks.

We both look at the expansion ranch where the landscapers are doing their weekly maintenance.

"As long as you're with me."

Her hand fits in mine. "I'm always with you."

"Because after this, you're driving me to the airport." She crinkles those perfectly styled eyebrows, and I add, "I'm going home."

"You're telling me something I said got through to you?"

I laugh and hug her. "Yes. I love you. Thank you."

"I'm so giddy that my words of wisdom helped you through your brain fart."

We pull back from the embrace. "Well, let's not go too far."

Our feet fall on the cobblestone driveway.

"I'm not letting this go for a long time," she says, but I say nothing because my heart is beating like a drum in a rock band. "You got this." Bridget opens the front door. "Dad! Violet!"

"They're probably out back," I say.

She nods and we head through the foyer, through the cook's kitchen to the dining room, and out to the covered porch. As I assumed, Phil and my mom are on the porch, drinking Bloody Marys and eating their lunch. They don't turn when we open the doors, Phil engrossed in his magazine and my mom on her phone.

"Girls?"

We jump and spin around.

"Audrina!" Bridget touches her arm. "You scared us."

"Cleo, you're back?" She hugs me to her large chest. "Too quick."

"She had a mental lapse, but she's going back tonight," Bridget says.

Audrina, Phil's maid, isn't blood, but she always knew what was going on with Bridget and me.

"The boy?" Audrina asks.

See what I mean? But in this instance, I think Bridget had something to do with her telepathy.

Bridget slides her arm through Audrina's like she always does mine. "She's in love."

"Love? Too young." Audrina waves it off as if it's not true.

I don't say that I am. Bridget suspects, but there's one person who needs to hear it first.

"Go, go, your parents are heading out in an hour." She shoos us out the door. Bridget goes first, but Audrina grabs my arm to keep me by her. "You okay? Up there?"

I nod. "Yeah."

She smiles, and her wrinkled hands cup my cheeks. "I'm proud of you. It took a lot to go up there like you did. See, I'm always telling you, taking chances pays off in gold sometimes."

I rush into her arms, hugging her tightly because after what I'm about to do, I might never be welcome back here again. "I miss you like crazy."

"I miss you. Bridget is never around. The house is quiet."

"Cleo," Bridget whispers. "You're doing a group hug without me?"

Audrina and I open our arms, and Bridget falls into our embrace. When we all draw back, each of us has tears in our eyes.

"Now go. I need to work." Audrina pats us forward.

Before we say anything, she shuts the door behind us.

I look at Bridget, and she links her hand with mine.

My mom must finally notice us because she turns. She taps Phil's arm, causing him to turn in our direction. Neither of them slides out of their chairs though. Phil turns to his paper one last time before folding it and setting it next to his plate.

"Cleo?" my mom asks.

"Hey," I say.

"Dad, do you want to go for a walk?" Bridget asks.

He flicks his wrist to look at his watch. "I don't have a ton of time, sweetie."

"What are you doing back? Why didn't you call?" My mom is still not standing to pull me into an embrace. She never was one for displays of affection.

"Dad." Bridget pulls out the voice that gets Phil to do just about anything for his little girl.

He rises from the table and touches my shoulder. "Nice to see you, Cleo. I'm sure I'll find out what this is all about later."

"Thanks, Phil."

He lowers his head, probably understanding that this mother-and-daughter conversation is long overdue. Phil and Bridget head off toward the stables, and I sit in the vacant chair on the other side of my mom.

"Cleo, what's that look on your face about?" She waves her hand in the air.

"How could you not tell me?"

She arches an eyebrow. "Tell you what? You need to be more specific."

"I found the paperwork. He left me a letter."

Her jaw clenches and she pulls in a deep breath. "What paperwork?"

"Seriously?"

"I'm not sure what you're here looking for."

"I'm looking for answers, Mom. How could you let me believe he was my dad all this time? I could maybe understand if you'd stayed married to him. Or if you'd allowed me to see him more than two weeks a year. But you let him adopt me, you took his money, and denied him a relationship with me."

She leans back and crosses her legs. "We were married when he adopted you. He wanted to pay for everything because he was your dad. And as far as seeing you, I don't remember him ever asking for more than two weeks."

I'm not sure how I thought I'd get any answers from her. "He tried to get full custody of me at fourteen."

"I don't remember that at all." She waves off the accusation as if it's a pesky insect.

"Never mind." I walk back toward the house. I'll wait for Bridget outside.

Her chair screeches along the concrete. "What do you want from me?"

I turn around. "Not to sound like Jack Nicholson from *A Few Good Men*, but I want the truth. I want to know why you conned a man into adopting me to hide what I assume was an unplanned pregnancy. Why you stole his money with the promise of a relationship. Why you let me believe Phil was buying everything for me when, in fact, it was Chip. Tell me why you never thought I should know." My voice increases in volume the longer I go on.

Her fists clench, the first sign of any emotion I've gotten from her. "I got pregnant and met Chip right after. He loved me and wanted to adopt you. It was better that way. Would you rather know that your father was a man who could never have supported you emotionally or financially? I did what was best for you. Best for us." Her eyes narrow.

"You did what was best for you." I stab my index finger in her direction. "If you did what was best for me, you wouldn't have run from Lake Starlight. You would've allowed me to see Chip, whether he was my biological father or not. And you would've sat me down when I was old enough and told me the truth. All you've ever cared about is yourself!"

She scoffs. "What? You grew a backbone up there in Small Town, USA? He might've paid for some things, but Phil put a roof over your head and food on the table. He bought you designer clothes. Expensive vacations. So Chip did some stuff. So did Phil." She crosses her arms.

"Because you never allowed Chip to do more. You were so selfish."

I spot Phil and Bridget walking back up the pathway. Bridget holds Phil back, but his eyes are on us, and he looks concerned.

"What do you want to get out of this, Cleo? To make me feel like a bad mother?"

"You *were* a bad mother. Look at me, Mom. I'm messed up. I just ran away from the one place where I fit. From the first man I've ever…" I leave it there because she doesn't care nor deserve to know how much Denver has changed me.

My phone dings in my purse.

"You're always so dramatic. You think this is a hard life." She opens her arms to indicate the house and the ranch.

It wasn't. I'm not saying that. I always had more than enough food and clothes, but emotionally, it scarred me. She scarred me.

"You have no idea what a hard life is," she says.

"Do you even care that I found out? Does it matter at all to you that I'm standing here and you've yet to apologize or talk to me about who my biological father is?"

She throws her arms in the air. "He was a drug addict who died when you were two. There. Does that make you feel better?"

I stand there, absorbing the information, because when I walk out of this house, I won't have a parent. At least not one that I talk to. "Thank you for that. It's the least you could do." I turn to leave.

"Cleo!" she yells, and I spin back around.

Phil and Bridget come up onto the porch, and Bridget

looks at me. My phone dings again. Mom shakes her head, but not one tear, not one apology. The woman I share blood with isn't half as concerned as the people standing near her who don't hold one drop of the same blood as me.

"Have a great life, Mom."

"Hold up, Cleo!" Bridget runs after me, but I'm already through the cook's kitchen when she catches up. "Not good, huh?" She puts her arm around me as my phone dings for a third time.

"No." I pull out my phone.

Phoenix: *Private plane. Dallas Love Field. Arrives at nine o'clock tonight.*

"He's coming," I say.

"Who?" She looks over my shoulder then kisses my temple. "Oh, him."

I laugh.

"Then I need to spend the day getting you ready for him."

"No," I say. "You've already done so much."

"One last splurge on my sister before she moves away forever," she says and opens the front door of Phil's house.

Outside, I stare back at the house. "I'll miss it."

Bridget heads to the driver's side of her car. "No, you won't."

We climb into the car and she pulls away. I never turn around for one last look. I'm on to the next chapter of my life now.

THIRTY-SIX

Denver

The plane lands and I unbuckle my seatbelt. On the way, I found Phil's house on my phone. That has to be where she's at.

"Rental car?" I ask the flight attendant.

"An Uber should be waiting for you when you land."

"Okay, thanks."

While the plane is taxiing, I pace. When it finally comes to a stop, the stairs descend and I run down and into the terminal, not stopping for anything. I follow the signs to the third-party pick-up area. It's a small private airport, so there's barely anyone here.

"Denver?" someone says from behind me, and I must be crazy because it sounded like Cleo.

I continue jogging and put my hands on the door to push it open.

"*Denver!*"

I turn, thinking I forgot something on the plane, but there she is, as if I conjured her.

"Cleo?" I say as if I could put my hand out and she'd vanish.

I can tell that she's been crying at some point. She looks a little worse for wear but nonetheless the sight of her warms my insides and I already feel more at peace, even though I don't know how this is gonna go.

I jog over to her. "What are you doing here?" The open expression on her face gives me hope.

She smiles. "I live here. Or I used to anyway."

It doesn't matter why she's here. I can't wait any longer to say what I need to to her. "I'm sorry. I'm such an idiot. How much time do you need down here? I can stay, or I can go back to Lake Starlight and wait for you. Whatever you want, but please, I don't want to break up."

She steps closer and puts her finger to my lips.

"That's my move," I whisper, and she laughs again.

These have to be great signs, right?

"I'm sorry. I don't want time to think. I was stupid for blowing up. Can you forgive me?" She removes her finger from my mouth.

"No, I was wrong. That's a lot you were handed, but I just..." The small voice inside me says it's time. "I love you, Cleo. I fucking love you so much and I took you leaving as a rejection of me—of us. My heart was imploding while watching you pack that suitcase. I reacted badly. I should've let you go and given you space to come back to me."

"No." She takes my hands, entwining our fingers. "We're partners. We're in this together. I never should've run."

I tighten my fingers in hers. "So you're saying we were both wrong?"

She chuckles and nods. "I love you, Denver."

I close my eyes, savoring the sound of the words that

ignite pure bliss inside me. I imagine my heart like those Glo Worm dolls from the eighties.

"Hey." Cleo steps forward, and I cup her face with my hands.

"What?"

"Can you do something for me?" she whispers.

"Anything."

"Take me home."

I bend down and my lips press to hers.

"Sorry, kiddos, but you're not going anywhere until tomorrow morning," Bridget interrupts.

I wave her off, sliding my tongue into Cleo's mouth. I didn't even realize she was here.

Turns out Bridget's right. So Cleo and I go to a hotel, and our makeup sex is the next level. I might have to start a few fights every now and then.

The next morning, we board Griffin's plane, and I take Cleo Dawson home where she belongs.

Denver

"That was an awesome flight. I think you can go solo next time."

Cleo looks at me from the pilot seat of Chip's plane. "I don't think I ever want to go solo."

I understand what she means. I used to love flying solo but now I prefer when she's with me.

Our show started airing four months ago. So far ratings are good, and Selma called about another season. Lifetime Adventures is improving every day, and this year we're starting family excursions. Yeah, Cleo got her way.

We're still living at Savannah's, but I actually pay her rent now. Phoenix is still there too. I couldn't kick her out, and thankfully Cleo felt the same way. We got Phoenix a pair of AirPods for Christmas that she uses every night though. Okay, not every night.

The hangar opens and it's pitch black.

"Did Nancy not turn on the lights?" she asks.

"Kill the engine. Maybe the circuit went bad or something."

She stops the engine, and I jump on the wing and down to the ground. She does the same on her side. "I was eager to pull it in the hangar."

"You can as soon as we see what's going on."

The minute we cross into the hangar, the lights flick on and everyone yells, "Happy birthday!"

Cleo looks at me. Most of my family is in attendance, along with Bridget, Nancy, Luther Lloyd, the guys from Smokin' Guns. Pretty much everyone in Lake Starlight who has met Cleo, because everyone fell in love with her. Sedona is still in New York and the newest member to the family, baby Phoebe, is strapped to Rome's chest while Dion toddles around, Calista running circles around him. Savannah is busy showing her engagement ring to everyone who hasn't seen it yet, while Liam stands at her side taking in the praise from all the women about what a good job he did choosing the perfect ring.

Cleo makes the rounds and hugs everyone. I watch her cheeks indent further with each hug. Her eyes light up with each happy birthday.

"Sometimes it's a long road and sometimes it's a short road," G'ma D says next to me, handing me a beer.

"Are those your words of wisdom?"

"She's glowing. It took her a long time to feel what she is now. Some get it quick, but something tells me that Cleo doesn't take it for granted."

"I don't either."

G'ma Dori puts her arm behind my back to hug me. "It took a lot of loss for you to get where you are. But it's kind of unbelievable, right?"

"Yeah." I kiss the top of her blue hair. "Thanks for kicking me in the ass."

"You would have realized it at some point, but this way you weren't hurting for too long."

I can't believe it's been a year with Cleo. Weren't we just in Dallas, making up in a hotel room? I've had a year of sleeping next to her. A year of her laughter. A year of her smiles. A year of her kisses. And I can't wait to see what the future holds for us.

G'ma D walks away when she sees Cleo approaching.

"Hey, you," Cleo says, putting her arms around my body. "What are you thinking about, over here all on your own?"

I kiss the top of her head. "You."

"Let me guess. Me naked in your bed tonight."

"No. You naked in our bed." She laughs, and I say, "But also how much I love you."

She squeezes me tighter. "Love you. We could sneak into the office." She bats her eyelashes.

"Another reason I love you." I slide my hand in hers and we head toward the office.

Phoenix jumps in front of us. "Where is he?"

"Who?"

Cleo laughs that I'm even asking who.

"You know who," Phoenix says.

I pat her shoulder to appease her. "Don't worry, he's moving here this summer, but don't tell anyone. He doesn't want anyone to find out."

She rolls her eyes. "Um, I would never do that because I don't want any competition. So you're going to introduce me finally?"

"Once he's settled, of course. He's on the hunt for a

nanny right now. I promise, Phoenix, I'm not bullshitting. After he's moved in, I'm inviting him to dinner."

"A nanny? He has a kid?" she asks.

"Yeah, now excuse us. Cleo would like to properly thank me for this great party." I drag Cleo away.

"Um, I did most of the work," Phoenix yells.

"Nobody likes a bragger," I yell back.

Opening the office door, I let Cleo walk in first, then I flip the lock.

"Time for your real birthday present."

She laughs, hopping up on her desk. "Let's see what you got, big guy."

"Oh, I'm going to rock your world."

"I don't doubt it in the least."

I descend on her, and in the back office while everyone is drinking and eating, I discover yet another thing that drives Cleo to the brink. Never a dull moment with us. I'd say this is the good life.

The End

COCKAMAMIE UNICORN RAMBLINGS

Now come on. Admit it. Denver won you over.

The book title fit him well. He had a hard and long road to get him where he needed to be.

Truth be told, Denver and Cleo's story changed on us. Originally, Cleo was a highly professional lawyer (or something like that) who hires Denver to fly her into the mountains of Alaska to spread the ashes of her late husband. They were going to be stuck in a snowstorm and that's where their love would spark. Then Cleo was going to be Chip's younger wife who inherits the company with Denver and they fall in love.

Then we realized a few things. If they're in the mountains, there's no Lake Starlight, no Buzz Wheel, no other Baileys and especially no Grandma Dori (although we don't doubt she might have strapped on a pair of snow shoes just to meddle). And we'd have to push forward too far in order for

Denver to fall for Cleo if she was indeed Chip's wife. Plus, we liked the whole fish out of water element for Cleo.

So while we wrote Falling for my Brother's Best Friend, we decided to change Denver's entire story, weaving in Chip and Lifetime Adventures. Let's just say there's a reason Chip never saw the page. Neither one us like to kill characters so it was better for all involved if he died off page and none of us grew too attached. You're welcome. ;)

This was one of Rayne's favorites of the series. She has something for reformed playboys. Those are the stories of ours she loves the most.

SUPER HUGE THANKS to our team who if not for them, we'd never be able to finish these books!

- Danielle Sanchez and the entire Wildfire Marketing Solutions!
- Cassie from Joy Editing for line edits.
- Ellie from My Brother's Editor for line edits.
- Shawna from Behind the Writer for proofreading.
- Sarah from Okay Creations for the cover and branding for the entire series.
- Sara from Sara Eirew Photography for the sexy and steamy Denver and Cleo.
- Bloggers who consistently carve out time to read, review and/or promote us.
- Piper Rayne Unicorns who shout from the rooftops about our new releases and love our characters like we do.

- Readers who took a chance on our book with so many choices out there.

Next up... You met her when she was only seventeen and about to graduate high school. She was a thorn in Austin's side. But now she's all grown up but hasn't lost her mischievous side as you'll see when she pretends to be a nanny! Phoenix Bailey is next and as you've probably figured out, Griffin Thorne is going to surprise her in more ways than one.

Xo

Piper & Rayne

ABOUT PIPER & RAYNE

Piper Rayne is a USA Today Bestselling Author duo who write "heartwarming humor with a side of sizzle" about families, whether that be blood or found. They both have e-readers full of one-clickable books, they're married to husbands who drive them to drink, and they're both chauffeurs to their kids. Most of all, they love hot heroes and quirky heroines who make them laugh, and they hope you do, too!

My Famous Frenemy

The Greene Family Vacation

My Scorned Best Friend

My Fake Fiancé

My Brother's Forbidden Friend

The Modern Love World

Charmed by the Bartender

Hooked by the Boxer

Mad about the Banker

Complete Set (all 3 books)

The Single Dad's Club

Real Deal

Dirty Talker

Sexy Beast

Complete Set (all 3 books)

Hollywood Hearts

Mister Mom

Animal Attraction

Domestic Bliss

Bedroom Games

Cold as Ice

On Thin Ice

Break the Ice

Complete Set (all 3 books +)

Charity Case

Manic Monday

Afternoon Delight

Happy Hour

Complete Set (all 3 books)

Blue Collar Brothers

Flirting with Fire

Crushing on the Cop

Engaged to the EMT

Complete Set (All 3 books)

White Collar Brothers

Sexy Filthy Boss

Dirty Flirty Enemy

Wild Steamy Hook-up

The Rooftop Crew

My Bestie's Ex

A Royal Mistake

The Rival Roomies

Our Star-Crossed Kiss

The Do-Over

A Co-Workers Crush

Hockey Hotties

Countdown to a Kiss (Free Novella)

My Lucky #13

The Trouble with #9

Faking it with #41

Sneaking around with #34

Second Shot with #76

Offside with #55

www.ingramcontent.com/pod-product-compliance
Lightning Source LLC
Chambersburg PA
CBHW061223310726
48971CB00007B/1920